The Executioner had a promise to keep

It had been made long ago to Galen Starke, when they were fighting for their lives in that strategic hamlet, outnumbered ten to one. Between artillery barrages and assaults on the perimeter, they had affirmed the Special Forces vow.

Alive or dead, no comrade left behind.

In one sense, Starke had been abandoned long ago. Whether his discharge from the service was a frame-up or a whitewash when he should have gone to prison, Starke had been cut adrift. The service and the war had moved on, leaving him behind.

From half a world away, one of his comrades had been sent to make it right. Bolan would see the mission through this time, for both of them.

MACK BOLAN ®
The Executioner

DON PENDLETON'S
THE EXECUTIONER®
ROGUE WARRIOR

A GOLD EAGLE BOOK FROM
W❂RLDWIDE®

TORONTO • NEW YORK • LONDON
AMSTERDAM • PARIS • SYDNEY • HAMBURG
STOCKHOLM • ATHENS • TOKYO • MILAN
MADRID • WARSAW • BUDAPEST • AUCKLAND

First edition October 2002
ISBN 0-373-64287-3

Special thanks and acknowledgment to
Mike Newton for his contribution to this work.

ROGUE WARRIOR

Printed in U.S.A.

If a man is in doubt whether it would be better
for him to expose himself to martyrdom or not, he
should not do it. He must be convinced that he has
a delegation from heaven.

—Samuel Johnson

Here's an object more of dread
Than aught the grave contains
A human form with reason fled,
While wretched life remains.

—Abraham Lincoln

A would-be martyr who extends his sacrifice
to innocent, unwilling victims is a threat to any
civilized society. He needs to be stopped, by any
means available. If that fulfills his dream of
martyrdom, so be it.

—Mack Bolan

For the sailors of the *USS Cole,* murdered in a terrorist attack in Yemen, 15 October 2000. God keep.

Hull Maintenance Technician 3rd class
  Kenneth Clodfelter

Electronics Technician 1st class Richard Costelow

Mess Management Specialist Lakeina Francis

Information Systems Technician Tim Gauna

Signalman Seaman Recruit Cherone Gunn

Seaman James McDaniels

Engineman 2nd class Marc Nieto

Electronics Warfare Technician 3rd class
  Ronald Owens

Seaman Recruit Lakiba Palmer

Engineman Fireman Joshua Parlett

Fireman Apprentice Patrick Roy

Electronics Warfare Technician Kevin Rux

Petty Officer 3rd class Rochester Santiago

Operations Specialist 2nd class Timothy Saunders

Fireman Gary Swenchonis Jr.

Ensign Andrew Triplett

Seaman Apprentice Craig Wibberly

Prologue

It was a pleasure to destroy the weak and useless members of so-called society. Each time he was dispatched to raid another village and eliminate the parasites who spent their wasted lives tilling the soil or herding scrawny cattle, Roshani Malinke felt a surge of pride.

Farmers and herdsmen were necessary, of course, but only those who served the Lord's Vanguard had any value, and their worth accrued from service to the cause. Those who thought only of themselves and their pathetic families were fair game to Malinke and his hunters.

They would also serve the cause, albeit grudgingly.

In death, they made a contribution vastly greater than themselves.

The village of Isala had been dusted eight days earlier. The Mil Mi-24 Hind helicopter had made its pass an hour before dawn while most of the villagers were huddled on their sleeping mats, beneath thatch roofs that had no hope of shielding them from silent, drifting death. Some would have wakened long enough to shudder at the sound of rotors overhead, fearing an armed assault. Perhaps a few had stepped outside to scan the heavens, thereby hastening their death.

Malinke hoped that some of them were still alive.

If not, he would be cheated of the sport that he loved best. Returning to the village of Isala, he wouldn't employ the helicopter. Fuel was scarce just now, with convoys under heavy guard, but he was more concerned with the advantage of surprise. If any of the human guinea pigs were still alive, Malinke meant to catch them in their nests before they could escape.

He would leave nothing in his wake but death.

Two dozen members of the Lord's Vanguard had been selected from among 450 volunteers to join Malinke on his mission to Isala. Village raids were always coveted assignments, since they offered a diversion from the day-to-day routine of any military force. Veterans appreciated the excitement, whereas green recruits were anxious for an opportunity to prove themselves. And what better way to do that than by wading in the blood of enemies?

That very blood was dangerous this time, but Malinke and his men were prepared. Each soldier carried in his pockets a gauze surgical mask and two pairs of latex gloves that would be worn on entering the village to prevent infection from contact with the dead or dying. Four members of the raiding team were armed with flamethrowers, their mission to obliterate Isala and its occupants.

The village was located on a tributary of the Okere River, fifty miles north of Moroto, the capital of Karamoja Province. Eight days earlier, it had been home to some 350 men, women and children, dwelling in the bliss of ignorance and sloth. Isala had no school, no hospital, no telephone or TV set—no link of any substance to the outside world. Twice yearly, crops and cattle were transported to Loyoro, sold or traded there for manufactured goods, but for most of the year Isala was a relatively closed society, like countless other rural villages across the length and breadth of Africa.

As such, it was the perfect killing ground. Who in the world would give Isala's inhabitants more than a passing thought when they were gone? How many would remember they had ever lived at all?

It was a two-day march from the remote headquarters of

the Lord's Vanguard to the Isala killing ground, thick jungle all the way, with crocodile-infested streams to cross and swampland where a man who lost his way could vanish in a heartbeat, never to be seen again. It was a challenge, but Malinke's troops were all of rural stock, inured to hardship in their struggle for the cause. They would accept the challenge and prevail, as much from keen anticipation of the kill as from the sense of duty hammered into them by their commanding officers.

Grim death awaited them, but it was someone else's death this time. They were the chosen few, anointed bearers of the cleansing fire.

It made Malinke proud.

With barely two kilometers to go before they reached Isala, Malinke told his men to halt. He waited for the stragglers to catch up, each man attired in camouflage fatigues and armed—except for those who carried flamethrowers—with Belgian FNC assault rifles imported from the Congo. In addition to the rifles, each man carried twelve spare magazines with a total of 390 5.56 mm NATO rounds per man, canteens, enough dried meat for five days on the trail, a first-aid kit, a poncho that could double as a blanket in the rain and a machete or survival knife. Malinke, as the only officer present, also wore a Browning Hi-Power semiautomatic pistol on his hip.

The side arm was Malinke's only badge of rank, but no insignia was needed to impress the troops with his authority. Each man on the patrol knew Malinke by sight, and most had felt the lash of his tongue at one time or another. All knew that disobedience to a superior meant swift and certain punishment.

In combat, it meant certain death.

Malinke surveyed the faces of his men. Their features showed determination carved in ebony, some of them daubed with tribal war paint, three or four with teeth filed down to jagged points in front. Though half of them had lobes or noses pierced, their jewelry had been left behind, strictly forbidden on the march. There was a time and place for such displays, but killing called for discipline.

"Isala lies within our reach," Malinke told his troops and jabbed a finger toward the east. "That way. Within an hour we shall smell the enemy."

There was a shifting in the ranks, but no one spoke. Such disrespect wouldn't be tolerated by the deputy commander of the Lord's Vanguard.

"Most of the parasites should probably be dead by now," Malinke said. He spoke in English, the official language of Uganda, though a number of his men were doubtless more familiar with Swahili or Luganda. "Those who still survive must be dispatched before they can escape. Surprise is critical. From this point on, no man shall speak for any reason unless I have ordered it. You understand?"

Heads nodded. No sound was uttered in response.

Perfect.

Malinke had expected nothing less.

"You must be cautious in the village," he went on. "The enemy has been infected with a vile disease, highly contagious. It is spread primarily by contact. Do not touch the dead or dying if you can avoid it. Any man contaminated will be left behind."

Malinke didn't have to clarify that statement. They could read the explanation in his eyes.

"Questions?" he asked.

No hands were raised. No soldier spoke.

"Put on your masks and gloves," Malinke ordered, setting the example as he removed his cap, slipped the elastic band of a surgical mask over his shaved scalp and settled the mask in place. The double gloves came next, one pair over the other for extra protection, taking care not to rip the latex.

When all his troops were masked and gloved, Malinke graced them with a smile. They couldn't see it, covered by his mask, but the ferocious grin was mirrored in his eyes.

"We have an opportunity to strike a great blow for the

Lord's Vanguard," he said. "I know each one of you will do his duty. Have no fear. Remember that God's strength is yours when you are fighting for His cause."

Bright eyes regarded him with something close to hero-worship. It was nothing less, Malinke thought, than what he rightfully deserved.

"Come then," he told his troops, "and follow me. We have work to do."

JIRI BIKO WAS running for his life. It was no easy task, on legs that sometimes felt like wood, with rubber in the knees, but he kept going, lurching through the jungle, jolted every few yards by collision with another tree.

His eyesight was going—nearly gone, in fact—and Biko's sense of balance was disrupted by the ringing in his ears. At least he wasn't bleeding at the moment, thanks to the *orishas* for small favors, but his normal strength and stamina were badly undermined by recent bouts of vomiting and bloody flux.

Biko suspected he was dying, yet he ran to save himself from what may well have been a quicker, simpler death.

He had been squatting in the brush a few yards from his hut, praying for mercy and a respite from the churning pain inside him, when he heard the strangers coming. It wasn't so much an error on their part, as cautious as they were, but simply that a lifelong native of Isala knew the countryside surrounding it, the jungle's every sight and sound.

Strangers were coming in the darkness before dawn, and Biko knew there could be no innocent reason for their stealthy approach. In better health, his mind would have made the connection between their arrival and the helicopter overflight of eight days earlier, bookends with living hell between the two. He didn't make the link, but Biko was alert enough to know that he must flee or die.

In other circumstances—if his head hadn't been pounding, if his eyesight had been better, if his trousers weren't stained with bloody muck that sapped his strength with each discharge—Biko might have remained to warn the village. With so many already dead or dying, all that he could think of was to save himself.

As if he could do that by running from the guns.

Biko already carried death inside him, but some instinct balked at letting him surrender quietly. However little life remained for him, Biko wasn't prepared to let it go without a struggle. Even if the best that he could do to save himself was running blindly through the forest, he would do that much and give it everything he had.

Biko was several hundred yards west of the village when the shooting started, automatic weapons crackling in the night. He stopped dead in his tracks—or would have, if his balance had been there. A final lurching step and he collided with a tree trunk wrapped in strangling vines. Some unseen creature scuttled out from underneath his feet, Biko ignoring it as he turned back to face Isala.

He had traveled too far through the jungle to see muzzle-flashes from the weapons, but his blurry vision did pick out a glow of firelight that appeared to sway and ripple, like a living thing. Biko heard screams, more gunfire and then an explosion.

There were no explosives in Isala, only five or six firearms for hunting and defense against the larger forest predators. He wondered whether any of the villagers who owned a weapon would be able to defend themselves. Were any of them even still alive, or had the bleeding fever claimed them all? What hope was there for those already weakened or disabled to survive a predawn military strike?

A wave of nausea struck Biko and nearly brought him to his knees. His stomach, long since empty, twisted in a brutal spasm and gave up a little blood-flecked bile. Biko stood gasping, both hands braced against a mighty tree, until the seizure passed and he could breathe again.

How long before one of the spasms knocked him down and finally snuffed out the spark of life? Could he survive the night? Another day?

Guilt nagged at him as he turned his back on the chaotic sounds of slaughter and resumed his awkward, shambling run. He had no destination fixed in mind, knew only that he felt a driving urge to get away. Those he had left behind would have no chance to think of him before they died, much less to curse his memory for failure to transmit a useless warning. He had only strength enough to save himself, and even that appeared to be a futile exercise.

At least, he thought, the raiders were unlikely to come after him. Arriving in darkness, uncertain of how many villagers occupied Isala or who among those still lived, the killers wouldn't miss one man. They were busy razing the village, by the sound of it, and Biko had seen enough of warfare in his thirty-seven years to understand that final body counts would be problematic, at best. Tracking a solitary runner through the jungle, even if the raiders knew he had escaped, would be another problem. How much time could they afford to spend in the vicinity if they were rebels hunted by the government?

If the were not...

Biko didn't believe Kampala would send troops to wipe his village off the map because its people suffered from the bleeding fever. The government sent doctors rather than extermination teams into the countryside when plagues broke out.

It occurred to Biko that he had a mission. As a survivor of Isala—and perhaps the only one—he had to report the tragedy that had engulfed his people. All he had to do was stay alive until he met another person who could hear his tale and carry it to someone in authority.

The ground gave way beneath his feet. Arms flailing, Biko tried to keep his balance, but to no avail. He plunged head-first into the darkness, somersaulted down a muddy slope and splashed into the swift, cool water of a jungle stream.

It seemed to Biko for a moment that he was about to drown, but then he thrashed back to the surface, retching water from his burning sinuses and lungs. The ringing in his ears had to have disguised the sound of flowing water, and his failing eyesight had allowed Biko to stumble off the bluff above. Now he was drifting with the current, floating downstream on his back.

He thought of swimming toward the shore, but realized instinctively that any strength he still possessed would be exhausted in that struggle. On the other hand, if he could stay afloat and somehow manage to avoid the scrutiny of crocodiles, the stream would carry Biko to the Okere River, passing several villages where he might make his way to shore and spread the word of what had happened in Isala.

The path of least resistance beckoned him and Biko spread his arms for greater buoyancy, letting the current carry him. Above him, in the gaps that separated overhanging trees, the first gray light of dawn was challenging a field of stars.

A new day was about to break.

Biko could only wonder whether he would live to see its end.

THE FLAMETHROWERS were busy, spewing brilliant arcs of liquid fire across the ruins of Isala, leaving desolation in their wake. Now and again, a high-pitched squeal would issue from a hut as it went up in flames, but those Malinke's riflemen had left for dead were roasted on their sleeping pallets. None of them emerged to give his soldiers any further sport.

Malinke's raiders had achieved complete surprise, the village sleeping as they entered and began the work of finishing the people who still survived. A number of the villagers had tried to run, but they were cut down in their tracks by automatic rifle fire. Others apparently believed that their thatched huts could shelter them from bullets, hand grenades and flamethrowers.

They were mistaken.

Basking in the heat from burning homes, Malinke watched his soldiers as they went about their final task of rounding up the dead. It was a risky business, touching those who bore the fever's taint. It took two men to drag the corpse of each person who was shot down in the street, dragging the body to the middle of the village, careful in the firelight not to soil their gloves or uniforms with poisoned blood. Another six or seven bodies, and the work would be complete.

The final burning could begin.

A woman's breathless scream distracted Malinke from his survey of the cleanup operation. Turning toward the sound, he expected to see another hut doused in flame, but instead he saw one of his soldiers grappling with a teenage girl, man-handling her toward the body dump. The girl's nightdress was torn, exposing her breasts. The soldier's shirt had lost some of its buttons, and his face mask was askew. Fresh scratches glistened on the soldier's chest.

Malinke moved to intercept the couple, blocking access to the body pile. The solider, Ari Lusala, blinked at his commander in apparent surprise.

"Sir, I—"

A quick burst from Malinke's FNC assault rifle spun the girl as if she were dancing, wrenched her from Lusala's grasp and dropped her facedown in the dust. Across Lusala's mask and sweaty cheek, a streamer of her blood reflected crimson firelight.

"You have disobeyed my standing order, Private."

"No, sir! She—"

"You are contaminated now," Malinke said.

Lusala raised one latex-covered hand to swipe the fresh blood from his face. "Sir, I can bathe! I'm not infected!"

"What about these?" Malinke asked, using the muzzle of his FNC to indicate the bloody scratches on Lusala's chest. "You have defiled yourself for pleasure's sake."

Lusala glanced down at his chest, seeming to notice his wounds for the first time. He raised his head and was about to speak when Malinke fired another burst of 5.56 mm rounds at point-blank range.

The impact of those bullets punched Lusala backward, airborne for an instant, before he landed sprawling on his back. The body shuddered once before it slackened into death.

Malinke turned to find the other members of his raiding party watching him. The masks they wore disguised their expressions, but he felt their eyes boring into him. Malinke faced them down, his finger ready on the rifle's trigger, just in case some comrade of Lusala's yielded to an impulse for revenge.

"This man thought nothing of himself," Malinke told them. "He thought nothing of the Lord's Vanguard, his mission or of you. He dallied with this parasite, against my orders, and was tainted with the bleeding fever in return. What can we do with such a weakling?"

For a moment there was no response, but then a voice was raised in answer. "Burn him!"

"Yes," another called out. "Burn him!"

"Burn them all!" a third voice cried.

It turned into a chanting chorus. Malinke knew he had them as his men went back to dragging corpses. Even in their zeal to please him they were cautious not to soil themselves with blood from those who had been shot. Lusala's body and the nameless girl's were added to the heap before Malinke's soldiers backed away.

"Burn them!" the chant went on.

The soldiers armed with flamethrowers awaited Malinke's signal. He nodded to them, and four streams of liquid fire gushed out to douse the body heap. One of the "corpses" leaped erect and tried to bat the flames away with flailing hands, but its pathetic screams were smothered by another fiery torrent. Raising blistered arms to heaven, it collapsed into a drifting pall of smoke.

Malinke watched the body burn, smelling the roasted-flesh odor of the funeral pyre. He didn't know if the contagion of the bleeding fever could be spread by ashes on the wind, but he was thankful for the gauze that swathed his mouth and nostrils, all the same. There was no point in taking chances when he planned to live and fight another day.

Another day...

Malinke realized that dawn was breaking. Darkness wouldn't shelter them as they retreated from the smoking ruins of Isala. He had no reason to think that government patrols were in the area or that Kampala's troops would tumble out of bed this early in the morning, but Malinke made a point of shunning all unnecessary risks. It was one thing to risk life in combat, but to dawdle needlessly on hostile ground was inexcusable. It courted ruin, and a fighting man who threw his life away to no result deserved unmitigated scorn.

Malinke shouted orders to his troops, commanding them to fall in line. Without Lusala they couldn't form even ranks with two abreast until Malinke chose a point man from the troop and sent him on ahead to scout the way.

They would return along the same trail that had brought them to Isala. It should offer them safe passage, although assumptions often ended in disaster. Roshani Malinke had faith in the Lord's Vanguard and his destiny, but it hadn't escaped his notice that God frequently punished conceit and overconfidence. Pride went before a fall, and for a combat soldier, any slip was a potential ticket to the cemetery.

Malinke's raiders were victorious this day, and now he meant to see them safely home. The jungle would assist them, covering their tracks and shielding them from airborne spies. They had avoided peasant farmers on the forced march to Isala and would do the same, if possible, on their return. If they met someone in the forest who shouldn't be there, someone who might betray them to the enemy, swift action would be taken to eradicate the threat.

Despite the weariness that dogged him, Malinke couldn't help smiling as he hiked through the brooding rain forest, following his scout. The experiment, from all indications, had been a resounding success.

Starke would be pleased.

THE REVEREND Mr. Hezekiah Rafferty believed himself to be a patient man. Patience was known, after all, as the cardinal virtue of saints. And while he might not qualify for sainthood in his present state, Rafferty honestly believed that he had done the best he could with what he had.

That very morning he had offered up another round of prayers, beseeching God Almighty to take time and light a fire under the sluggish stewards of the New Life Global Ministry in Oklahoma City. It had been almost six months since the ministry had promised Rafferty a water purifier for his humble parsonage at Melfi, twenty hard miles north of Loyoro. Without the purifier Rafferty was left to boil the water that he hauled in buckets from the nearby river, morning, noon and night. Failure to boil the water could result in sundry tropical diseases that would make the suffering of Job seem like a picnic by comparison.

It was a beastly place, this heathen Africa, for godly men. The climate was nothing short of hellish—although Rafferty had always pictured Hell as radiating what the desert dwellers of his native Arizona called a dry heat. The humidity in Africa was punishing, oppressive, and the swarms of biting insects made it that much worse—but if he had to tell God's honest truth, the thing that troubled Rafferty the most about his African assignment was the people.

It wasn't that they were heathens. He had come expecting that, prepared to save their wretched souls for Jesus Christ at any cost. He had arrived in Africa prepared to deal with cults and cannibals, wearing the armor of the Lord. If necessary for his mission, Rafferty had pledged himself to be a martyr for God's word—although he felt no shame in hoping it would not be necessary.

It wasn't fear that made Rafferty's sojourn in Africa a test of faith. A man got used to scorpions and spiders, snakes and crocodiles, even the threat of rebel soldiers waging war against the church.

It was temptation of the flesh that troubled him the worst.

Nothing in Rafferty's instruction had prepared him for the way the native peoples flaunted themselves, displaying their bodies as if public nudity were the most natural thing in the world. Some of the men made Rafferty believe that he had been short-changed by Mother Nature—not that such a thing should matter to a man of God, committed in all things to purity of body, heart and soul. Why should he feel inferior if all men were created in the image of the Lord?

And some, each day reminded him, had been created more equal than others.

Still, the sin of envy set aside, it was the native women who tormented Rafferty the most. He did his best to teach them modesty, convince them that the Lord would frown upon their bare breasts, but tradition and the jungle climate worked against him. While a handful of his dusky-skinned parishioners agreed to wear the secondhand garments shipped sporadically from Oklahoma City, most preferred their freedom, even in the midst of singing hymns. When Rafferty announced that females had to be fully clothed in order to attend his Sunday services, two-thirds of them had turned their backs on him. He had been driven to a series of embarrassing apologies, sweating through his wilted collar, struggling to maintain eye contact and stop his gaze from wandering below the shoulders of those he would save from Lucifer's toils.

Temptation.

Rafferty had never sown wild oats. He was a preacher's son who had the lessons of the Good Book hammered into him from infancy. He felt such guilt at the idea of straying from God's path that no real punishment had ever been required of his God-fearing parents. Although the New Life Global Ministry didn't require its ministers to swear a vow of chastity, he had imposed that grim restriction on himself, for fear that once he tasted pleasures of the flesh there would be no turning back.

Temptation gnawed at him with jagged rodent's teeth, and when the village women—some of them no more than budding adolescents—smiled at him in passing, Rafferty imagined that they would surrender to his touch, responding with a heathen ardor that would match his own.

That way lay madness—and disease, of course. Throughout the range of sub-Saharan Africa, venereal disease was epidemic, with AIDS ranked among the leading causes of natural death. That fact didn't surprise Rafferty, nor did it unduly alarm him. It reaffirmed his lifelong belief that death was the wages of sin.

And the fear of disease helped him, too.

There were days—and more often nights—when only fear of pustulating sores, the shame they carried with them, or the dread of bitter, wasting death kept Rafferty from yielding to temptations of the flesh. Sometimes he'd huddle on his cot and pray for strength to vanquish lust, his hands clenched beneath his chin to keep them from soothing the ache in his loins.

It nearly always worked, and on the rare occasions when prayer failed him, Rafferty was always eager to repent.

By day, he lost himself in work. There was a great deal more to saving souls in Africa than simply preaching Sunday sermons and arguing with native girls about the need to wear a blouse. God's house was constantly in need of maintenance, a silent victim to the jungle rot that was a bane of living in the tropics. Insects and mildew were relentless enemies, attacking everything from lumber to fabric and the printed pages of God's holy word.

Rafferty knew that he couldn't defeat the elements, but neither would he yield before them. He was obviously meant to struggle in this heathen land, whether contending with temptations of the flesh or battling termites in the rafters. He wouldn't surrender, even when it seemed that all his efforts, all his sacrifices, were in vain.

This morning after his devotions Rafferty had fetched his bucket for the short walk to the river, where he would retrieve the water he required for tea. It was the only stimulant that Rafferty allowed himself: two cups each morning, two more in the hour or so before he went to bed.

He saw the body as he reached the river bank.

The man was floating on his back, arms spread, making no effort to propel himself along. Something about his form, its stillness, told the minister that he was either dead or gravely injured.

Checking up and down the river bank for lurking crocodiles, spying none, Rafferty waded out to intercept the floater, dog-paddling the last few yards when the bottom fell away beneath his feet. Unthinking, he threw one slender arm around the stranger's neck, as they had taught him in lifesaving class long years ago, and tugged him back to shore.

Only when he had beached the man and started to examine him did Rafferty make out the lesions that marked the dead man's face and throat. It seemed almost as if he had exploded from within, his blood staining Rafferty's white shirt and sunburned arms.

"Oh, God!" The preacher plunged his crimsoned hands into the river, scrubbing frantically. "Oh, Jesus! Jesus Christ!"

1

"We're almost there. Are you absolutely sure this trip is necessary?"

Seated to the pilot's left, well clear of the controls, Mack Bolan flashed a smile. "I'm sure."

"I don't like HALO jumps on principle," the pilot, Jack Grimaldi, said, "We're clear on that?"

"We're clear," Bolan confirmed.

For all his experience with airborne warfare, as a member of the U.S. Army Special Forces and beyond, Bolan was no great fan of high-altitude, low-opening parachute jumps. The method had been pioneered for combat drops, letting paratroopers bail out at an altitude where they would be invisible to watchers on the ground, free-falling for thousands of feet, then snapping their special chutes open at the last moment, minimizing observation time as they came down on target.

Hopefully.

Parachute jumping was risky, with the potential for equipment failure that could send a jumper screaming into fatal impact with the earth, winds that could carry whole platoons a mile or more off target, unseen obstacles like swamps and jagged boulders, lakes and rivers, forests and high-voltage lines. With HALO drops, reaction time once the rip cord was pulled was reduced to seconds. HALO jumpers either got it right or paid the price.

The good news, Bolan thought, is that there won't be any power lines down there. It made him smile again.

"What's funny?" Grimaldi asked.

"Nothing," Bolan replied.

"You're damned right." Grimaldi had been unhappy with the drop since he was briefed on Bolan's plan, angered that he couldn't offer an alternative. "You realize that with these clouds, you won't see anything until you're damn near treetop level?"

That was an exaggeration, but he got the point. "Are we off course?" the man known as the Executioner inquired.

"Hell, no! I checked the instruments myself before we left Kitale."

"Then we're fine."

"Correction, pal. *I'm* fine. I know exactly where I am, and I'll be staying in the airplane when it turns around to head for home. You, on the other hand—"

"Had better get my tail in gear," Bolan replied, cutting off Grimaldi.

The aircraft was a twin-engine Cessna 402C. It cruised contentedly around twelve thousand feet, above a solid floor of murky-looking clouds, and Grimaldi held it near the top-end speed of some 200 miles per hour. He would slow a bit when it was time for Bolan to unload, then throttle up again and point the Cessna eastward, back to Kenya.

Leaving Bolan to his assignment.

The combat and survival gear he wore weighed close to eighty pounds, not counting the parachutes strapped to his back and chest. His lead weapon, a compact Steyr AUG assault rifle, accounted for eight pounds of that load with a 30-round box magazine in place. His side arm was an old friend, the Beretta Model 92, with fifteen 9 mm Parabellum rounds in its magazine and one in the chamber. He carried two knives: a nineteen-inch machete for jungle clearance, and a Ka-bar for the close-up work that ranged from killing men to cleaning fish. The rest of his burden was a mixed bag, including a GPS direction finder, a compact transmitter with collapsible dish antenna for satellite uplinks, night-vision goggles, two canteens, a first-aid kit, spare magazines for both weapons, high-explosive rifle grenades for the AUG, fragmentation and incendiary hand grenades, a block of C-4 plastic explosive with timers, a poncho, field rations and a spare set of fatigues.

The Executioner had come prepared for damn near anything—and still he knew that something else could well be waiting for him underneath that bank of brooding clouds.

The flight from Kitale, Kenya, across the Ugandan frontier into Karamoja Province, had taken just over an hour with the Cessna cruising near top speed. An hour back, and Grimaldi would doubtless use the time to worry helplessly about his friend.

"What should I tell the man?" the pilot asked, as Bolan rose and shifted toward the Cessna's passenger compartment.

Bolan frowned. The man was Hal Brognola, the director of the Justice Department's Sensitive Operations Group. He was waiting back in Washington for periodic updates on the progress of the mission.

"Tell him insertion was accomplished by the numbers," Bolan said. "Beyond that, nothing. I'll check in as circumstances and satellite availability allow."

"He won't like that," Grimaldi responded.

"They don't have phone booths where I'm going," Bolan said. "I got the gear from Stony Man Farm, and Hal knows what it's for."

"I didn't say he wouldn't understand it, Sarge. I just hate to piss him off."

Grimaldi seemed to have another retort on the tip of his tongue, but he thought better of it and kept quiet. Bolan slapped his old friend on the shoulder and moved back along the central aisle to reach the Cessna's door on the port side.

"It's time for oxygen," he called back to Grimaldi, as he stood before the door.

His own tank, good for half an hour, was fastened horizontally across the top of the reserve chute strapped to Bolan's chest. In theory, it wasn't supposed to crack him underneath the chin on touchdown, but it could break his jaw or snap his neck. The rubber mask that covered Bolan's mouth and nose was held in place by an elastic band, as were the goggles worn to keep his eyes from being frozen shut or scorched by rushing wind. The canned air tasted stale, but still gave him the tingling prelude to a rush.

Bolan confirmed that Grimaldi had donned his mask, then cranked the door open and slid it aside. A sudden drop in temperature reminded Bolan why he wore long thermal underwear beneath his camouflage fatigues. The Cessna's engine noise was suddenly, almost violently amplified, as if Bolan were trapped in a chamber with wraparound speakers all belching the racket full-blast. The first shock of in-rushing air staggered Bolan, but he kept his footing and leaned into it, advancing toward the darkness.

Grimaldi had slowed the Cessna to about 150 miles per hour for the jump. Once Bolan bailed, Grimaldi would engage the automatic pilot, come back long enough to shut the door and then resume his flight back to Kitale. It would eat away at the pilot until he heard that Bolan was alive and well, but there had been no other way to do the job.

No other way to find the human target hiding down there, somewhere in the jungle, underneath the clouds.

Bolan launched himself headfirst into the void, arms flush against his sides until the Cessna's slipstream caught him in its grip and swept him clear of any chance collision with the plane. The wind tore at him like a wild thing armed with talons, rattling Bolan's skeleton and threatening to spin him like a scrap of paper in a cyclone.

Bolan spread his arms, hands cupped, to keep his equilibrium. The rush of free fall held no terrors for him, after all his practice runs and combat jumps, but he would readily admit to some concern about the cloud cover. It shielded him from earthbound watchers, while it lasted, but he had no way of knowing when—or if—the clouds would break and let him see the jungle canopy below. The largest of the trees might stand two hundred feet above the forest floor, although one-third of that imposing height was typically composed of leaves and slender branches that could flay a hurtling body without doing much to slow it.

The soldier brought both hands together in front of his face, thumbing a button to illuminate the altimeter on his right wrist. He had already dropped six hundred feet. Four hundred more would plunge him into clinging mist, enveloped by the clouds.

He spread his arms again and watched the smoky billows rushing up to meet him. So vast were they, spreading out as far as he could see in all directions, that they scarcely seemed to move. Repeated weather checks had reassured him that there were no thunderstorms in the vicinity, so he wouldn't be flash-fried by a bolt of lightning in midair before he had a chance to face the perils waiting for him on the ground.

He burst into the cloud bank at eleven thousand feet. There was no buoyancy, as rookie sky divers sometimes expected. Rather, it was like free-falling through a smoke screen, but with icy condensation droplets peppering his face, splashing his clothes and soaking through. It might be seventy degrees below him, underneath the jungle canopy, but there was never any heat up among the clouds.

The good news: In his thermal underwear and gloves, with the velocity of his descent, there was no reason to believe that hypothermia would cripple him before he pulled the rip cord and began his hazardous descent into the rain forest.

He used the next six thousand feet, while dropping blindly through the cloud layer, to recite some of the perils waiting for him, if he made it to the forest floor intact. Leopards. Wart-hogs. Crocodiles. Pythons—which probably couldn't devour a man, though that wouldn't prevent a good-sized specimen from crushing him to death if given half a chance. Green and black mambas. An assortment of cobras and vipers. Various scorpions, spiders and disease-bearing insects.

The usual.

On top of Mother Nature's booby traps, toss in the dual threats of government military patrols and marauding guerrillas, either of which might fire at will on strangers—especially white strangers—found trespassing on their turf.

If he survived all that, perhaps he could touch base with Brognola and put his old friend's mind at ease before he started on the next leg of his journey.

Either way, the trek could only end in death. Hopefully not his.

He punched out of the cloud bank at five thousand feet and counting. He saw the jungle spread below him like a carpet, nearly jet black on this night without a moon. It had a soft look to it, almost welcoming. Who would have guessed that it was waiting for an opportunity to lacerate his flesh and shatter Bolan's bones before the predators came out to feast on his remains?

He felt an urge to yank the rip cord, but restrained himself. Not yet. His HALO chute had been designed to take the impact—barely—at six hundred feet or so. Allowing for the giant trees below him, jutting skyward like an endless field of punji stakes, Bolan had to time the deployment precisely.

Another glance at the altimeter.

His ears were full of rushing thunder as he hurtled toward the unforgiving earth.

OMARI NYASORE WASN'T afraid of heights. From childhood, he had loved to climb the jungle trees and scamper through their branches like a monkey. When he fell from time to time, as every climber must, he took the pain and the laughter of his friends in stride. The falling didn't frighten him. If anything, it made him crave heights all the more.

Nyasore was afraid of snakes, however. In his seventh year, a baby mamba's bite had nearly killed him, and he still had vicious headaches every other month or so, which he attributed, without the benefit of medical opinion, to the mamba. Although he had been forced to leave his FNC assault rifle behind to make the climb, Nyasore carried two long knives to deal with any of the several serpent species that lived out their whole lives fifty feet or more above the forest floor.

So far he had seen nothing but a hairy-legged tarantula,

which he had skewered with a blade and flicked away, smiling as he imagined what would happen down below if it should land on someone's head.

Eleven men waited 150 feet below him, killing time. They had been waiting close to ninety minutes, and they wouldn't relax their vigil until Nyasore spied their quarry or the dawn arrived to tell them they had failed. So far, the walkie-talkie clipped onto Nyasore's belt had been deadweight, crackling periodically with demands to know if he were still awake.

And if he was watching for a soldier from the sky.

The mahogany's massive trunk was bare of branches for the first hundred feet or so. Climbing would have been extremely difficult, except for the ropelike lianas that hugged the bark on every side, anchored with thousands of tendrils far above, in the canopy. Barefoot, climbing hand over hand, Nyasore had made good time on his ascent, settling himself on a solid perch fifteen minutes after he left his friends behind. He kept a slender liana looped around his waist in case he lost his balance and began to fall.

But he wasn't the least bit sleepy on his roost, so far above the forest floor. He loved the altitude, the cool breeze on his face that those below him couldn't feel, the calls of night birds and the jerky fluttering of bats.

More to the point, he was excited by their mission.

By their quest.

It was routine for them to rove in search of government patrols, lay mines and booby traps, snipe at policemen in the rural villages, but this was different. For one thing, they were told the man they hunted would be white, a European or American. And he wouldn't be riding in a convoy from Kampala, staring through binoculars at the countryside he traveled.

He would be dropping from the clouds.

One man, plunging to earth in darkness. They could never find him, waiting on the ground, because the territory was too vast and giant trees obscured all but the smallest fragments of the sky above. The quarry might be dressed in black to take advantage of the night, it was explained. His parachute would probably be black, as well. Perhaps invisible.

Nyasore had been selected as the eyes of the Allied Democratic Forces patrol because he knew the canopy, he felt at home there, and his vision was acute. Time after time, he was the first among his ADF comrades to detect a trip wire or a footprint, first to see one of the hated snakes coiled up and poised to strike beside a game trail.

Ninety minutes now, and he had nothing to show for his vigil but a stiffness in his lower back and chafing where his buttocks met the branch that was his resting place. At one point, not too long ago, he had believed he heard the muted sound of airplane engines somewhere far above the clouds, but that meant nothing. Day and night, aircraft flew back and forth across the sky, pilots and passengers no more aware of what went on beneath the jungle canopy than crewmen on an ocean liner knew what crept or glided along the bottom of the sea.

A soldier from the sky.

Nyasore hadn't asked his leaders how they knew that such a man was coming, much less the vicinity in which he would descend. Such things weren't for common soldiers to debate, and insubordination carried rigid penalties within the ADF. Officers knew best, and orders were obeyed without question.

Which brought Nyasore to his aerie in the jungle canopy, watching the dark sky for any hint of a plummeting figure, a parachute—anything that might give the search a more precise direction.

His position let him scan 180 degrees of the horizon without shifting from his perch. An awkward turn that put cramps in his neck muscles would let him see another ten degrees on either side. The rest was blocked by trunk and limbs, unless he worked his way around the tree, perpetually circling like a spider spinning web, but Nyasore had quickly rejected that plan. Aside from multiplying the risk of accident, frequent movement would be detrimental to his observation. There would always be a pillar of mahogany between Nyasore and approximately half the forest. As he made his cautious way from branch to branch, he would be forced to concentrate on hand- and footholds rather than the sky he was assigned to watch.

So he sat still and cranked his head around to left or right from time to time. If someone fell to earth behind him, maybe miles away, who would suggest that he had failed to do his duty to the best of his ability?

He almost missed the swooping shadow, even so.

A flicker of dark movement at the corner of one eye caused him to whip his head around with suddenness that drove a white-hot lance into the left side of his neck. Nyasore grimaced, but he kept his eyes open.

What was it? Where was—

There!

He had a good feel for perspective, even in the darkness. Closer in, it might have been a fruit bat or an eagle hunting for a midnight snack. Farther away, it could have been the legendary dragon, Kongamato, which his ancestors believed was prone to dine on native fishermen and children.

No.

This was a parachute. He saw the boxy cut of it, rectangular in shape before it bellied with a scoop of wind inside. Beneath it, drifting and manipulating guidelines, was a human figure.

Nyasore took the walkie-talkie from his belt and keyed the switch to let him speak. "I have him," he announced.

"You're sure?" A hint of doubt in the lieutenant's voice.

"Yes, sir."

"Which way from here? How far?"

Nyasore made a rapid calculation. "South by southwest," he replied. "Perhaps two kilometers. If I stay here and watch him land—"

A squawk of static overrode Nyasore's voice. "No time for that," the lieutenant said. "We are leaving now, as soon as you come down. Hurry!"

Climbing down a tree was sometimes harder than ascending, if the tangled branches served as ladder rungs, but the lianas made it simpler on a great tree such as this. Nyasore's palms and soles were thick with calluses, permitting him to slide for ten or fifteen feet along his vine of preference, with only minor damage to his knuckles from the bark, before he caught himself, then poised and slid again.

The troops were clearly restless when he reached the ground, milling about and double-checking weapons without need. Rifles were always loaded, unless they were being cleaned. Knives were kept razor-sharp, since dull blades in the jungle were no blades at all.

Nyasore's rifle stood between two giant buttress roots of the mahogany, beside his boots. He sat and pulled on the boots, quickly laced them and grabbed a dangling liana to haul himself upright. The rifle felt good in his hands, a solid, re-assuring weight.

"This way?" The squad's commander wanted to confirm it, pointing through the trees.

"Yes, sir."

They set off in the darkness, hunters long accustomed with the jungle, stalking unfamiliar prey. Nyasore had seen white men, of course, but he had never faced one in battle. Who among his comrades had?

He wondered who this soldier from the sky might be, what brought him here and why he thought it worth the risk. Most Europeans and Americans ignored the wars and plagues of Africa. Soldiers might be dispatched from time to time when there was oil or gold involved, but Nyasore's homeland had little of either. Foreign investors in coffee, tea and cotton kept to their banks and offices and fine homes in Kampala. Tourists anxious for a glimpse of native wildlife traveled under guard and seldom penetrated Karamoja Province.

This man dropping from the sky on silent wings was something else.

It shamed Nyasore that despite the jungle's warmth, he felt a sudden chill of fear.

TOUCHDOWN AT NIGHT on unfamiliar forested terrain is the second most dangerous landing a parachutist can make, after hostile gun emplacements in broad daylight. Snowy moun-

tain crags and shark-infested seas are more forgiving, in their
way, than massive trees with their chaotic branches that can
snag a chute or snap a spine with equal ease, while wicked
thorns and bark like sandpaper draw blood to summon predators.

Some jumpers into jungle never make it past the topmost
canopy, unconscious from the impact of their landing or hung
up in lines they dare not cut, for fear of plummeting a hundred feet or more without a net. Others are broken in the fall,
clotheslined by limbs, battered about like pinballs as they
drop. A handful are impaled. Some lose their chutes entirely
in the canopy and tumble shrieking to the earth.

The broken men, if they are lucky, will be dead before the
ants or wild dogs find them and devour them alive. Or worse,
before their human enemies arrive and introduce them to the
tortures men reserve for one another, after they are "civilized."

Bolan was lucky on the drop, as such things went. He
pierced the jungle canopy and plunged another seventy or
eighty feet before his chute got snagged and jerked him to a
halt, thumping his back against a massive tree trunk. Cush-
ioned somewhat by his gear and padded harness, Bolan took
a moment to relax and get his bearings, testing arms and legs
to reassure himself that nothing vital had been broken,
sprained or dislocated.

All okay.

He pushed off with one foot, twirled ninety degrees on the
line, until his left shoulder was braced against the trunk. It was
impossible to miss the hanging lianas, some as thick as hawser
lines, others as fat as well-fed pythons. Bolan chose one, grip-
ping it in both hands, snugging it around one leg before climbing six or seven feet to put slack in the parachute lines and let
the vine take his full weight.

It was solid.

Bolan didn't have to ask if his descent rope reached the forest floor. Liana vines were climbers. Unless severed by some

outside force, they always trailed to earth. Before he made his final move, the soldier unsnapped a padded pouch that held his night-vision goggles and tugged the device over his head. The flip of a switch, and the world went green. It was surrealistic, but at least he had a better chance of picking out the details and potential dangers that surrounded him.

Slipping the vine across his back and underneath one thigh like a rappelling line, Bolan gripped it in his left hand while his right attacked the quick-release buckles of his parachute harness, shrugging out of it in seconds. Normally, if he had landed on the ground, Bolan would have paused to bury or conceal the chute. As it was, suspended twenty yards above the forest floor, he left it to the apes and roosting birds.

Bolan descended cautiously, trying to minimize the sound of boots scraping bark, still conscious of the fact that time was slipping through his fingers. He scanned the forest floor that now seemed lit by green lights from above. A living emerald moved across the field of Bolan's vision and he focused on it, making out some kind of rodent on its nightly rounds. There was no signature denoting body heat for any man-sized predators as he completed his descent and stepped clear of the clinging vine.

But there was someone on the way.

He couldn't see the hunters yet, but Bolan heard them coming, working more or less toward his position from the northeast. Someone was hacking brush with a machete, taking no great pains to cover the approach. Speed counted more than stealth apparently, and unless it was a troop of villagers out hunting forest hogs, Bolan suspected that the searchers had to be after him.

Someone had seen the drop.

Dammit!

A quick glance at his watch and at the compact global positioning satellite monitor told Bolan he had fifty minutes in which to reach his scheduled rendezvous, three-quarters of a mile due west. Evading hot pursuit would make it dicey, and he didn't care for the idea of bringing heat down on his contact before they even met. Still, there was no alternative.

He had to move.

There was a risk in heading westward, since it brought him closer to the midnight hunting party, but evasive tactics in the present circumstances were an even greater risk. If Bolan missed the rendezvous, he would be short one crucial contact and his mission could be scuttled on the launching pad. Uganda's official language was English, granted, but he harbored no illusions about completing his journey unaided.

Another risk was simply getting lost on unfamiliar ground. The GPS could tell him where he was, in terms of latitude and longitude, but that was little consolation in the middle of trackless jungle wholly new to him, with hunters following his every move. Location was one thing: The GPS could tell him almost to the yard how far he was from any town or village on the map, but it couldn't forewarn him if a cliff or quicksand lay across his path. Or if other hunting parties were converging in a move to cut him off.

West, then, to meet his contact, if that still remained an option. He would turn and fight if necessary, but perhaps he could evade the trackers if they fixed on the location of his drop and didn't know in which direction he was traveling.

The goggles helped, in terms of spotting roots and branches, vines and fallen trees that might have snagged a foot or otherwise delayed him. Bolan traveled without using his machete, saving it in case he hit a patch of jungle where he couldn't shoulder through or wriggle underneath. The less noise he made now, the fewer trees or bushes that he marked in passing, the better his chance of eluding pursuit.

Or so he thought.

Bolan had covered no more than one hundred yards when he realized that the hunters had changed course. They were closer now, by the sound of their progress, moving on an interception course. He couldn't plot their track precisely, but Bolan trusted his senses to tell him when danger was nearby. If he continued on his present course and speed, he estimated contact with the unknown stalkers somewhere within the next two hundred yards. The night-vision glasses could give him an edge, assuming that the trackers weren't similarly equipped, but they could also hamper him if it came down to fighting. Muzzle-flashes or explosions would be amplified on infrared, resulting in a short-term blindness that could get him killed.

Change course. Speed up.

It didn't have to be a drastic change. Indeed, it couldn't be if he meant to arrive on schedule at the rendezvous. But if he had a chance to miss the hunting party, even by a matter of yards—lie silent in the weeds and watch them pass him by—it could be worth the risk.

Contact would slow him down a great deal more, assuming that he ever reached the rendezvous at all.

Bolan veered northward and picked up his pace. He kept a firm grip on the Steyr AUG and thumbed off the rifle's safety. If he couldn't avoid hard contact with the trackers, he would do his best to stop them cold, with minimal delay.

Five minutes gone, and Bolan noted that the sounds of pursuit seemed closer rather than farther away. Had he underestimated the number of trackers? Had the hunting party split to try a pincers movement? Was he being driven headlong into an ambush?

The question was answered when two green-limned figures suddenly appeared in front of Bolan, resembling Hollywood aliens in the light of his infrared goggles. Both carried automatic rifles, but only one of them swung his weapon toward Bolan, leveling the muzzle.

The soldier didn't wait for him to fire, stroking a short burst from the AUG that sent the shooter spinning out of frame. His sidekick dived for cover in the shadow of a looming tree.

Bolan followed his example, waiting for the jungle to explode with incoming fire. Instead, what he heard was a man's angry voice, barking commands in English. "Hold your fire!" it ordered, echoing among the trees. "Cease fire!"

Bolan couldn't have said to whom the order was addressed,

and while he didn't let his opposition dictate battle tactics, this was strange enough to make him hesitate, his left hand resting on the smooth girth of a frag grenade.

"Hello, my friend!" the stranger called out through the darkness. "Don't shoot me, please!"

A glance around the roots that sheltered him showed Bolan an advancing figure, male and seemingly alone. The man wore camouflage fatigues and high-topped boots, an OD cap atop his head. He kept his rifle slung across one shoulder, muzzle pointed toward the ground, and there appeared to be no other weapon in his hands.

"Before we kill each other," he continued, drawing nearer, "may I introduce myself? I am Gabra Ezana, a lieutenant of the Allied Democratic Forces. And you, I think, were sent from the United States to help us solve a problem of some mutual concern."

2

Six days before Mack Bolan made his HALO drop into the humid heart of Africa, Hal Brognola set out from his Arlington, Virginia, home on a cool, misty Saturday morning. He had a ninety-minute drive ahead of him to reach his destination in rural Nelson County, and he took no chances with the traffic that might slow him. He made good time and watched his back, pausing for coffee twice along the way to reassure himself that he hadn't been tailed.

His getaway had been a hunting cabin, once upon a time, but the big Fed had hunted men for most of his adult life, and he took no pleasure in the "sport" of stalking helpless creatures.

The cabin had been built sometime between V-J Day and the outbreak of hostilities in South Korea. It was old, yet built to last, with stout log walls to keep the winter chill outside— or soak up automatic weapons fire, in case the heat was on. It hadn't come to that so far, and Brognola hoped that it never would...but he was ready, just in case.

Brognola wore the standard-issue federal agent's Smith & Wesson Model 4006 semiauto pistol on his right hip, in a thumb-break holster, with two spare magazines of .40-caliber rounds snug in the small of his back. Behind the driver's seat, stowed in a duffel bag, were an Ithaca 12-gauge riot gun, loaded with an 8-round alternating mix of deer slugs and double-aught buckshot, and a Ruger AC-556, a military version of the classic Mini-14 rifle with an eighteen and a half inch barrel and a folding stock.

Brognola's cabin was located on a private parcel of land in the midst of the Washington national forest, purchased years before on a whim and cherished ever since as a personal island of solitude. Brognola's wife had been there half a dozen times, but she was wise enough to know when her man needed private time, and as the only secrets kept between them were official ones, she offered no objections on the five or six weekends a year when the head Fed took off alone to find some space.

This morning, though, he wouldn't be alone. A visitor was coming, hopefully to help him deal with a disturbing, unexpected problem that had landed on his desk two days before.

Brognola kept a sharp eye on the rearview mirror as he left the highway, picking up the access road that would eventually dead-end at his cabin. Anyone who turned up on his bumper was suspect, unless he or she was wearing a park ranger's uniform. Trying to shake a tail at this point would be hopeless. On the other hand, intruders who checked into Brognola's private domain might not check out again.

The cabin was located forty miles southwest of the ultracovert Stony Man Farm and predated the establishment of Brognola's Sensitive Operations headquarters by a decade. If anything, the cabin and its solitude had given him the notion of a more secure, disguised facility on federal land, complete with all the bells and whistles in defensive preparations and communications gear.

He could have held this morning's meeting at the Farm, but the big Fed had sought more privacy. Selected members of the Stony Man contingent were conversant with the problem, naturally, and they would monitor the mission's progress day by day—assuming it proceeded—but he didn't want to make the pitch before an audience in the Stony Man War Room.

This one was personal, to an extent that he couldn't recall

in more than one or two preceding missions, and he thought the briefing should be handled one-on-one.

From one friend to another.

How else could he ask Mack Bolan to assassinate a fellow warrior, one to whom Bolan literally owed his life?

Brognola had no tail as he approached the cabin. Even so, he drove around in back and parked his Chevy Blazer where it wouldn't be immediately visible to anyone approaching on the access road. Bolan would know that he was there and waiting. Any trespassers could do with a surprise.

He took the duffel bag of weapons and a briefcase with him when he went inside, pausing to lock the Blazer. Just in case.

He checked the propane stove, then fired it up, put coffee on and settled back to wait. An hour and change remained before the Executioner was scheduled to arrive, and Brognola had planned it that way. Even after two full days of chewing on the problem, he wasn't convinced that he had found the right approach to win Bolan's cooperation.

Brognola had never asked Bolan to kill a treasured comrade from his Special Forces days. If he decided not to take the mission...

Brognola poured himself a mug of coffee and sat back to drink it black. What would *he* do if the positions were reversed? Could he have dropped the hammer on Agent Terry O'Reilley, who had saved his bacon from desperate bank robbers during his first year as an FBI agent?

Damn right, if the stakes were high enough.

And this time, they were through the roof.

The coffee needed something, a little kick, but the big Fed resisted the urge to spike it from the bottle of Bushmills Black Label he kept in the cabin as an occasional sleep aid.

He wanted a clear head, no lingering tang of alcohol on his breath when he pitched the mission to Bolan. It was wild enough already, without tempting Bolan to ask if the details had come from a shot glass.

Brognola felt an urge to check his watch but stopped

himself. Bolan was punctual to a fault. If his progress had been stalled for any reason, he could reach the head Fed on the cell phone.

The rest of it should be so simple.

There were alternatives if Bolan turned him down. Brognola didn't want to think about them at this juncture. He had come up through the Bureau ranks believing that defeatist thinking jeopardized performance, and while he couldn't exactly *will* the Executioner to fly halfway around the world to waste a lifelong friend, at least he had to sell the notion with a positive outlook.

Brognola laughed aloud at that, mocking himself.

There was nothing positive about the damned situation from start to finish, nothing in his plan or its diverse potential outcomes that could be described as uplifting or rewarding.

Nothing except the chance to head off an epic disaster in the making.

Brognola heard a vehicle approaching on the access road. He drained his coffee mug, rose from his chair and moved to watch his yard from the nearest window. Even with the coffee warm inside him, he could feel a chill race down his spine.

BOLAN HAD DRIVEN UP to Hal Brognola's cabin before. That last trip was strictly R & R, unlike the present case, but Bolan felt no pressing sense of apprehension as he turned his rented Ford Explorer onto gravel that could charitably be described as one lane with a dash of wiggle room.

He took his time, sparing the rental vehicle's paint job and enjoying how the sunlight slanted down through trees no logging company would ever touch. It was a day to relish for the very fact that he was still alive to see it, feel the sun's warmth on his face and smell the tang of pine trees in the air. Something he learned from his friend within the next half hour might send him off to risk his life for strangers, but this peaceful moment had already been indelibly recorded in his memory.

Like Brognola before him, Bolan had been cautious on his

morning drive. He had flown into Richmond on Friday night, picked up the SUV rented under a pseudonym with valid plastic to support it and crashed for the night at a generic suburban motel. Before sunup that morning he had risen, showered, packed his hardware and consumed the largest breakfast offered at a local Denny's. Hot food was a luxury to soldiers on the line, and since the Executioner was always in a state of combat readiness, he never knew when he might have to do without.

Driving past towns that dwindled in direct relation to their distance from Virginia's capital, Bolan kept up his guard and took nothing for granted. No one in the state was looking for him, as far as he knew, and the odds against a chance encounter with a rare surviving enemy who knew his face were astronomical, but Bolan stayed alive by planning for the unexpected, running down oblique alternatives and long shots to their logical conclusion.

He hadn't been followed from the airport the past night, or from the motel that morning. There was always a billions-to-one chance that someone had planted a homing device on the Ford, but Bolan placed no credit in it and he had no tools or time to strip the vehicle, in any case. If hostiles were intent on tracking him, he would confront them with the weapons that he carried and the skills he had acquired in a lifetime of mortal combat against killer odds.

The Executioner wouldn't go quietly, and he wouldn't go down alone.

He stopped once on the gravel track and let his dust plume settle, showing him a hundred yards of empty road in the rearview mirror, before he eased off the Explorer's brake and drove on to Brognola's cabin. He drove past the cabin, rolled by the porch and small front windows to let Brognola make visual ID and parked on the north side, where his Explorer wouldn't block their field of fire spanning the access road.

Precautions.

The big Fed came out to greet him on the porch as Bolan

locked and left his vehicle. His old friend's handshake was solid, firm, but there was something in his eyes that the soldier didn't like. Concern? Worry? Brognola was levelheaded, not the kind to blanch at any problem, but his voice was somber as they moved inside.

"You made good time," he said.

"I caught a break on traffic."

"Coffee?"

"Please."

They sat across from each other at a redwood table, stubby benches in the place of chairs. Between them, a manila file had been positioned squarely in the center of the table. It was tied with twine, two inches fat with documents and photographs. Its cover had been stenciled with the letters *EHF*.

Uncomfortable silence stretched between them for a moment until Bolan pitched the icebreaker. "I'm wondering," he said, "what's so important or so secret that we need to talk about it here instead of meeting at the Farm."

"I haven't cut the team out of it," Brognola replied, "but it occurred to me you'd rather hear about this privately. In case you want to turn it down."

The frown on Brognola's face said there was a chance he thought Bolan would do exactly that. It was a fact that Bolan had insisted on free agency when he agreed to work with the big Fed and his support team at the Farm. He could decline missions at will, and he was free to move on targets he selected for himself without consulting Brognola or any of the others in advance. And while he had pursued the freelance route on several campaigns, Bolan couldn't recall an instance where he had rejected any task Brognola viewed as critical.

Because the man was nearly always right.

"Let's hear about it," Bolan said. He took another sip of coffee, waiting.

Brognola leaned forward on his elbows, folding his big hands on top of the file. "We have a situation in Uganda," he began. "Maybe you heard about it on the news? Recurring outbreaks of Ebola hemorrhagic fever?"

EHF.

The label on the file now made sense. Bolan felt a shifting of the short hairs on his nape.

"Ebola."

Brognola nodded and stated, "We both know how bad it can get."

"Yeah. It's a virus, often fatal, with no known cure. There was talk of a vaccine last year, but it's still in the testing stage."

The big Fed tapped the folder with an index finger. "We have reason to believe the outbreaks in Uganda are deliberate, a piece of military strategy."

"Germ warfare?"

"In a nutshell," Brognola said, "with emphasis on the *nut.*"

"You've lost me."

"According to the information I've received—" he tapped the file again for emphasis "—we have a wild card operating in Uganda who was once a highly decorated Green Beret."

A niggling worm of apprehension twitched in the soldier's gut. A former Green Beret. Brognola's cabin. Unaccustomed privacy.

"Someone I know?" he asked.

"You served with him," Brognola said, "if I recall correctly. Galen Arthur Starke."

THE NAME CALLED UP disjointed images of paddies and jungle, beer and laughter, life and death in a demented atmosphere where it was often difficult to tell your friends and enemies apart. It was a challenge just to stay alive. Winning, as confirmed by history, was out of the question.

Bolan and Starke had been assigned to different A-teams, thrown together in defense of a "strategic hamlet" whose name never rated so much as a footnote in official histories of Bolan's first war. Thirty Americans and some 250 native allies held the line against three thousand enemies with full artillery support, fighting through a monsoon that grounded supply choppers and made air support hit-or-miss, when it got through at all. Seven days and nights of hell on earth until Mother Nature relented and gave the F-14 Phantoms blue skies to dive from, turning five square miles of jungle into a smoking charnel house.

Inside the hamlet—no longer strategic, unless blasted ruins had some value to the war effort—nine Americans and eighty-six native troopers survived, nearly all of them wounded. Bolan and Starke, somehow unscathed except for minor cuts and bruises, drew a long weekend of R & R behind the lines and spent most of that time together, strangers transformed into friends by their baptism of fire. Their triumph in the field turned out to be a Pyrrhic victory. The hamlet they had saved was subsequently razed by Army engineers, its former residents dispersed to other villages, left to make their way among strangers.

But Bolan's friendship with Starke had endured. With their old units shattered, both were reassigned to other A-teams, but they kept in touch. Communication was sporadic—all the more so when Bolan was off on long-range search-and-destroy missions, earning the "Executioner" label—but the U.S. Army Special Forces is a closed fraternity. Word gets around. Bolan kept track of Starke through the exploits of his unit, catching up on details when they met from time to time, on leave or in the forward base camps that were launching pads for Green Beret excursions into hostile territory.

He remembered Starke in those days: brash, impetuous and quick to smile, invincible in combat. A battlefield promotion to lieutenant made Starke Bolan's superior, but he was never the kind to pull rank. Instead he pulled his own weight with the best of them, and near the end of his second tour, after another brutal action in the bush, word filtered through the ranks that Starke had been nominated for America's highest military decoration, the Congressional Medal of Honor.

Two days later, Bolan had been summoned home to find

his life in ruins, his parents and younger sister dead, while his brother Johnny lingered in intensive care. It was a new and unexpected war for Bolan, facing unfamiliar enemies, and he had plunged into the bloody heart of it with everything he had. He had heard nothing more of Starke since shipping home, but once, while dawdling in a bookstore on surveillance, he had spotted a massive volume listing those who had won the Medal of Honor throughout history. He scanned the index for Starke's name while waiting for his target to move on.

Nothing.

Apparently the nomination had been vetoed somewhere further up the ladder of command, perhaps even in Washington. A moment later, Bolan's mark had finished off his bagel in the bookstore's coffee shop, and it was time to go. Starke's face and name had drifted back into the past.

Until this day.

"I KNOW HIM," Bolan said and then corrected it. "*Knew* him, I mean. It's been a while."

Brognola took a pair of reading glasses from his pocket, slipped them on and opened the manila folder, thumbing quickly through the first few pages. Looking at them upside down, Bolan could see Department of the Army printed at the top of the first page. Some kind of personnel file, from the look of it.

When he was half a dozen pages deep into the file, the big Fed paused and raised his eyes. "He was a soldier's soldier."

"That he was."

"You heard about the Medal of Honor?"

"I knew he was flagged for it," Bolan replied. "Right before I came home."

"The nomination was rescinded two weeks later," Brognola went on. "According to the CID reports, he shot and killed two friendlies, one of them a full-bird colonel, at a brothel where—he claimed—they were delivering strategic secrets to the enemy."

"Were they?" Bolan asked.

Brognola shrugged. "Beats me. The stink was bad enough,

it carried all the way to Washington, but quietly. Nobody wanted an in-depth investigation, least of all the Oval Office at that time. Instead of filing charges, CID gave Starke the option to resign. They dumped him with a general discharge."

The kiss of death.

There are various kinds of discharge from military service in America, but only one that counted. If the exit paperwork said anything but honorable, it was all the same, an indelible stain that could slam doors in state or civilian employment, scuttle security clearances, and—at least in prior generations—brand the bearer of the mark as unfit for mingling in polite society. Starke would have left the service without pension or other benefits, taking only his skills when he left, effectively barred from regular enlistment with the armed forces of any friendly nation.

And that left...what?

Brognola supplied the answer, as if reading Bolan's mind. "He turned mercenary after that." More pages riffling. "We have reports of him in South America, the Middle East, Sri Lanka, East Timor. He didn't seem to care much which side he was on."

Why would he? Bolan thought, but kept it to himself. He was prepared to take for granted that the friendlies Starke had killed before his discharge were the traitors Starke alleged. Such executions had been commonplace in Bolan's war, but they were generally carried out with marginal finesse—a suicide or accident, a stray round fired in combat, where it was untraceable or could be foisted on the enemy. In any case, "low profile" and "deniability" had always been the watchwords. Starke had known that going in, but something had gone wrong.

Or had he simply snapped?

"He's now in Uganda?"

"Affirmative. He has been for at least two years apparently. His first gig was training insurgents for the Allied Democratic Forces. That's the rebel force opposed to Kampala's elected regime. From training and logistics, Starke apparently began to lead the ADF commandos on their raids, mostly hijacking military convoys. Then about a year ago it seems he had some kind of an epiphany."

The choice of terms made Bolan blink.

"What?"

"Details are few and far between, as you'd imagine," Brognola replied. "From what we hear—I'm talking CIA and DIA, primarily, a footnote here and there, from State—it would appear that Starke has found religion in the jungle. I have no idea what triggered it, but after thirteen months of coaching and direction operations for the ADF, he split with his employers and went independent. Two or three hundred hardcore ADF commandos followed him. These days, they call themselves the Lord's Vanguard and target both sides of the insurrection as their enemies. They published two or three communiqués, but that was early on. Here's one that sums up their thinking."

Brognola extracted a sheet from the file and slid it across the table to Bolan. It was a photocopy of a crudely typed announcement. The caps-lock key was stuck on someone's typewriter, and the author had a thing for exclamation points.

THE LORD'S VANGUARD ANNOUNCES ITS IN-
TENTION TO RESOLVE THE STRUGGLE IN
UGANDA AND OF SUBJECT PEOPLES ALL OVER
THE WORLD! GOD'S HOLY PATIENCE IS EX-
HAUSTED! TIME AND TIME AGAIN MAN DIS-
APPOINTS HIS MAKER! THE WAY OF SIN IS
DEATH AND EVERLASTING FIRE! MANKIND
MUST BE HUMBLE! BECAUSE MEN CANNOT
LIVE IN PEACE, PEACE WILL BE FORCED UPON
THEM WITH THE SWORD OF RIGHTEOUSNESS!
THE PLAGUES OF REVELATION ARE UPON
YOU! RECOGNIZE YOUR FAILING AND REPENT!
YOUR SECOND CHANCE IS NOW! IT IS YOUR

LAST AND ONLY CHANCE! WHO SO PROVOKES
HIS WRATH SHALL BE LEFT DESOLATE! HE IS
A JEALOUS GOD! WE TRIUMPH IN *HIS* NAME!
BEWARE THE DAY WHEN YOUR REPENTANCE
COMES TOO LATE!—L.V.

"The sign-off," Bolan said. "Lord's Vanguard?"

"Right. Fliers like that one were distributed all over
Karamoja Province, in the northeast of Uganda, when the
Vanguard set up shop. It lasted for a month or so. Since then
they seem to think actions speak louder than words."

"What's the connection to the Ebola outbreaks?" Bolan
asked.

"It's circumstantial," Brognola admitted. "First, Uganda
hasn't had a problem with the virus in recent years, although
her neighbors in the Congo and Sudan have seen their share.
That could be coincidence, of course. It starts with monkeys,
and they aren't well-known for recognizing borders. On the
other hand, the first outbreak came down within a week of the
Lord's Vanguard putting out their last communiqué, and that's
a bit too much coincidence for me."

"There's more," Bolan remarked, reading his old friend's
face.

"There is. We have reports from patients who survived the
virus in three different villages, all saying that a helicopter
made a pass at them a day or so before the virus made its
symptoms known. Kampala has admitted that the ADF has
captured some of its equipment, several whirlybirds included,
and the ADF reports that one of them went missing at the time
of Starke's defection to create the Lord's Vanguard."

"You're in communication with the rebels?"

"They reached out to us, ironically," Brognola said. "They
grabbed one of the CIA's men in Kampala and detained him
long enough to say they needed help. The Company couldn't
ignore a lure like that. Some meetings were arranged. Turns

out the ADF is trying to eliminate the Lords' Vanguard, before Starke's people go too far and start some kind of epidemic that could sweep the country."

"What's to say the ADF is playing straight on this? They could be angling for a split between Kampala and the State Department that would boost their stock in Washington."

"That's been considered," the big Fed acknowledged, "but we found out that they made their first approach directly to Kampala. What I'm told, and the reports here back it up—" he tapped the file again "—the ADF tried several times to liquidate the problem on their own, but every time they sent teams out the hunters disappeared. Kampala mounted two campaigns, with similar results. The first team got wiped out, the second found their headless bodies, but no trace of Starke or any of his people from the Lord's Vanguard. They did find something, though."

A stack of half a dozen glossy eight-by-tens changed hands. Bolan examined them. The photos showed a Spartan laboratory, walls of corrugated metal, with a thatch roof overhead. The workbench held its share of beakers, test tubes neatly racked, a butane torch and other standard implements. Something that might have been an air compressor occupied the space beneath the bench. Off to one side, dour monkeys glared at the photographer from cages fashioned out of chicken wire.

"The monkeys were infected with Ebola?"

"That's affirmative," Brognola said. "We can't tell whether they were naturally infected or deliberately injected with the virus, but they tested positive across the board. The CDC confirms it was your basic virus factory. Draw blood from the infected monkeys, get your cultures started, it goes 'round and 'round."

"And how much of the virus was recovered?"

"None," Brognola stated, "except for what was still inside the monkeys. Whatever the Vanguard had been cultivating, it was gone before the cavalry arrived."

"Where was this?" Bolan asked.

"In Karamoja Province, fifty-odd miles north of some-place called Patonga. Jungle country, rugged. You could hide an army there. Apparently Starke's done precisely that."

"While cooking up the plagues of Revelation?"

"That's the consensus."

"What about the helicopter overflights?" Bolan asked. "Ebola's spread by contact with the body fluids of infected subjects."

"Right. Aside from rural villages in Africa," Brognola said, "the worst outbreaks have been in hospitals and clinics where the hygiene leaves a lot to be desired. But the CDC and World Health Organization are nervous as hell. They're afraid some backwoods Frankenstein may have been tinkering around on Starke's behalf. We may have a mutated strain that can sur-vive on other media or even one that travels on the breeze. If that's the case, infected monkeys are superfluous. You could unleash it anywhere on Earth, at any time, and let it spread from there."

A plague of biblical proportions.

"I understand the problem," Bolan said, returning to the question that had nagged him from the moment Brognola had mentioned Galen Starke. "I don't see how I qualify as the solution."

"There's a fair degree of panic brewing in Uganda as we speak," the head Fed said. "You've got a more or less pro-gressive government in place. The ADF guerrillas don't be-lieve that national reforms are going far enough or moving fast enough, but in their way, they're patriots. Nobody profits if an epidemic decimates the population, right?"

"Why me?" Bolan repeated. "Someone in the ADF should know Starke's moves and motives, who supports him, where he can be found. I haven't seen the man in years. The person you're describing is a total stranger."

"I agree," Brognola said. "It's a long shot, and then some. I should tell you that the panic's not confined to Africa, right now. I'm hearing echoes all the way to Washington. If there's disaster brewing, broadcast live on CNN, we'd hate to see the talking heads tell everybody in the world that it was caused by a psychotic former Green Beret from Texas."

"Starke was born in Oklahoma."

"Whatever. The PR angle sucks, but it's a big part of the game these days. Perceptions matter. At the bottom line, though, if we take Starke out *before* he has a chance to play the Armageddon rag, we're covered all the way around. No epidemic, no bad press. There's even feeling in Kampala that the government might open up negotiations with the ADF if rebel leaders help eliminate the Lord's Vanguard."

"He's running rings around Ugandan troops and rebels in their own backyard. What makes you think that I can find him?" Bolan asked.

"You know how that works," Brognola replied. "An army marching through the jungle telegraphs its moves, no matter how well trained the soldiers are. Starke's men are natives too, remember. Most of them are from Karamoja Province. They have friends and family among the rural villages, a built-in early-warning system."

"Stage an air strike," Bolan said. "Pinpoint the Vanguard's headquarters and blast if off the map. If you're concerned about the virus spreading, take them out with fuel-air bombs."

"It's Starke," Brognola said. "We need an on-site confirmation that he's done. Can't have him popping up in Kenya or Sudan six months from now, to start the whole thing up again from scratch. He's legend-building every day. We can't afford a second coming."

Bolan thought about it for another moment. "I don't know the ground," he said at last.

"You'd have a guide. The ADF has somebody lined up," Brognola said. "Two men, no fuss. No warning. No comebacks."

No such luck, the soldier thought.

"When do I leave?"

3

The ADF patrol leader, Gabra Ezana, advanced cautiously. Behind him, two of his soldiers were tending to the man Bolan had wounded, while the rest were clearly on alert. None of them aimed a rifle Bolan's way, as he emerged from cover, but Ezana noticed fingers ready inside trigger guards, prepared to open fire at the first provocation.

Bolan offered none, slinging his rifle as he stepped around the tree to meet their leader. Ezana was thirty-something, an athletic-looking five foot eight or nine, with a complexion that was burnished ebony. His smile was bright and seemed sincere, despite palpable tension and a tang of cordite in the air.

There was a ritual yet to be completed. "Before we start to chat," Bolan remarked, "I need to ask the number of the beast."

"It is the number of a man," Ezana replied on cue. "Six hundred threescore and six."

Brognola had taken the coded exchange from Revelation, in deference to propaganda references from the Lord's Vanguard. Archaic as it was, the scripture had a certain resonance in the midst of the brooding rain forest, with death close at hand.

"Mike Belasko," Bolan said, introducing himself, and shook Ezana's hand. "I guess you had me spotted from the drop?"

"Indeed," the lieutenant said. "We had a late start for the

rendezvous, evading government patrols. I judged it preferable to watch and wait for your arrival, rather than risk missing you."

"Sorry about your man."

Ezana turned to find the wounded soldier sitting upright now, bare-chested, while his comrades bound a shoulder wound. The man winced, but he let no sound betray his pain.

"He will survive," Ezana stated. "It is an object lesson in obedience. My men were told to offer you no threat of any kind."

"It was still a bad start."

"We'll make a better ending," Ezana said, and flashed another brilliant smile. "My camp is six kilometers due north. We should be there in time for breakfast if we leave at once."

"Suits me," Bolan replied.

In fact, it took a few more minutes for the medics to complete their work and get the wounded soldier back in uniform. Ezana took the man aside and spoke to him in muted tones, the soldier nodding periodically to register assent. At last he followed his commander back to where Bolan stood waiting, thrusting out a callused hand with knobby fingers.

"No hurt feelings," he declared.

"Same here," Bolan replied, and shook the hand that felt like whittled wood.

They set off marching northward moments later, two scouts ranging out ahead of them a hundred yards or so, while Bolan and Ezana took the middle of the column, four men in front of them and five behind. Despite the password, Bolan couldn't altogether shake a certain feeling of discomfort, surrounded as he was by strangers, moving over unfamiliar ground, but every yard they covered put him a little more at ease.

Conversation was impractical and ill-advised while they were moving through the jungle. Bolan kept his questions to himself, biding his time. They weren't hunting Starke. Not yet. Wherever Starke might be, Bolan could only hope the prophet of the Lord's Vanguard would have no premonition of his nemesis approaching, drawing nearer by the day. It would be better if he had no clue, prepared no obstacles. Bolan didn't believe his one-time friend possessed a psychic gift, but he had martial skills that rivaled Bolan's own. Surprising Starke would be a challenge.

If Starke knew someone was coming for him, it might be impossible.

Bolan accepted the importance of his mission—he wouldn't have had Brognola summon Jack Grimaldi for the night drop otherwise—but he wasn't a wild-eyed kamikaze looking for an opportunity to sacrifice himself. He recognized that Starke had lost it and should be removed before he caused more tragedy to innocents, but Bolan also hoped to understand what had befallen his old friend and left him mad.

What turned a soldier's soldier into a demented prophet of doom? Where was the line, and if he saw it coming at him, was there any way to keep from crossing over it?

Would there by any chance for him to speak with Starke, before the end? Would it even be possible to find him, hidden in the vast up-country jungle of Uganda, with the frontiers of Sudan and Kenya close at hand?

Bolan would have to wait and see.

And if the journey was for nothing...then, what?

Wait and try again, he told himself.

It was a trait of messianic madmen that they didn't simply fold their tents and disappear. Invested with a sacred mission from on high, as they supposed, determination was their strong suit. Prison might contain them, but it wouldn't break their will. Adversity only convinced them that their cause was just, that it would triumph in the end.

Some lunatic messiahs self-destructed, taking their disciples with them. Jim Jones and the People's Temple in Guyana. Marshall Appelwhite and Heaven's Gate in California. Luc Jouret and the Order of the Solar Temple in Belgium. Dead and gone, along with the believers who had pledged them everything they had to give.

Other demented saviors, from Adolf Hitler to Iran's Ayatollah Khomeini, mobilized the faithful for crusades against outsiders, infidels, the scapegoats of the moment. Ultimately, those self-styled messiahs were destroyed as well, but whereas self-destructive cults killed dozens, sometimes hundreds, of their own, crusaders liked to share, spreading the carnage until thousands—even millions—were consumed.

All things considered, Bolan wished that Starke had picked a different sort of madness to pursue—or better yet that he had fallen on the field of battle, with his memory and honor still intact.

A pang of guilt surprised him at the thought, but Bolan shrugged it off. If Starke had died fighting his enemies, when he still wore the Green Beret with pride, there likely would have been no Lord's Vanguard, no threat of plagues sweeping the countryside. Some three hundred victims of Ebola hemorrhagic fever in Uganda might still be alive, along with untold others Starke had doubtless taken out in his career as a soldier of fortune.

How many of those had been innocents?

Where would it end?

They had been comrades in another life, shared common attitudes toward life and death, duty and honor, God and country. Both of them had suffered trauma and been separated from the service, spinning off into their private wars. Bolan's had taken him around the world, confronting predators in human form, defending innocents as he had done in uniform. Starke had pursued a different path, at first for profit, later, seemingly, in service to some grand design that Bolan couldn't grasp.

If there was time, he hoped that he could ask Starke what had happened, how they came to this.

But if he got a clean shot from a distance, that was fine.

The Executioner had work to do and promises to keep. One of those promises had been made long ago to Starke when they were fighting for their lives in that strategic hamlet, outnumbered ten-to-one. Between artillery barrages and assaults on the perimeter, they had affirmed the Special Forces vow.

Alive or dead, no comrade left behind.

In one sense, Starke had been abandoned long ago. Whether his discharge from the service was a frame-up or a whitewash when he should have gone to prison, Starke had been cut adrift. The service and the war had moved on, leaving him behind. He was as much a prisoner of war as any U.S. pilot caged inside the Hanoi Hilton, but there had been no reprieve for him, no armistice.

From half a world away, one of his comrades had been sent to make it right.

Bolan would see the mission through this time, for both of them.

But first he had to find his friend, his target. And for that, he had to put his faith in strangers, trusting them to guide him, put him on Starke's track.

The Executioner would carry it from there.

He owed Starke that much, at the very least. In fact, Bolan owed Galen Starke his life.

Given the chance, he would repay that dept with swift, clean death.

And Starke would thank him for it, if he understood.

GABRA EZANA KEPT a sharp eye on the white man as they walked together through the jungle, flanked by soldiers. He fancied himself a fair judge of character, and certain things were obvious about this stranger, even to the untrained eye.

He was a warrior with sufficient nerve and ample skills to keep himself alive in killing situations. Trim and fit, he was the tallest of their number by at least three inches. He was older than Ezana and the rest, but it was difficult to guess his age, between the darkness and the camouflage war paint that stained his face. Rash soldiers seldom lived to reach maturity, which told Ezana that the man was a survivor who could pull his weight.

He was American. Ezana would have known it from his accent, even if he didn't have the information in advance. A soldier from the States had been assigned to dispatch another soldier from America. There was a synchronicity to it that made the lieutenant smile.

For once, the white man would be cleaning up his own mess there, in Africa.

Ezana only hoped that it wasn't too late.

A night march through the jungle called for somewhat different skills than traveling the same route by daylight. Darkness multiplied the jungle's dangers for unwary passersby. A whole new set of predators and scavengers emerged from hiding at sundown to forage on the jungle floor or glide across the canopy, forever ravenous. Darkness also concealed the inert obstacles a man would automatically avoid in daylight: roots and dangling vines, burrows to snap an ankle, fallen trees, quicksand.

Ezana's soldiers didn't rush, but neither were they wasting any time. Spread out along the game trail that would take them back to camp, they held a fairly steady pace, trusting the point men to alert them one way or another if they met some danger up ahead.

Another glance at the American showed that he was keeping up the pace without apparent difficulty. After parachuting in, trying to dodge the ADF's patrol, and the mistaken clash in which he could have been gunned down, the man seemed perfectly relaxed, at ease with his companions and surroundings. That, in turn, bespoke experience in jungle fighting and survival skills.

Ezana wondered what was going on inside the white man's mind. Who was he, really?

Never mind the American's name. Ezana took for granted that it had been manufactured, maybe buttressed by such trappings as a birth certificate, a driver's license, credit cards, back in the world where those things mattered. There, in Karamoja Province, the important things were what a man could do, and whether Ezana could trust him at his back when there was killing to be done.

The lieutenant couldn't have explained it, didn't really understand it yet, but he did trust this stranger.

To a point, at least.

He trusted that the men who sent the American were concerned about the repercussions for themselves if the Lord's Vanguard was allowed to run amok, led by one of their own. He trusted that they would help him destroy the renegade, if only to protect their public image, tarnished and bedraggled as it was. Ezana trusted the Americans to serve their own self-interest and to help his people if the action also helped themselves.

As for the man who walked beside him through the darkness now, Ezana couldn't read his mind. A soldier went where he was told to go and fought the enemies who were selected for him by commanding officers or politicians. Some would do anything that they were told to do, while others drew a line and wouldn't cross it. Which kind was Belasko? Did it even matter?

The lieutenant took for granted that the white man wouldn't be there if he was opposed to liquidating Starke. Duplicity wasn't unknown in dealings with America, of course, but if the CIA or someone else in Washington desired to *help* Starke for some reason, it would be no use to send a single man. What could one soldier do to help the Lord's Vanguard?

Ezana frowned as his subconscious turned the question upside down. What could one man do to destroy the private army Starke had gathered to himself?

Cut off the head, the viper died.

For all its trappings of religion and communiqués sprinkled with scripture, the Lord's Vanguard was still a cult of personality. For reasons best known to themselves, a bloc of soldiers from the Allied Democratic Forces had defected, following the white man—an American, no less—as if he were their Moses or their Christ. That they believed in him and took his every word to heart could not be doubted. Thus far, since the rift within the ADF, not one of Starke's disciples had returned to ask for pardon or to volunteer as living eyes and ears inside the Lord's Vanguard. The wall of silence seemed impenetrable. No one leaked the Vanguard's plans ahead of time or pointed out its sympathizers in the countryside at large. Between abject devotion and the fear of grim reprisals, Starke had been secure.

Ezana wondered if the tall American beside him could dispose of Starke before Starke kept his promise of a coming plague and spread the bleeding fever throughout Karamoja Province, maybe all throughout Uganda. He was no physician, but Ezana understood enough to realize that Starke had somehow tampered with the way in which the bleeding fever spread. He could infect whole villages, advancing progress of the plague beyond its normal pace.

Tomorrow, why not Moroto or Kampala?

After that, why not Nairobi or Johannesburg? Why not Madrid or Paris, London or Los Angeles?

Distracted, Ezana stumbled on a root and nearly fell. The American caught him by one arm and hauled him back, the power in his grip surprising. Silence was the rule of march, but Ezana flashed a smile of thanks and saw the white man's teeth glint briefly in his painted face.

A strange one—and cautious, too. Ezana noted that his rifle was an Austrian design, his side arm Italian. Loss of either one along the trail wouldn't identify their owner as American. If, on the other hand, he should be killed or captured, those who had dispatched him on this mission would undoubtedly deny all knowledge of the man.

He would be on his own.

And yet, was that not true of life in general? Ezana thought that each man died alone, even when he was cut down on a busy street or crowded battlefield. Death was a personal experience that no one who remained behind, alive, could ever truly share.

Watching his step to save himself embarrassment, Ezana thought ahead to the impending journey he would take with the American. It was entirely possible that both of them would simply vanish, never to be seen again. The jungle swallowed men as if it were a hungry, living thing. Sometimes it spit them out again, pathetic living wrecks or bleached-out bones, but many others disappeared without a trace.

It was the way of nature, with a bit of help from man.

If only they could—

The explosive sound of gunfire startled the lieutenant, but he kept his wits about him, leaping off the trail in search of cover. The American got there first, a blur of motion in the darkness, crouched behind the great bole of a forest giant. Bellied down beside him, screened by ferns, Ezana peered across the sights of his assault rifle and watched for muzzle-flashes in the night.

Another burst of fire, and this one closer to them. Bullets rippled through the air and fanned the undergrowth, a yard or so above Ezana's head. Unless the shooters had night scopes, Ezana knew they couldn't have him zeroed in—and they should be more accurate if they were using infrared.

A burst of random fire, then, strafing down the trail.

Ezana thought about his scouts, their failure to detect the ambush. Were they dead? Cut down by the initial shots? Or had the ambush party let them pass, waiting to jump the larger squad?

Ezana spied a muzzle-flash and squeezed off three rounds from his FNC, on semiautomatic. It was impossible to tell if he had scored, but there was no immediate return fire from the point where he had aimed his rounds. A lucky hit, perhaps, and one down on the other side, but he wouldn't take anything for granted. At the moment, Ezana couldn't say how many guns were ranged against his soldiers, where the shooters were or even who they were.

It was unusual—but not unknown—for army regulars to stage nocturnal raids in Karamoja Province, where the ADF and the Lord's Vanguard had many friends among the rural populace. Daytime patrols were common, as a show of force, but as a rule Kampala's soldiers didn't open fire unless they were attacked. Custom aside, there was the unofficial truce that had prevailed for nearly two weeks now, begun when leaders of the ADF agreed to help Kampala deal with Galen Starke.

This ambush either meant the cease-fire was revoked or else they had been confronted with a unit of the Lord's Vanguard, prowling the night in search of human prey.

Ezana turned to speak with Bolan, startled for an instance by a change in the American's appearance. He had donned the strange-looking night-vision goggles that gave him an insect's profile. His mouth below the goggles was a grim, straight line.

"We need to get around behind these guys," Bolan said. "They'll keep us pinned down, otherwise, and finish us at dawn."

Another burst of automatic fire served as a punctuation for Bolan's statement. "I'll go with you," Ezana said.

"I don't have eyes for two."

"I have my own."

"Your funeral," the American said. "Before we go, you want to tell me who my guide is for the trip up-country? Just in case."

"That would be me," Ezana said, flashing another smile. "I will endeavor to remain alive."

"Do that," Bolan said, slipping away into the shadows like a wraith. The lieutenant scrambled after him, already thinking that this might be the worst mistake he'd ever made.

SPEED AND SILENCE in the jungle weren't usually compatible. With automatic weapons tearing up the night, however, stealth was less important at the moment than decisive action. If the ambush party kept them pinned down until dawn, there was a decent chance Bolan would die before he had a chance to match his wits with Starke's.

The emerald field of Bolan's vision jerked and wavered as he high-stepped through the undergrowth, seeking contact with the enemy. He knew their general locations—two or three of them, at least—but there were others, some of them no doubt encircling Ezana's squad right now. If they were able to triangulate their fire, precision shooting would become superfluous. They could begin to sweep the trail from front and back, both sides at once, and cut Ezana's men to pieces where they lay.

Unless somebody stopped them first.

Ten seconds into his advance, Bolan scored his first heat signature. The sniper was twenty yards ahead of him, crouched behind a tree as he replaced an empty magazine. The goggles Bolan wore prevented him from lining up the Steyr's optic sight for a precision shot, but at the present range it was unnecessary.

Bolan stroked a quick burst out of the AUG and watched his target shudder with the impact of the 5.56 mm rounds. Advancing on the supine form, he verified the kill. Ezana joined him there and stooped to take the dead man's weapon, slinging it across his back.

"Waste not, want not," the rebel said, flashing his trademark smile.

"Then we don't want to waste our time," Bolan replied.

Ezana caught his sleeve, restraining him as he stooped to roll the dead man onto his back. "I must see something first," he said.

Another heartbeat, and the rebel leader straightened, his teeth flashing in what could have been a grimace or a smile. "These are not army regulars," he said with confidence. "They may be bandits or a party from the Lord's Vanguard."

The news lifted a weight from Bolan's shoulders. He hadn't come here to clash with the Ugandan military or the ADF, if either conflict was avoidable. The covert nature of his mission presented certain built-in risks—foremost among them the persistent threat of being taken for a rebel by whatever trigger-happy government patrols they might encounter in the bush while he was traveling with native guides. This time, at least, he was relieved to know his adversaries weren't soldiers on assignment from the capital.

He moved on past the corpse, Ezana keeping pace. The jungle was alive with muzzle-flashes and the sounds of gunfire, bullets whispering through foliage, sometimes slapping into flesh or bark. Bolan had no idea if any members of the ADF patrol were down, and he had no time to concern himself with that.

Survival was the first priority.

He would do everything within his power to stay alive.

The goggles led him to another target and his AUG rapped out another burst. The spectral man-shape staggered, reeling, squeezing off wild rounds into the air as he collapsed. Ezana snagged the dead man's weapon, adding it to his collection, before jogging to keep pace with Bolan in the dark.

As they approached the point where Ezana's scouts had to have been ambushed, Bolan paused and listened to the night. Despite the sounds of combat echoing around him, he could still hear bodies crashing through the undergrowth, a group of men advancing in a hurry, moving toward confrontation with their enemy. It took another moment for the night glasses to pick them out, and Ezana seemed to spot them more or less at the same time.

It looked like seven, maybe eight men, moving in to the attack. They held no strict formation, following the paths of least resistance, compromising stealth for speed now that the battle had been joined. Clearly they gave no thought to a reverse ambush, believing that their targets were pinned down and relatively helpless on the trail.

They were about to get a rude surprise.

Bolan dropped to a crouch and braced the Steyr's stock against his shoulder. The lieutenant knelt beside him, shouldering a rifle, while the other two lay easily within his reach. Bolan was hoping not to need four magazines, but he could never tell until the shooting started and his adversaries went to ground.

"Not yet!" he whispered, hoping that Ezana heard him and possessed the self-control to wait. A few more yards. Five seconds, maybe ten...

Ezana held his fire, waiting for Bolan's cue. Their enemies were barely fifteen yards away when the Executioner opened fire, his first rounds drilling through the point man's chest to slam him over backward in a clumsy somersault.

All hell broke loose at that, the shadow figures firing

blindly in various directions, hoping for a lucky hit before they glimpsed the wink of hostile muzzle-flashes. By the time they got a fix on Bolan and Ezana, four of them were dead or dying, cut down by short bursts that dropped them in their tracks. The others sought whatever cover they could find, clinging to shadows as a last resort, returning fire as they attempted to retreat.

In other circumstances, Bolan might have been content to let them go, but he didn't want adversaries lurking in the dark just now or shadowing Ezana's troops back to the base camp. If their attackers disengaged and fled, there was a chance they would come back with reinforcements and the odds would shift again. The only way to seal off that option was to annihilate the ambush party before it scattered.

Bolan unclipped a fragmentation grenade, yanked the pin and lobbed the bomb overhand toward the erratic muzzle-flashes of two automatic rifles. As the egg was airborne, Bolan closed his eyes and waited for the flare of the explosion that would blind him if he kept them open, peering through the goggles.

Five...four...three...

Ezana emptied one rifle and dropped it, snatched another to his shoulder and resumed firing. Bullets zipped through the air on either side of Bolan like a swarm of angry hornets seeking flesh to sting.

Two...one...

The blast rocked Bolan, ringing screams erupting out of the night. Two of the hostile guns were silenced, whether permanently or for but a moment, Bolan couldn't tell. He took advantage of the shock and rushed the last position where he had observed a living enemy, braced for the impact of a bullet if it came his way.

Ezana caught up with him on the run, spare rifles slung on either shoulder, slapping at his flanks with every step he took. They were together when they reached ground zero and discovered one of Bolan's targets still alive, but barely.

Ezana knelt beside the wounded man and grabbed him by the hair, giving his head a shake. He said something that sounded like a question, in a language Bolan didn't understand, and got a muttered answer from the enemy. Another question, but with no reply this time. Ezana rose, stepped back a pace and pumped a round into the dying gunner's chest.

"Lord's Vanguard," he explained. "I don't know whether they were sent for us or if we meet by chance."

Bolan had no chance to respond before a rifle cracked and sent a bullet hissing past his face. His left eye registered a muzzle-flash at the periphery of vision, and he spun in that direction as he dropped into a crouch, returning fire. Ezana joined him, pouring rounds into the darkness, lifting off the trigger when they were rewarded with a gargling scream.

"I'll check," Ezana said, moving into the darkness, Bolan covering. A single shot rang out a moment later, and he doubled back. "All done," he said, flashing another smile.

"Not yet," Bolan reminded him, cocking his head in the direction of continued gunfire, ranging up and down the game trail.

There were no distinctive weapons in the firefight, all feeding the same 5.56 mm ammunition that was standard for Uganda's military rifles. Bolan had no way of knowing, from a distance, in the dark, which of those guns were fired by friends, and which by enemies. The only way to tell was to go back and check it out, up close and personal.

"You want the left side or the right?" he asked.

Ezana shrugged. "The right will do."

"Take care."

They separated, moving through the darkness, back in the direction of Ezana's squad. Along the way, Bolan passed Ezana's scouts, cut down at something close to point-blank range before they had a chance to warn the column following along behind. Both men were dead.

He left collection of their guns to someone else.

Two members of the Lord's Vanguard were still alive and fighting on Bolan's side of the trail. He came up behind the first of them, ducking low to avoid friendly rounds, closing to twenty feet before he stroked the trigger of his AUG and took one shooter down with a head shot.

That left one more.

In the confusion, Bolan's final target didn't know his comrade had been liquidated. Focused on the enemy with a determination that bespoke fanaticism, he was spraying short bursts up and down the trail, dodging incoming fire, shifting from one tree to another as he tried to stay alive. It was a decent tactic, in the circumstances, but it wouldn't save him from a stalker at his back.

Bolan was ready when the gunner paused to fumble with an empty magazine. His AUG spit once and pitched the dead man over on his face, twitching.

"All clear on this side!" Bolan called out, safe behind a giant tree from the converging streams of fire that sought his voice.

"Cease fire!" Ezana shouted from the far side of the trail. "Cease fire!" When that had no effect, he started cursing at his troops by name until the shooting tapered off and died away.

"Four dead and three wounded," the rebel officer reported after counting heads. His voice was bitter as he added, "There aren't enough of us to take them home."

"Depends on how you look at it," Bolan said. "Some would say they're home already."

Ezana nodded, started barking orders at his troops. "Gather the weapons now and bring the wounded! It is nearly dawn!"

A brand-new day, already stained with blood.

4

The Allied Democratic Forces base camp was a clearing in the jungle, hacked out of the trees and undergrowth by sheer brute strength, concealed from airborne eyes by camo netting mounted thirty feet above the ground. Lianas were entangled with the netting, providing more authentic cover for the soldiers sheltering beneath. Heat-seeking gear would pick out human beings and their camp fires down below, but such equipment was apparently in short supply.

Bolan was welcomed by the troops in camp with the affection normally reserved for process servers or freeloading in-laws. Most of them avoided him as if *he* had the plague. The few besides Gabra Ezana who addressed him kept it short and not so sweet. The sight of wounded comrades, coupled with the news that four more had been left behind, clearly did nothing to enhance Bolan's standing with the rank and file.

"They *do* know I'm a friendly, right?" he asked Ezana, as they ate a stew composed of boiled potatoes, corn, and meat that he couldn't identify by taste.

Ezana shrugged. "You are a stranger," he replied. "And you are white."

That said it all, and Bolan had retired to catch four hours' rest before they started their journey north. It was a testament to practice and experience that he dropped of almost immediately into dreamless sleep. Bolan could only trust Ezana to protect him from the others while his guard was down—but he still kept his AUG close by, with one hand curled around the pistol grip.

When Bolan woke, the camp was bustling. It was time to eat again, another steaming bowl of spuds and mystery meat. The lieutenant sat beside a loaded military pack, his chest crisscrossed by bandoliers that held two dozen spare mags for his FNC. He also wore a long machete on his belt, thrust out behind him at the moment like a rigid, lethal tail.

"What kind of distance are we looking at?" Bolan asked between mouthfuls of stew.

"No more than eighty kilometers," Ezana answered. "Perhaps not quite so far...unless the camp has moved, of course."

"Of course."

"It is unlikely," Ezana said, as if to put his mind at ease, "but I can't rule it out."

"And if it has moved," Bolan asked, "how do we find it?"

Ezana frowned and swallowed, freeing up his tongue. "Ah, well," he said at last, "that could require some time."

Terrific.

Hiking eighty klicks through jungle like the bit they had traversed that morning might consume three days—longer, if there were cliffs, rivers or mountains to negotiate along the way. If they ran into any kind of organized resistance, it could well turn out to be impossible.

Bolan rejected that idea immediately. He had never pandered to depression, and this didn't seem the wisest time to start. He had a job to do, and he would get it done.

He kept one eye on his watch as they were eating and finished up in time to break out his communications gear. He had a clear five-minute window to the satellite that would receive his coded message and eventually bounce it back to Stony Man. The collapsible antenna, made of a reflective fabric, opened to umbrella size, braced on a telescoping spike that Bolan plunged into the earth. His transmitter was smaller than the average cigar box and recorded messages on microchips instead of tape. A built-in scrambler and compressor took his cryptic words, relating safe arrival at the contact point, and fired them skyward in a pulse of silent energy two seconds long. If all went well, the message would arrive at the Farm within the hour.

And if it failed, Bolan might never know.

They set off on their journey shortly after noon. Soldiers lined up to wish Ezana well, a handful nodding to Bolan, while the majority made a point of ignoring him. The frosty send-off made no difference, though, as long as Bolan's guide could lead him to the camp where Starke had based the Lord's Vanguard. The soldier had no need to return this way when he was finished with his mission, but he memorized landmarks from force of habit.

All the information Bolan had absorbed about Uganda's climate, forest-dwelling predators and plant life was consigned to muted background noise as he followed his guide through perpetual twilight. A hundred feet or more above their heads, the forest canopy and understory growth screened out most of the sunlight, even at high noon. Accordingly, the flora of the jungle floor was sparse and stunted, dominated by shade-loving ferns and staggering varieties of fungi. Only from the sky or where a river broke up the forest and let the sun shine on its banks, was the "impenetrable" jungle of boyhood adventure tales a physical reality.

That helped, in terms of making time, but there were also drawbacks. Heat and near-hundred-percent humidity conspired to sap a hiker's strength before he covered half a mile, the forest operating like a giant pressure cooker with the steamy atmosphere trapped underneath the canopy. It was a teeming paradise for wildlife born and raised to take the heat, but fragile man could find himself dehydrated as rapidly in a rain forest as he could in the Sahara or Death Valley.

Open space between the looming, giant trees also provided fields of fire for snipers who might have Ezana's route staked out. Bolan wasn't surrendering to paranoia, but the thought had crossed his mind that Starke might easily have eyes and ears inside the ADF, from which the Lord's Vanguard had sprung. Why not? It would explain the ambush they had faced that morning, and there was no reason to believe the opposition, once defeated, would throw in its hand without a second try.

It was impossible for Starke to know that Bolan had been sent for him. The Executioner had been reported dead and wore a new face since the last time Starke had seen him. On the other hand, Starke was a hunted man and lived with that reality daily. It would be no great stretch of the imagination for him to surmise that an American dropped in to join the ADF in Karamoja Province may have come to do him harm.

And he wouldn't be wrong.

They were on notice, therefore, from the moment they began their journey, that the enemy might lie in wait for them at any point along the way.

Bolan and Ezana spoke in whispers on the trail, when they were moved to speak at all. Sound carried in the jungle, and it didn't have to be the screech of a macaw or howler monkey. There were tricks to the acoustics, Bolan knew, that would let him eavesdrop on a distant conversation, while at other times he might not hear the twig snap underneath a boot before its owner drove a knife into his back.

The forest was a lot like life in general, that way. He had to keep his eyes wide open, all sense on alert.

And sometimes, even that wasn't enough.

JULIENNE MARCEAU WASN'T a great believer in despair, but she had reached a point where happy upbeat thoughts turned sour and made her scowl. Looking around the camp, she knew there was no way that she could carry all the gear. Her personal equipment, with the food and water she required to stay alive, would tax her nearly to the point of physical collapse. As for her tent and sleeping bag, the propane stove and cookware, that and all the rest of it would have to be discarded.

The reality of her situation struck Marceau like a slap across the face, and she sat on the mossy trunk of a huge, fallen tree. She closed her eyes, and when she opened them again to study the deserted camp, despair was that much closer, looking better all the time.

It made no difference, she realized, if she was strong enough to carry all of the abandoned gear or if she struck off through the jungle empty-handed, travelling with nothing but the clothing on her back.

It made no difference because she couldn't plot her final destination on a map and had no realistic hope of reaching it alone, in any case. She would be lost within an hour, wandering off course until her water, food and hope were finally exhausted.

At which point—if not before—the jungle would consume her, flesh and bone, body and soul.

She would be lucky to survive the weekend.

"Merde!"

Her guide and porters had been missing when she woke that morning, gone without a trace. She gave them points for slipping away silently, but their escape had been facilitated by the fact that they had taken none of the equipment purchased for her trek into the bush.

It could be worse, she thought. They could have stolen everything, including food and the canteens.

More to the point, they could have taken her or slipped into her tent and killed her while she slept. It would have been a moment's work for any one of them with a machete—slightly more, perhaps, if he had used bare hands.

But now she was alone and going nowhere. It disgusted Marceau that she couldn't even retrace with any certainty the route that she had traveled for the past four days. She knew the general direction of the small town they had started from, but what did that mean? Without landmarks, she would soon be lost.

I'm lost right now.

She cursed again and slapped her forehead with an open

palm. The stinging blow did nothing to resolve her difficulty, but it helped to vent a little of her anger and frustration.

It didn't help with the fear.

She was alone, abandoned in the heart of darkest Africa. It was a wild and savage land that swallowed individuals, and sometimes whole safaris. Even now, with all the news about Mandela and redemption, AIDS and famine, civil wars and economic opportunities, the tropic heart of Africa was still a place where Mother Nature hunted men and ate them raw.

She had a small fire burning in the middle of the clearing, and she had a pistol, smuggled in her luggage past a customs officer more interested in her cleavage and the scent of her perfume than anything she might have hidden in her bags. It was an 8-shot Mauser Model HSC, which she imagined would do more to irritate a charging leopard than to stop him in his tracks. Eight shots, and no spare magazine.

The great white hunter.

"Merde, merde, merde!"

She was about to slap herself again, but the first blow had sparked a throbbing pain behind her eyes. Instead, she smacked the open palm against her thigh.

Enough! She had sufficient trouble as it was, without beating and bruising herself.

The worst of it, Marceau thought, was watching the break of a lifetime slip through her fingers like water. Disappointment was a leaden weight, smothering frail hope.

And if the opportunity was slipping through her hands, so was her life.

Abandoned.

She had sensed a certain nervousness about her guide and porters, but she had believed that doubling their normal fee for the safari would have overcome what Marceau regarded as illogical and baseless fear.

Apparently she had been wrong.

Damned cowards.

She had carefully explained the nature of her mission to

the guide and porters, guaranteed safe passage for them as her own safety was guaranteed. All she required of them was transportation and delivery. They didn't even have to wait and take her back.

Now they were gone, and the chance of a lifetime looked more like the *end* of her lifetime. There was a certain poetry about it if she read between the lines. What journalist, deep down, wouldn't prefer to die in the pursuit of an amazing and important story, rather than succumbing to the bottle, the cocaine spoon or some tedious disease?

Stop it, she thought. I don't want to die.

How long could she stay alive in the jungle on her own? If she was frugal with her food, she had a week's worth, maybe more. Her canteen would be empty long before then, but this was a rain forest, for God's sake. Even if the water she had access to wasn't the purest, most delicious Evian, it would be ample for her needs.

In fact, she realized, the pressing problem wasn't sustenance or water. Left to wander through the jungle on her own, she doubted whether she would last until the food ran out. In this dark, unforgiving world, she might turn out to *be* the food for any of a dozen different predators. A host of other forest denizens too small to eat her still posed a mortal threat, with deadly bites and stings.

Or she might simply blunder through the murky woods until she had an accident. It wouldn't take a broken leg or hip to cripple her. A twisted ankle would do very nicely. Even minor cuts would breed infection, lure biting flies with their loathsome diseases. There were plants whose sap was venomous, whose lightest touch would scald her flesh.

Where's Tarzan when you needed him?

That thought made her laugh, the sound surprising her and shocking her to cautious silence. She didn't want to attract undue attention.

What's that?

A muffled but familiar sound brought Marceau to her feet.

Voices? Yes! She was sure of it. Male voices, by the sound, and for a conversation to occur there had to be two, at least.

The porters coming back? And if so, why?

She drew the Mauser, racked the slide and held it against the right leg of her denim pants. If they were enemies, she might surprise them.

With forest all around her, Julienne Marceau wished she could find a place to hide.

GABRA EZANA FROZE in place and waited for the sound of laughter to repeat itself. He knew that there were jungle birds who mimicked human sounds, but the laugh had sounded real.

He glanced back at Bolan, found the tall man watching him.

The American kept his voice pitched low. "A woman?"

Ezana shrugged. "There is no village within seven or eight kilometers," he answered, whispering. "It would be strange to find a woman here."

"We should check it out," Bolan said.

"It could be trouble."

"Do you smell that?"

Ezana flared his nostrils, sampling the breeze.

Wood smoke. He had detected it on a subconscious level, but it hadn't registered. There was no scarcity of lightning strikes in tropic Africa, although rain forest rarely burned, except when fires were helped along by man.

"A camp," he stated.

"Your call," Bolan said.

"Hunters, perhaps."

"We don't want them behind us if they're hostile."

There were only two ways to approach a jungle camp. "Quiet or loud?" Ezana asked.

"Let's take a chance."

Ezana nodded, thumbing the safety switch of his FNC rifle into the off position. He deliberately raised his voice as he replied, "Of course. Why not?"

"It isn't like we mean them any harm," Bolan said, following the lieutenant as he started in the general direction of the wood smoke and the peal of laughter.

"By no means," Ezana said, but kept his finger on the automatic rifle's trigger, just in case.

He lost track of the small talk after that, responding automatically. A moment later, he could see the smoke, as well as smell it. In a forest clearing stood three tents—one blue, the others olive drab. The campfire was a small one, poorly tended, with no evidence that any food had been prepared.

He saw the woman standing by herself, facing Ezana's general direction. She was tall for a female, and slender in her khaki shirt and denim pants, feet planted well apart in sturdy hiking boots. She wore a wide-brimmed bush hat, but it didn't hide the spill of auburn hair that fell across her shoulders. She was quite attractive.

"Hello in camp!" Ezana called out. "We mean no harm."

He scanned the trees beyond the camp and off to either side. Three tents, and only one person? A woman in the forest, all alone? A white woman?

The redhead focused on their weapons first, then their faces, as they stepped into the clearing. Stepping back a pace, she raised a pistol in her right hand, while the left came up to brace her wrist.

"That's close enough," she said.

Ezana tried to place her accent as he said again, "We truly mean no harm."

"You're French," Bolan offered, nailing it.

"And you're American," she answered.

"We're a long way from home," Bolan said. "You really don't need that."

"Do you need those?" she asked, eyeing their rifles.

"Not for you," Bolan replied. "They may be useful, where we're going."

The woman frowned, then shrugged and let the pistol drop back to her side. "You're going north?"

"We are," Ezana stated. "And you?"

"I was," she said. "My guide and porters have deserted me. I gave them double wages, but they still—"

"You paid them in advance?" Ezana asked, interrupting.

"Half in advance."

He couldn't quite disguise his smile. "So, they go home with pay for a job half-done, and you are left alone."

"Yes, I suppose that's right."

"Where were you going, ma'am, if I may ask?"

Her look was cagey now. "North, like yourself," she responded.

"But north of here lies only Kenya and Sudan, ma'am. Would it not be easier to fly?"

"I have a job to do," she said defensively.

"And that's a camera bag," Bolan said. "You're a photographer?"

"A freelance journalist," she said. "My name is Julienne Marceau. I'm on assignment from *Paris Match*."

"Because French readers are so fascinated with Uganda's wildlife?"

She ignored the question and replied in kind. "What brings you here, with all these weapons? Are you soldiers?"

"We're Boy Scouts," Bolan said. "You know the motto— Be Prepared."

The redhead actually smiled at that. "I'll risk a guess," she said, "that you and I may share a final destination."

Ezana frowned at that. Bolan said nothing.

"You're not hunters," she went on. "Hunters don't use military rifles, and they certainly don't carry hand grenades. You're obviously not Ugandan," she addressed Bolan, "and if you were from Kampala, on official business, there wouldn't be two of you alone. You're looking for someone, I think. A man. Perhaps the same man I have come to see."

"If that's the case," Bolan said, "we'll tell him you ran into trouble on the trail."

The woman blinked. Ezana thought she lost a bit of color from her face.

"You mean to leave me here?" she asked, a hint of panic in her voice.

"You must have a compass in your gear."

"Yes, but—"

"You walk due south," the Executioner said. "You'll hit a village day after tomorrow. Keep the pistol handy, but don't waste your shots on shadows."

"You can't do this!" she protested.

"Dragging you along with us is worse," he said. "Instead of helping you, it stands to finish off all three of us."

"But I can help you! Don't you see?"

"It's dim from where I stand."

The woman hesitated, gathering her nerve, then blurted out, "You seek a man named Galen Starke. He leads the Lord's Vanguard. Am I correct?"

Ezana's frown became a scowl, matching the one on Bolan's face.

"What do you know about the Lord's Vanguard?" the American asked her.

"It's the subject of my article," she said. "Starke has agreed to an exclusive interview. I have safe passage to his camp— or did, until my porters left me here alone."

"They weren't Starke's men?" Bolan asked.

She shook her head. "I hired them in Loyoro."

"But you don't know where Starke is, exactly?"

Now the woman smiled. "I have the map coordinates. Of course, without a guide..."

Ezana turned and met the American's glance. The white man raised one eyebrow, questioning.

"Hold on," Bolan told the woman. Then, to Ezana he said, "Can we have a word?"

They paced off several yards, keeping the woman and his pistol well in sight as they conferred.

"What do you think her chances are of finding the way south?" Bolan asked.

"I would not wager that she lives two days," Ezana said.

"And if she goes with us it may help get us past Starke's guards."

"If she speaks truthfully, perhaps."

Bolan obviously didn't like the thought of taking Marceau along, but he was even less inclined to leave her in the jungle on her own.

"Why don't we try to make the best of it?" he said.

"If that is what you wish?"

Bolan turned back toward the woman as he said, "Okay, you've got an escort. We won't ditch you on the way, and you won't steer us wrong."

"I wouldn't think of it," she answered, with a smile.

"I wasn't asking," Bolan said. "If you try to set us up, I guarantee you'll wish we'd never met."

THE WOMAN TALKED nonstop while she broke camp, leaving the tents and other clumsy gear behind. She wouldn't leave her camera or her laptop with the solar-powered battery, and Bolan didn't offer to help lug her gear across the countryside.

If Julienne Marceau was bound to join the trek, the very least that she could do was pull her weight.

Before they hit the trail again, Bolan had heard the background story of her trip to Africa. It seemed—if he could trust her version of events—that Starke had somehow reached across the miles to find a voice in Europe, some outlet that would relay his message to the world. A spokesman for the Lord's Vanguard had been rejected by *Der Spiegel* and the London *Times* before he tried his luck in France and caught a break with someone on the staff at *Paris Match*. Marceau had been selected for the trip because she had experience in Africa, reporting from Biafra and Sudan. She spoke Swahili, and her vaccination card was up-to-date.

The rest was history.

She had flown in from Paris to Kampala, chartered a bush flight to Loyoro and recruited the native staff for her safari. Several guides had turned her down, apparently frightened of trespassing on Starke's domain. The crew she finally secured has asked for double pay and half up front. In retrospect, she readily admitted that she should have seen the warning flags.

"You live and learn," Bolan suggested. He saw no point in reminding her that sometimes people also learned hard lessons in the split second before they died.

It was the lesser of two evils, bringing Marceau along. If Bolan and Ezana hadn't crossed her path, he understood, there was a likelihood—call it a probability—that she wouldn't have left the rain forest alive. Her death, unknown to Bolan, would have meant nothing to him or to his mission. Having met her and assessed her life-or-death predicament, however, the soldier couldn't bring himself to simply leave her stranded there. Retreating to Ezana's camp with Marceau wasn't an option, so he had decided to make the best of a bad situation.

If she truly had a pinpoint fix on Starke's location, that would be an unexpected bonus, but he wasn't wholly in accord with Marceau's apparent plan. Bolan had no need or desire to find Starke's hardsite, unless it proved impossible to drop him from a distance, quick and clean.

Still, it would do no harm to let the woman think her plan had been accepted. There was no point telling her the truth, when it would only frighten her—or worse, prompt her to undermine his own design, try warning Starke before the ax could fall.

They hiked in single file, with Ezana at the point and Bolan bringing up the rear. It helped discourage conversation while they were in motion, when the threat of stumbling over human enemies or jungle predators was greatest, and it gave Bolan a chance to study Marceau.

She had a trim, athletic figure and appeared to have no trouble keeping up with Ezana's pace, although the weight of her combined backpack, laptop and camera produced a slight stoop in her shoulders. When she turned to glance at Bolan, every hundred yards or so, as if to reassure herself that he was still behind her, she invariably flashed a smile that showed him straight, white teeth.

The friendly type...or was it something that reporters did to gain a stranger's confidence before they started asking questions? Marceau had already begun, while she was breaking camp, inquiring as to why Bolan and Ezana were en route to visit Starke. Bolan had told her it was need-to-know, and he had firmly vetoed her attempt to photograph them for her scrapbook. He would have to watch that, as the trek went on, and more particularly after they had found Starke's base of operations. Marceau had come to write one kind of story, but she was about to find herself caught up in something very different.

The last thing Bolan needed in his life was a dramatic photo spread depicting him in action, maybe picked up by wire services around the world.

He had changed faces twice since the beginning of his private war, and he wasn't convinced that a third time would be the charm.

Bolan was mulling over ways to lose or break the lady's camera, perhaps expose her film, when Ezana raised a hand to halt their march. Marceau was unfamiliar with the military gesture, and she moved up to his side, anxious to see what their point man had found.

Her squeal was quickly stifled, cut off on a rising note as the lieutenant clapped his hand across her mouth.

"No noise," Ezana cautioned her, keeping his hand in place until she gave a jerky little nod.

Bolan moved up behind them. He was tall enough to look across Ezana's shoulder at the object that had been arranged to greet them on the trail.

It was—or had once been—a man. Not much of him remained, where jungle rot, insects and scavengers had done their work. The tattered clothes he wore were denim, and deeply stained with blood. His race was indeterminate and irrelevant. The cause of death appeared to be decapitation—not so much because the head itself was missing, as because it had been artfully replaced.

A large gourd had been mounted on the dead man's shoulders, skewered with a wooden stake whose other end was planted deeply in the stub of mutilated neck.

The gourd was painted yellow, marked with two black dots for eyes and a dark crescent frown.

It was the grim reversal of a classic Smiley Face.

To keep the gourd-head squarely in its place, the corpse had been wrapped tightly in barbed wire, secured to a stout tree trunk.

"Somebody put out the unwelcome mat," Bolan remarked.

From this point on, he knew, they might be watched, perhaps attacked at any time.

It gave the hunt an edge, knowing that Starke had lost none of his wit or skills.

His old friend might be crazy.

But he was still a warrior.

5

"There's no mistake?" Galen Starke asked.

His hands, rock steady, never deviated from their task. His right guided the blade of a straight razor backward, from his hairline to a point near the crown of his head, while the left followed after it, testing for stubble.

So far, there was none.

His scalp, bare and tan, was as smooth as a long shot of Bushmills.

"No mistake," Roshani Malinke assured him. "I have questioned the traitors myself. They held nothing back."

Starke believed that without asking details. Malinke had a gift for persuasion. The only problem was that he could sometimes be a trifle too persuasive. If he asked the subject leading questions, then began to ply his blade or crank up the generator, there was a risk that he would get an answer...but that it might not be the truth.

"You didn't make them any promises?"

Malinke shook his dark, bald head. "They know what must become of them," he said.

"You didn't slip and feed them any lines?"

"No, sir."

"In that case," Starke replied, "we really have no choice. You'll see to the arrangements?"

"Yes, sir!" Malinke eagerly responded.

"That's all for now. Call me when you're ready."

"Yes, sir." With a brisk salute to his commanding officer, Malinke turned and marched off to complete the preparations for a double execution.

Staring at his own reflection in a polished Cadillac hubcap, Starke frowned and told himself, "I don't need this today."

In fact, he didn't need it any day.

Contrary to the legend Starke had fashioned for himself in Karamoja Province, this wasn't the first time traitors had been found within the Lord's Vanguard. Such parasites were few and far between, but some sort of betrayal was inevitable, he supposed, when dealing with the human species.

All the more reason to get the cleansing back on track and escalate the pace.

His problem children in the past—no more than half a dozen out of hundreds, in the year and change since he had organized the Lord's Vanguard—had suffered from the sins of pride and avarice. They watched Starke, envied his command of men and coveted the power he possessed without a grasp of what it took to earn that power, that abiding trust.

The traitors had all been soldiers who believed they could replace Starke, turn the Vanguard to personal advantage and forsake its holy mission.

They were wrong. And each of them had paid for the mistake in blood.

These two, apparently, were different. Instead of pride or envy, these two carried malice in their hearts. They had been sent to infiltrate the Lord's Vanguard and undermine Starke's mission, possibly report his movements as the opportunity arose, and thereby help Kampala's ruling elite to prepare a lethal trap for him.

It was a mark of clumsy training and their personal bankruptcy of the spirit that their treachery had been discovered only three or four weeks after they came straggling into camp, claiming that one of Starke's fliers had moved them to enlist.

Such things weren't unknown, and Starke didn't reject new converts out of hand.

Instead he charged his second in command to watch the new meat and be ready with the cleaver if they looked like going bad.

Which they had done, apparently, although Malinke had secured them for questioning before they could do any lasting harm.

Now they had to pay.

Starke took no pleasure in dispensing justice to his children, but he didn't shirk the duty, either. Having laid down rules and consequences, he was bound to follow through with those who disobeyed him or disgraced the Lord's Vanguard in any way. There was no room in camp for any law except his own, and he could spare no men for guarding prisoners.

The one and only penalty for any crime against the brotherhood was death.

And this one would be memorable.

It would sear the message of obedience into the hearts and minds of his disciples for all time.

Examples were required from time to time. If God had not provided him with these, Starke might have had to pick some on his own, for illustrative purposes.

Waste not, want not.

Finished, Starke rinsed his razor in the plastic pail that served him as a sink, then wiped the blade meticulously, taking care to leave no moisture on its polished surface.

He had so many dreams and visions spinning in his head, filling his heart until Starke thought that it would burst. He carried so much love inside him, so much blazing wrath, sometimes Starke wondered how much longer all the white-hot energy he generated could be physically contained.

He might explode someday, and nothing crafted by the hands of men would stand before that blast.

What would become of him in that event? Starke wondered if his soul would be launched heavenward and seek reunion with his Maker at the speed of light.

Or would he have some other mission to complete, perhaps the cleansing of another world, where he would be reborn in flesh and start anew?

The possibilities were endless. Starke looked forward to the great adventure with an eagerness he hadn't felt since childhood, shaking presents underneath the Christmas tree.

But first, he had a sacred mission to complete in this world. He was getting closer, step by step, but it would take more time.

Still so much cleansing left to do, before the world was made pristine.

He would begin with those who had betrayed him in his own backyard.

Starke ran a callused hand across his naked chest, tracing the tattoos etched into his flesh. He bore the marks with pride. They were inscrutable, his own design.

I am the Lord thy God.

Thou shalt place no gods over Me.

Thou shalt not take My name in vain.

Thou shalt prepare the Earth for being cleansed.

Or words to that effect.

The Lord's message was clearer on some days than others. Starke accepted that, took it for granted. Sometimes, when he had to find his way alone, a worm of doubt began to gnaw away inside his heart, but he could always pluck it out and cauterize the wound.

No fire this time.

This time, when the cleansing was accomplished, it would start within each human parasite and burst forth into glory, into blood.

And by the time the parasites knew what was happening to them, it would already be too late.

Amen.

JULIENNE MARCEAU was weary by the time her two escorts decided it was time to camp. Aside from carrying more weight than previously, when she had the porters to assist her, she had traveled farther, at a faster pace, than during any of her first three days in the jungle. She realized that her companions on the first leg of her journey had been dragging their feet deliberately, and Marceau was once again embarrassed by her own naïveté.

She wasn't sure how many miles they had traversed that day, but from the painful protest lodged by muscles in her back and legs, the distance had to have been substantial. The journalist felt optimistic now, albeit cautiously. She didn't think her escorts meant her any harm—they could have treated her as harshly as they wished a hundred times by now, and left her dead along the trail—but there was still a nagging doubt as to the purpose of their search for Galen Starke.

She smelled a story in the making, and her nose for news was almost never wrong.

Her motive for traveling so far from home and trekking through the jungle to interrogate a man who might well be insane was straightforward. She was a reporter, with her reputation on the rise in Western Europe, and the Starke interview—if she survived it—would advance that reputation greatly. She was thinking of a book about the Lord's Vanguard, already had her agent feeling out some big-name publishers, and if it went well, there might even be a movie sale.

She had a sense of something hidden, held back in reserve by her two benefactors. There was obviously something that they didn't wish to share with her, and they had quickly laid down rigid rules against her taking any photographs of them along the march. She hoped to sneak some later, risk it even if she never chose to publish the photos, but this wasn't the time to press her luck.

If they turned against her—even if they simply left her in the forest, as her former guide had done—Marceau knew she would never reach Starke's camp or see her Paris flat again.

She had been surprised by all the open space beneath the jungle canopy, where she had expected an impenetrable wall of flora to obstruct her every move. Instead, it almost felt like walking in a palace that had gone to ruin, with the massive pillars still in place and holding up a leafy roof.

The campsite was another forest clearing, with a river situated one hundred and fifty meters to the north. It was too late to ford the river when they reached it, the men had agreed, so they retreated to the clearing noted earlier and pitched their camp.

"Why so far from the river?" she had asked them, as they shrugged off packs and weapons, spread small tarps as meager sleeping pallets.

"It's insulation," Bolan said.

"Pardon me?"

"The most important element for life on earth is water," he explained. "It doesn't matter if you're in the middle of a desert or a jungle. Sooner or later, everything and everyone comes to the water. We don't want to meet them in the middle of the night."

"Ah. Insulation."

"Right."

"I'll get wood for the fire," she said.

"No fire," Ezana told her, frowning.

"What?"

"We're camping cold from now on," Bolan responded.

"Why?"

"Because a predator—human or otherwise—can see the fire a long way off at night. The smell would carry even farther." Watching Marceau, he said, "We smelled your camp before we heard you laughing at yourself."

She felt the rush of color to her cheeks, determined not to let him shake her. "What about—"

"There's more," Bolan said, interrupting. "If we pick up a tail, trackers can check the ashes and find out when we broke camp. That lets them know what kind of lead we have, how fast they need to move to overtake or get ahead of us."

"I understand," she said, "but what about food?"

"You brought some, didn't you?" The American frowned. "I asked you twice before we left your camp."

"Of course. I brought some canned things." She could feel their weight, where backpack straps had cut into her shoulders. "But to eat them cold—"

"You'll learn to love it," the American replied, and she could see Ezana grinning in the background. "Canned stuff always tastes about the same, whether it's hot or cold."

The journalist could recognize a losing argument and knew when to concede defeat. "All right, then. But my canteen's nearly empty." She removed it from its belt pouch as she spoke and shook it at Bolan to produce a feeble sloshing sound. "You can't intend for me to go without the most important element of life on earth?"

His ice-blue eyes locked on her face and held there for a moment, studying her. "You know where the river is," he said at last. "Try for clean water. If you get sick out here, we've got no medicine to give you and no time to play doctor."

"I'll be fine, I'm sure," she replied.

"Suit yourself," he said. "Try not to get lost."

She swallowed her reply to that and turned away from him, moving past Ezana toward the river. She had gone no more than half a dozen paces when the American called out after her, "And watch out for the neighbors."

She hesitated, glancing back. "Neighbors?"

"There may be crocodiles, perhaps a hippopotamus. Mambas and tree cobras are not uncommon. Leopards sometimes go to drink before the twilight comes," Ezana replied.

Marceau refused to let the two men see her tremble. "It's a good thing that I have my pistol, then," she said.

"No careless shooting," the American instructed her. "We can't afford the noise." Bolan unsheathed his machete and delivered it to Marceau. "If you run into anything, use this."

"Thank you. I will."

She held the heavy knife in one hand and her canteen in the other, as she left the camp. Marceau imagined the two men watching her, perhaps smiling at her discomfiture, but she refused to give them the satisfaction of looking back.

What could be so difficult about retrieving water from the river?

Crocodiles. Tree cobras. Leopards.

It was a long fifty meters to the river, even with the Mauser on her hip and the machete in her hand. She stopped midway and turned back toward the camp, fighting a surge of panic when she could see nothing of her two companions.

Try not to get lost.

"Damn you!" she muttered. "I will *not* get lost!"

Fuming, she turned and marched on through the trees as twilight fell.

TWO WOODEN STAKES had been erected in the middle of the camp. The seat reserved for Galen Starke, a massive throne of woven cane, was placed directly opposite the stakes, a dozen paces back. He could see everything, without suffering too much from the heat.

Roshani Malinke supervised the preparations, dispatching a party for kindling and firewood. His sergeants rounded up the spectators. Attendance at executions was mandatory, with the sole exemption being major injury or illness. Since the two traitors were the only members of the unit at death's door, 347 others would assemble on command and watch the show.

Malinke relished weeding traitors from the ranks. It would be better, theoretically, if there was none to punish, but he recognized that this was an imperfect world. The Lord's Vanguard wouldn't have been required to cleanse the earth, if it was otherwise. This way, the traitors had an opportunity to serve the cause they had betrayed and stiffen the resolve of those loyal soldiers whom they left behind.

Starke was, as usual, the last officer to arrive. Malinke waited for him patiently, without resentment. The two traitors weren't going anywhere. It didn't matter if their execution was delayed five minutes or five hours.

No one would complain, because Starke's word was law within the Vanguard. He could do no wrong.

Who else was there to tell Malinke and the others what their Lord required of them in order to secure their place in paradise?

A ripple in the ranks announced that Starke was on his way. Malinke heard the whispered conversations stifled and saw the troops stand at attention for their commander-in-chief. It was all the more amazing, watching them respond so to a white man, awed by his charisma, his vision, craving his approval, trembling in the shadow of his wrath.

It was a miracle. God's hand at work among the heathens to redeem their souls.

Malinke turned to watch Starke cross the compound and assume his throne. Starke wore his full-dress uniform, reserved for ceremonial occasions. It consisted of a crimson swallow-tailed coat with brass buttons and gold epaulets, beige riding breeches and brown knee-high boots spit-polished to a shine resembling patent leather. The ensemble was surmounted by a green beret, perched at a jaunty angle on Starke's clean-shaved scalp. The saber that he wore suspended from a Sam Browne rig was three feet long, with ivory grips and an elaborate gold-plated basket hilt.

Starke had to shift the saber forward, resting it across his knees when he sat. He scanned the ranks of his disciples as if memorizing faces, then favored Malinke with a somber nod.

"Proceed."

Malinke clicked his heels and bawled out toward the far side of the compound, "Bring out the traitors!"

The prisoners were leashed and led before the comrades they had betrayed, led toward the stakes with ropes around their necks. Hands bound behind their backs, with shackles on their feet, they moved with little shuffling steps, as if afraid they might fall and wind up being dragged.

The four-man escort wasted no time on the final preparations. One traitor was forced to kneel, a guard remaining at his side, while two more led the other to a waiting stake. The fourth fetched chains, and in another moment the first traitor was secured with fireproof bonds around his chest, waist, thighs and calves, immobilized. He started weeping, crying out for mercy as the escorts went for his companion.

The second traitor tried to fight, but it was hopeless. He could only snap his teeth and try to butt his handlers in the groin, but even that poor tactic was denied him as Malinke stepped in close and smashed a fist into his face.

He pulled the punch, using enough force to subdue the traitor without knocking him unconscious. There was no point in proceeding with the execution if the man wasn't able to repent.

Both prisoners were pleading for their worthless lives, in English and their tribal dialect, as half a dozen soldiers stacked brushwood around the stakes where they were bound. The pleas bled into inarticulate weeping as plastic cans of gasoline were shuttled forward and the contents sloshed around their feet.

Malinke signaled for the torches to be lit and handed to his chosen executioners. He stood before the traitors, with his back to Starke, as he pronounced their sentence for the benefit of the assembled troops.

"You have confessed and stand convicted of high treason to the Lord's Vanguard and your commanding officer." Malinke knew the script by heart. "As God expunges sin with fire, so shall you be expunged and your transgression purged. We now commend your souls to Him and to His judgment, while your sinful bodies are consigned to flame."

Malinke turned to face the executioners. "Proceed!" he ordered.

Stepping forward with their torches, the two men stooped and prodded at the wood piled up around each stake. Flames sprang up amid the twigs and branches, spreading as the executioners circled their subjects, working for an even burn.

The traitors had begun to scream. Malinke made no effort to decipher anything they said, most of it simply wailing as the fire began to lap around their feet and ankles. With a crisp salute to Starke, he turned once more to watch the spectacle.

One of the prisoners apparently remembered what he had been taught in basic training: if a death by fire appeared inevitable, needless suffering may often be averted by determined inhalation of the superheated air. It seared the lungs and starved the brain of oxygen in seconds flat, producing merciful unconsciousness.

The traitor on Malinke's left had stopped his screaming now, and seemed intent on hyperventilating as the fire raced up his legs. It may have worked, or possibly his heart gave out from fear. In either case, he slumped against the chains that held him fast and uttered no more sounds.

His fellow parasite wasn't as clever or so fortunate. Forgetting everything that he had learned, the traitor thrashed against his chains, as if mere flesh and bone could vanquish tempered steel. His lunging grew more agitated and spasmodic as the flames leaped higher while he screamed with enough force to lacerate his throat.

The second traitor lasted thirteen minutes by Malinke's watch. He set a record and provided an exemplary performance for his audience.

When it was done, Malinke turned toward his chief again. Starke's face, as always, was impassive and serene. Whatever might be going on behind those blue eyes, Starke kept it to himself. His nostrils flared a little, drawing in the scent of roasted flesh before he rose and marched back to his quarters, with the saber slapping at his flank.

Another job well done, Malinke thought.

The others would remember and exert themselves more ardently to please their officers.

"ONE OF US should have gone with her," Gabra Ezana said some twenty minutes after Marceau had left the clearing.

"You can catch her if you hurry," Bolan said, "or meet her coming back."

Ezana thought about it for a moment, then he frowned and shook his head. "White woman in the jungle," he replied. "I don't think so."

Bolan was working on an MRE—Meal, Ready to Eat, in

military jargon—that had thankfully replaced C-rations in the Army. Hesitating with the plastic spoon poised in midair, he said, "You think I need to go and find her."

"Only if you think there may be danger."

That was the hook, of course, for there was always danger in the jungle. At any given moment, an unwary traveler could die or suffer crippling injury in any one of several dozen different ways. A simple fall could be disastrous, if it proved disabling or produced infection from an open wound. Even the smell of blood could draw large predators.

"All right," he said, sealing the foil pack of his MRE before he tucked it back inside his pack. "I'll go see what she's doing."

"You'll feel better for it," Ezana told him, smiling.

"One of us will, anyway," Bolan replied.

He took the AUG and followed her path through the forest toward the river. Halfway there, Bolan could hear the faint sounds of running water. It would be enough for Marceau to fix on, navigating by the noise. The only way she could get lost was if she happened to be deaf.

How long should filling a canteen take, anyway? Two minutes? Three?

Say ten, he thought, to make allowances for scouting out the river bank, looking for ready access to the water. But if she had ranged along the riverbank and lost her fix on where the camp was located...

The splashing sounds reached Bolan's ears when he was twenty yards back from the river, closing in. He picked up his pace, thumbing off the Steyr's safety and wishing that he still had his machete, in case he had to hack through tangled vines and other plants along the river's edge. His mind offered an image of Marceau in trouble, grappling with a crocodile— perhaps so badly injured that she couldn't even find the strength to scream.

But what he found was something altogether different.

Marceau's shirt and pants were draped over a boulder, near the water's edge. Her boots stood beside the rock, with a hint of something mauve and frilly visible in one of them. Her pistol belt was curled around the boots like a deflated adder, with the gun still in its holster. Bolan's machete lay beside the boots, blade pointed toward the river.

Splashing sounds again.

He turned in the direction of the noise and caught his first glimpse of Marceau as she rose from the water, glistening. She stood within ten feet of shore, dark water deep enough to lap against her buttocks. She seemed to struggle with the current for a moment, almost lost her balance, then recovered it and raised both hands to pull wet hair back from her face. In profile there was more to her than met the eye when she was dressed up and outfitted for the trail.

She turned toward Bolan and he ducked back, put a massive tree between them, pressed his back against the trunk and slid down until he was sitting on his heels. He felt a momentary pang of guilt for spying, and as quickly shrugged it off.

Her foolhardy defiance put a scowl on Bolan's face. What was she thinking, wading in a river—much less wading naked, with her weapons out of reach—after the warnings Ezana had provided. Bolan didn't know if it was pure contrariness or something else, and he didn't intend to waste time analyzing her whims. He wasn't her psychiatrist or any kind of voluntary bodyguard, for that matter. She could do anything she damn well pleased, and if it got her into trouble, that was her problem.

Except it wasn't. Not since Bolan and Ezana had agreed to bring her on their jungle trek. Bolan had known the folly of assisting strangers while he had a mission under way, but he had made the choice. Now he had to live with it.

Rising, he cleared his throat with more volume than necessary, calling out, "Hello? Julienne?"

He was rewarded with a louder splash than any swimming stroke would justify. She answered, sputtering, "Who's that?"

"It's just me. Mike Belasko. Are you having trouble?"

"No!" More splashing, as she made her way to shore. "Stay where you are, please! I'll be with you in a moment."

"Okay," he said, smiling. "I was afraid you might have fallen in the river."

"No, I'm fine."

And slightly breathless, from the sound of it. He pictured Marceau, still wet from swimming, grappling with her clothes.

"That's good," he said. "The more I thought about it, I decided Gabra should have warned you about spiny candirus."

"Excuse me?" Muffled sounds, as if she might be hopping on one foot.

"The spiny candiru," Bolan repeated. "It's a tiny tropic fish, about two inches long, no thicker than a pencil lead."

"That doesn't sound so dangerous."

"The thing is," he went on, "it has these spiny fins—"

"But still, a fish so small—"

"—which it flares out, after it wriggles up into a swimmer's urinary tract."

Dead silence.

"I'm told it's agonizing," Bolan said. "You can't just pull it out, of course, because the spines point *backward*. That means surgery. It's not a pretty sight."

She hesitated for another moment, then replied, "You made that up."

"No, ma'am. It's gospel. The worst part's that the fish is so small, an infected swimmer may not know it's there until...well, until he has to..."

"Stop it!"

Marceau brushed through the lianas and stood before him, looking much as she had when she left the camp, except for wet hair slicked back from her face. Her shirt was buttoned crooked, too, but Bolan let it go. He could see places where the moisture on her skin had darkened fabric, soaking through.

"Tell me you made that up!" she challenged him, slapping the blade of his machete angrily against her boot.

"The spiny candiru?' He shook his head and smiled. "You'll find them by the thousands...up and down the Amazon."

"Oh, that's hilarious!" she stormed. "You frightened me back there, you...you..."

Bolan watched her search in vain for epithets a moment longer, then he said, "Relax. It won't happen again. One thing, though."

"What?" She spit the word between clenched teeth.

"Next time you feel the urge to swim with crocodiles, let Gabra have an address for your next of kin."

Bolan turned and left her there, without a backward glance, retreating toward the camp. He had progressed no more than thirty yards before he heard her, hurrying along behind him through the trees.

6

The village of Indrissa wasn't sleeping as the troops moved toward it, marching through the rain forest as quietly as they were able. It was time to cleanse another nest of parasites, and those who were about to die had no idea they had been chosen by the hand of God.

Roshani Malinke enjoyed his work.

The good Lord loved a happy warrior.

The name Indrissa meant "immortal." There was arrogance in such a name, but clearly not much prescience. Malinke and his soldiers were about to prove the name a lie.

He raised a hand to halt the troops when they were within an easy gunshot of Indrissa. Signals sent his men fanning off to either side for the encircling maneuver. They looked eager, hungry. Their enjoyment of the task had been increased by knowledge that there was no bleeding fever at Indrissa.

Simply parasites to be eradicated from the earth.

Malinke kept a sharp eye on his watch, giving the soldiers who had to travel farthest to surround the village ten full minutes. With each second blinking on the LED display he half expected warning cries to issue from the village.

Could these peasants really be so foolish, in this time and place, that they didn't post sentries for their own protection?

Live and learn, Malinke thought, then smiled at the delicious irony. Indrissa's residents would learn, but none of them would live.

Starke had ordered their extermination after speaking to the Lord. Malinke didn't understand why that village had been selected—and he didn't care. A man who asked too many questions, second-guessing God's design, was doomed to writhe in hellfire for eternity.

Malinke meant to claim a place in paradise.

The watch showed him it was time. Malinke raised his hand again and gave the signal to advance. He hung back slightly, as the others moved toward the village. As the field commander of the unit and second in command of the Lord's Vanguard, Malinke had a duty to protect himself from harm. There was no reason to expect these peasants would defend themselves, but just in case—

A woman's high-pitched scream knifed through the morning air, cut off a heartbeat later by a short burst from an automatic rifle. Malinke's skirmish line picked up its pace, the soldiers double-timing in their haste to join the action. They had missed first blood already, but there still should be enough to go around.

Malinke slowed his pace instead of jogging to keep up with them. He knew how troops behaved on cleansing raids, when there was no fear of the bleeding fever, and while such diversions weren't to his personal taste, neither would he discourage them.

More firing now. The rattle of FNC assault rifles was punctuated by the reports of other weapons. Shotguns, used primarily for putting small game on the table, sounded very different from the FNCs. Likewise, the sharp crack of a hunting rifle couldn't be mistaken for a military arm.

Malinke further slowed his pace, putting himself thirty meters behind the skirmish line. That meager distance wouldn't save him from a rifle shot, but it allowed him to explore Indrissa, watching as his men engaged the enemy, fighting from house to house.

And some of them were houses, in the sense that they had walls of corrugated metal or pressed wood supporting thatched roofs, as opposed to bundled reeds. Some of the better homes had square-cut windows with mosquito netting tacked across them in place of glass. None of them had been built with armed assault in mind, however, and he saw them falling to his troopers, one by one.

How many people in Indrissa? Perhaps four hundred. Malinke had brought forty men on the theory that ninety percent or more of the villagers would be unarmed, too frightened by the sight of soldiers to resist. He hoped that he wouldn't lose any men, but it was difficult to mourn for those who earned a place in paradise by giving up their earthly lives.

And besides, there were always more recruits where these came from.

When he was close enough to smell the cordite and to recognize his individual commandos dodging through Indrissa's streets, Malinke paused. The cleansing had begun in earnest now, and there was nothing he could do in terms of shepherding his men from one point to the next. Combat was chaos, for the most part, its outcome determined by the will of God and strength of men.

Malinke heard the boom of a grenade exploding and saw a dust cloud wafted skyward on the far side of the village. One more nest of parasites expunged. A second blast quickly followed the first, this time producing smoke as one of the shacks caught fire.

Malinke found a sturdy tree and crouched on his haunches, leaning back against the trunk, the FNC across his knees. It was as good a vantage point as any to enjoy the show. He would inspect the carnage more closely after the firing died down and the place was secure.

No point in rushing things. His soldiers needed time to do their jobs—and have their fun.

Malinke rested, breathed in the cordite as if it were the sweetest of perfumes. There was no hurry.

All things come to those who wait.

THE FIRST SHOTS could have come from anywhere. There was a sense of distance in that short burst. If that had been the end of it, Bolan couldn't have placed the sound.

But it wasn't the end.

A moment later, several automatic weapons opened up in unison. The shooters stuck with short bursts for the most part, and there was apparently no target shortage on the firing line.

"Northwest," he said.

Gabra Ezana nodded, scowling. "There's a village that way," he replied. "It's called Indrissa."

"How far?" Bolan asked.

"Less than two kilometers, I think."

Julienne Marceau was at his elbow, crowding him. "What is it?"

"Someone's getting killed," he answered bluntly.

Choices. Anything they did had to be done swiftly, without wasting time.

"How many people, Gabra?"

"I would guess four hundred."

Dammit!

"If we're going," Bolan said, "we don't have a lot of time."

Ezana nodded his agreement. One side of his mouth hitched upward in a kind of smile.

"What are we doing?" Marceau inquired.

"*You're* staying here," he said. "We'll come back for you later."

"Think again," she said. "If there's a story there—"

"There's only death," Bolan told her, "and we don't have time to talk about it."

"Good. It's settled, then."

"Suit yourself," Bolan said. "Keep up if you can, and stay out of the way."

He turned to Ezana. "Let's go!"

They ran double-time, a good ground-eating pace that still let Bolan watch for obstacles and dodge them. Marceau was taken by surprise and fell behind almost immediately, struggling with her pack and camera gear, but after staggering a bit she managed to maintain a fair pace of her own. Bolan didn't look back to see if she was keeping up.

The danger lay ahead.

After three-quarters of a mile, the gunfire had increased in volume to the point that Bolan knew they had to be close. On top of that, he *smelled* the battle, gunsmoke mixed with wood smoke on the breeze, together with a scent that may have been imaginary, but which he had smelled on every killing ground he had ever seen.

The scent of fear.

Screams wafted to Bolan as he slowed and took a stealthier approach. Ezana did likewise. They were stalking now, although they didn't know the name or number of their prey.

His first glimpse of the village was like staring back through time. Skin pigments may have changed, and architecture of the simple huts, but otherwise he could have been in Southeast Asia, watching recon troops perform a standard S&D.

Search and destroy.

Most of the villagers in this case were unarmed and had almost certainly done nothing to provoke the raid. It was a massacre in progress, and for many of the villagers, help had arrived too late.

"The Lord's Vanguard," Ezana said, speaking the name as if it were a curse.

"You in?" Bolan asked.

"Yes."

"I'm going to the right."

"I'll take the left."

And that was all. They had no time to formulate a battle plan, when each passing moment spelled death for another helpless villager.

Well, not all helpless, Bolan thought, as he picked out the sprawled form of a raider, faceless from the impact of a shotgun blast. He'd have to watch out for the villagers, as well as the guerrillas who were killing them. Bullets didn't discriminate when drilling flesh and bone. For all the frightened natives knew, he might be with their enemies.

Before that thought could put down roots, he was across the strip of open ground that separated village from jungle. Smoke was everywhere, and he could see a number of the dwellings half-consumed by fire. Dry thatch made perfect tinder for the flames. From one hut Bolan passed, the too-familiar smell of roasting flesh reached out to grab him by the throat.

His enemies were dressed in camouflage fatigues much like his own and Ezana's. Bolan made a mental note to double-check his moving targets if he had the time, and then the first one stood before him, obviously startled beyond measure to behold a white man in this place.

Bolan took full advantage of his adversary's hesitation, triggering a 3-round burst that cut a tidy pattern in the center of his chest and dropped him on his back.

One down. How many left to go?

He edged around the southeast corner of a plywood structure stitched with bullet holes. Mosquito netting on a small window had been torn along one side and drooped as if melting. Glancing inside, he saw a woman stretched out on the floor, still holding the small hands of children lying to her right and left.

If any of the three was breathing, Bolan couldn't make it out.

A hand grenade went off somewhere nearby. The soldier

kept moving, coming up behind two raiders as they took aim on a huddled group of six or seven unarmed villagers. Bolan shot them in the back, three rounds apiece, already moving past them as they hit the deck.

"Get out of here!" he told the startled villagers, hoping that at least one or two of them would understand.

They blinked at him and took off running toward the tree line. Bolan turned his back on them and went to find the war.

GABRA EZANA FRAMED one of the raiders in his rifle sights and squeezed off two quick rounds on semiauto fire. The target stumbled, dropped his weapon and collapsed onto his side.

Another saw his comrade fall and crouched beside the body, scanning left and right to find the source of gunfire. He was still looking when Ezana slammed a 5.56 mm bullet through his neck and pitched him over backward, crimson pumping from a clipped carotid artery.

Economy of fire. His mind kicked back the adage learned in basic training. Less was more.

Ezana stepped from cover, moving with a confidence he didn't truly feel. One small advantage gave him courage. He was of the same race as the raiders, dressed nearly the same and armed with the familiar FNC assault weapon his enemies were using. At first glance, they could mistake him for one of their own.

And by the time they stopped to double-check, with any luck at all, they would be dead.

Ezana didn't recognize the two men he had killed, but he knew others in the raiding party might turn out to be his former comrades, those who had deserted from the ADF and followed Galen Starke into the Lord's Vanguard. If so, he didn't relish killing them, but the lieutenant knew they wouldn't hesitate to drop him in his tracks at the first opportunity.

So much for friendship.

None of the comrades he had known and loved as brothers would participate in such a massacre as this one. Ezana thought they would have turned upon their officers if they were told to slaughter women, children and the elderly. Starke had to have warped their minds somehow, perhaps usurped their souls.

Which made Ezana hate him all the more.

He spotted two more raiders emerging from a thatch hut to his left. One of the men was zipping up his pants, the other wiping fresh blood from his knife blade on a swatch of brightly colored fabric. Something from a woman's garb, perhaps.

Ezana felt the anger surge inside him as he brought up the rifle to aim. The soldier on the left was grinning at his buddy when the bullet cracked his smile and snapped his head back at an angle that would certainly have made him scream if he were still alive.

The raider with the knife in hand gaped at his friend's collapsing corpse, then dropped his blade and fumbled with his slung FNC.

Too late.

Ezana shot him through the chest and watched his legs fold. The guerrilla was most likely dead before he landed on his knees, but there could be no harm in making sure. Another round opened a keyhole in his forehead, dropping him in the distorted posture of a limbo dancer who has lost his footing and collapsed, legs tucked beneath his buttocks.

The lieutenant didn't check the hut they had emerged from, knowing more or less what he would find. It would accomplish nothing if he knew the victim's age or memorized her features.

He had enough hate inside to see him through the battle as it was.

Moving on, he met another pair of raiders coming down Indrissa's secondary street. The men were firing into prostrate bodies, making sure that those their comrades shot and left behind were truly dead. One of them glanced up from his work, saw Ezana and began to raise a hand in greeting. At the final moment, though, he squinted, frowned and dropped the hand back to his weapon's pistol grip.

Ezana triggered two quick shots, tracking to pin the second target in his sights before the first one fell. He got there just in time, the wounded soldier's comrade dodging to the left, seeking the cover of a more-or-less undamaged hut.

They fired together. Ezana felt the hot wind of a passing bullet sear his cheek and saw his own shot slip the moving target's left shoulder. It was a simple flesh wound, but it staggered him. He lurched off balance, sprawling in the doorway of the hut. Before he had a chance to wriggle out of sight, Ezana fired off two more rounds and was rewarded with a splash of scarlet from the raider's thigh.

The thatch hut had no windows, and the simple door had been torn off its hinges sometime earlier. Ezana approached with caution, knowing that his wounded enemy could fire directly through the walls if he was so inclined. A careless sound might give him all the guidance he required to make a kill.

As he approached the hut, Ezana checked the first man he had shot. The raider was alive, but stunned. A sucking chest wound made it difficult for him to breathe. The lieutenant debated giving him a mercy round, but since the soldier's FNC had fallen out of reach, he let it go.

Why give his enemy inside the hut a fix on where to aim?

He stopped a few yards short and well off to one side, so that a wild shot through the open doorway wouldn't find him. He was pondering the best approach when suddenly it came to him. It might not work, but it was worth a try.

Ezana walked back to the dying soldier, sat him upright and then crouched behind him, lifting. When he had the raider on his feet, albeit barely capable of standing by himself, Ezana walked him toward the shadowed doorway of the hut. When they were half a dozen paces from the threshold, the lieutenant gave his human shield a mighty shove to get him started, trusting human instinct and the pull of gravity to do the rest.

The wounded raider stumbled forward, zombielike, until he sagged against the thatch frame of the doorway. Ezana thought he tried to speak, but only crimson bubbles passed his lips. Inside the hut, his wounded comrade saw a lurching silhouette and cut it down with half a magazine of 5.56 mm rounds.

The muzzle-flash helped Ezana aim. He fired off three quick rounds and watched the dim form of his target slump back into shadow.

Easy.

If his luck held for the next half hour, Ezana thought he just might make it out of Indrissa alive.

IT TOOK SOME TIME for Roshani Malinke to realize that a full-scale battle had erupted in the streets of Indrissa. He had listened with approval to the sounds of automatic weapons and grenades, the hungry crackling of flames, male shouts and curses, female screams, the squall of children.

It was music to his ears.

Long moments passed before he understood that not all the assault rifles firing through Indrissa's streets belonged to his soldiers. The first clue was a shout of "Retreat! Move back!" that snapped Malinke's drooping eyelids open to behold an unexpected sight.

Three of his men were running toward the tree line, more or less in his direction, as if death were on their heels. In fact, that proved to be the case, as one of them was struck by a bullet from behind, arms flailing in a hopeless effort to regain his balance, crashing facedown in the dirt. The other two turned back to face their enemy, clearly reluctant to engage the unseen adversary as they fired off ragged bursts along their track.

Malinke couldn't see who they were shooting at. He surged upright and sidestepped for a better view. The drifting smoke from several burning huts obscured much of the village on that side, but—

There!

A stocky African in camouflage fatigues, armed with an FNC assault rifle, was firing at Malinke's soldiers. Even as he watched the shooter dropped another member of the Lord's Vanguard, a spray of blood erupting from the wounded soldier's chest.

What madness was this?

At first, Malinke thought one of his own men had rebelled or gone berserk, turning upon his comrades, but a closer look revealed his error. Though their garb was similar, their choice of weapons identical, this gunman was a stranger to Malinke. He hadn't come to Indrissa with the raiding party and wasn't a member of the Vanguard.

That left two major possibilities, one of them eliminated as the gunman showed his profile, dodging toward the shelter of a nearby hut. He wore no shoulder patch or other regular insignia of the Ugandan army. That made him a guerrilla, possibly a member of the Allied Democratic Forces, and where there was one...

Malinke wasted no more time on speculation. Unfolding his FNC's stock, he shouldered it and tracked the moving figure, even as his target fired another burst and took down the last of his three troopers. The man was good, Malinke gave him that, but he had to die before he did more damage to the raiding party.

Thought translated into action, but it came a beat too late. Malinke stroked his weapon's trigger to unleash a swarm of 5.56 mm bullets, but his target ducked inside the hut and disappeared, leaving Malinke's wasted rounds to rustle through the thatch.

Just wait, he thought. The bastard had to come out sometime.

Were there others? Would one man dare to tackle thirty-five alone? Was this, perhaps, his village? Was he home on leave?

Distracted by the storm of questions raging in his mind, Malinke let his eyes shift back and forth, scanning the portion of Indrissa that was visible from where he stood. More smoke, with shadow-figures rushing to and fro, some firing weapons, others tumbling to the earth.

Which men were his? How many of the raiding party still remained alive?

There had been no contingency for solid opposition. He had counted on the peasants of Indrissa to defend themselves feebly, if at all. It was supposed to be a cleansing operation, not a firefight. Now, at least three of his men were down, and very likely more.

Malinke had no means of sounding a retreat order. The walkie-talkie on his belt was the only one his strike team carried. It was meant for contacting the base camp on their homeward march. He was too far from Starke to call for reinforcements, and it hardly mattered, since a rescue team that left the base camp now wouldn't arrive for seven hours.

Too late.

Blurred movement on the left periphery of vision brought Malinke's head around, his neck muscles cramping with the sudden move. He took the pain in stride, barely felt it in fact, as his eyes locked on the white man striding through Indrissa's smoky killing ground.

A white man?

By the time Malinke raised his weapon the spectral figure had retreated into smoke and shadow. There were gunshots from the general direction he had taken, someone cursing loudly in Swahili, just before another short burst cut him off.

Distracted as he was, Malinke missed his first target emerging from the hut where he had taken cover. A swarm of bullets rattled overhead, missing his scalp by inches as they plowed into surrounding trees.

Malinke bolted, dodging backward. The momentum seemed to carry him, and he kept running even when he knew that he was out of range, his adversary robbed of any clear shot from the village.

By the time he stopped at last, Malinke knew that he couldn't go back. He didn't have it in his heart.

The white man had unnerved him, and his black comrade had nearly finished off the double play.

What would become of his remaining soldiers now?

Malinke didn't know, and at the moment he wasn't concerned. He had to reach the base camp and report to Starke that there was danger on the way. He would devise a lie to cover his retreat.

And hope that Starke couldn't sniff out his fear.

IT TOOK SEVERAL moments for Julienne Marceau to understand that the battle was over. Screams and gunfire echoed in her head and kept her hiding in the forest until, suddenly, she realized that it was done. A deadly silence had descended on the village, as if God himself were stunned by what had happened there.

But what, exactly, had happened?

Bolan and Ezana had done their best to leave her behind as they ran toward the village, but Marceau had kept them in sight to avoid getting lost. She'd seen them disappear into the smoke and madness of the battle, watched a bit from cover, snapping photographs from a safe distance, but her mind had shut down after she saw a woman and two children shot down on the run. Their killer had been smiling as he kicked the corpses, grinning to the very moment when a bullet struck him in the face and took him down.

A bullet fired by Ezana? By the American?

She hadn't tried to track the gunshot's point of origin, afraid to see more, know more, as she ducked back under cover and sat trembling in the shadows with her camera clutched against her chest. Each burst of gunfire made her flinch, each explosion seemed to strike her like a slap across the face.

And she tried not to hear the screams.

No one was screaming now, but she began to pick out other sounds. The hungry fire, devouring simple homes, sounded like giant hands crumpling a massive sheet of cellophane. A child was crying out for someone who didn't reply. Voices of women, weeping as they searched the killing ground for scattered pieces of their lives. Men's voices that she recognized.

Bolan called out, "Clear, this side!"

Ezana answered from a distance, "Also here!"

Marceau rose trembling to her feet and forced herself to step from cover, moving toward the wreckage of a small community whose name she didn't even know. The people who had died there in the past few minutes, innocent or otherwise, were strangers. She would never know their names, would never understand their suddenly truncated hopes and dreams.

The camera was deadweight around her neck. Instinctively she lifted it and started snapping pictures of the carnage. This was something, even if she didn't know exactly what it meant right now and might not grasp the full importance of it while she lived.

A record should be kept. Someone should know.

"You're getting this?"

Bolan's voice surprised her, made her jump and blur the shot she was taking of a hut in flames. Turning, she found him watching her from several paces off. He had his rifle slung, and there was a smudge of dirt or ash on his left cheek.

"Would you prefer I not take photographs?" she asked him, not quite challenging.

The American shook his head. "I think you definitely should," he said. "You need to know what this is all about, before you have your little tête-é-tête with Galen Starke."

Her hands tightened around the camera. "I don't know what you mean," she said.

"Don't you?" His eyes were penetrating. There was something very close to anger in his frown. "You do your homework, right?"

"Of course."

"So you know all about the insurrection and the split within the rebel forces. You're aware of Starke's agenda and his methods."

"I'm not sure I—"

"Look around you, dammit! See beyond the camera! You're looking at a day's work for the Lord's Vanguard."

A sense of dread enveloped her, but Marceau wouldn't submit to it so easily. "You don't know that," she said. "You can't know that."

"Gabra!"

"Coming."

Behind her. It embarrassed Marceau that she was taken by surprise a second time.

"You make the soldiers?" Bolan asked.

"Two of them I recognize," Ezana replied. "I didn't know them well, before they left the ADF."

"To join the Lord's Vanguard?"

"Of course."

"That doesn't mean—" But she couldn't complete the lie, not with the American staring at her and the stench of burning corpses in her nostrils. "Why would he do this?" she asked, instead.

"Because God told him to," Bolan said. "Because he's on a mission." Something very much like sadness crept into his voice as he added, "Because he's lost his mind."

"All this," she said, "for nothing?"

"You can ask him when you see him," the American replied. "Maybe he'll tell you what it's like to have a conversation with the Lord."

His words affirmed what the journalist had suspected from the day of their meeting. "You don't plan to join him, then."

"Not quite."

"Why are you looking for him, Belasko?"

"We can talk about it on the way."

"And these people?" She fanned a helpless hand. "What can we do for them?"

"It's done," Bolan said, "unless you want to help us dig some graves."

7

Galen Starke was throwing knives and hatchets at a man-sized target when he heard the sentry's call from the perimeter. He took stock of the target, satisfied that if it were a man of flesh and blood, he would have scored at least three crippling hits. The hatchet sprouting from the wooden forehead would have been a kill.

Sometimes, when he was in the proper mood, Starke threw knives with his eyes closed. The results were inconsistent, but he scored more often than he missed, and there were no complaints from his disciples if they had to dodge a flying blade from time to time.

The master of the Lord's Vanguard was only human, after all...but he was on the sure road to becoming so much more.

Soon. When he had carried out his cleansing mission for Jehovah, Starke would claim his well-deserved reward.

There was a clamor in the camp, excited voices babbling questions, one voice snapping back at them to mind their business and be quiet. There was anger in that voice, but underneath the brittle rage lay stinking fear.

It was a gift of God, Starke thought, that let him smell the fear of other men. He could remember feeling fear before his life was changed forever, and he wondered who had smelled the stench on him.

Malinke had returned, and he was frightened. Obviously

How To Play:

1. With a coin, carefully scratch off the 3 gold areas on your Lucky Carnival Wheel. By doing so you have qualified to receive everything revealed—2 FREE books and a surprise gift—ABSOLUTELY FREE!

2. Send back this card and you'll receive two hot-off-the-press Gold Eagle® books. These books have a cover price of $4.75 or more each, but they are yours TOTALLY FREE!

3. There's no catch! You're under no obligation to buy anything. We charge nothing—ZERO—for your first shipment. And you don't have to make any minimum number of purchases—not even one!

4. The fact is thousands of readers enjoy receiving books by mail from the Gold Eagle Reader Service™ before they're available in stories. They like the convenience of home delivery and they love our discount prices!

5. We hope that after receiving your free books you'll want to remain a subscriber. But the choice is yours—to continue or cancel, anytime at all! So why not take us up on our invitation, with no risk of any kind. You'll be glad you did.

A surprise gift

FREE

We can't tell you what it is...but we're sure you'll like it! A

FREE GIFT!

just for playing LUCKY CARNIVAL WHEEL!

LUCKY
Carnival Wheel
Find Out Instantly The Gifts You Get Absolutely **FREE!**
Scratch-off Game

Scratch off ALL 3 Gold areas

LOSER

WINNER

♠

♥

WINNER

♣

LUCKY CARNIVAL WHEEL

LOSER

♣

◆

♥

WINNER

YES!
I have scratched off the 3 Gold Areas above. Please send me the 2 FREE books and gift for which I qualify! I understand I am under no obligation to purchase any books, as explained on the back and on the opposite page.

366 ADL DNXG   166 ADL DNXF

FIRST NAME   LAST NAME

ADDRESS

APT.#   CITY

STATE/PROV.   ZIP/POSTAL CODE

The Gold Eagle Reader Service™ —Here's how it works:

Accepting your 2 free books and gift places you under no obligation to buy anything. You may keep the books and gift and return the shipping statement marked "cancel." If you do not cancel, about a month later we'll send you 6 additional books and bill you just $29.94*—that's a savings of over 10% off the cover price of all 6 books! And there's no extra charge for shipping! You may cancel at any time, but if you choose to continue, every other month we'll send you 6 more books, which you may either purchase at the discount price or return to us and cancel your subscription.

*Terms and prices subject to change without notice. Sales tax applicable in N.Y. Canadian residents will be charged applicable provincial taxes and GST.

If offer card is missing write to: Gold Eagle Reader Service, 3010 Walden Ave., P.O. Box 1867, Buffalo, NY 14240-1867

BUSINESS REPLY MAIL
FIRST-CLASS MAIL   PERMIT NO. 717-003   BUFFALO, NY

POSTAGE WILL BE PAID BY ADDRESSEE

GOLD EAGLE READER SERVICE
3010 WALDEN AVE
PO BOX 1867
BUFFALO NY 14240-9952

NO POSTAGE
NECESSARY
IF MAILED
IN THE
UNITED STATES

he had bad news to share—so bad, in fact, that he believed he might be punished.

Starke stood waiting for his second in command, a hatchet dangling loosely from each hand. Stripped to the waist, he gleamed with sweat, as if his body had been oiled for exhibition. Muscles shifted underneath the deep bronze of his tan.

When Malinke was within earshot, Starke asked, "How many of my children have you lost?"

Malinke stopped there, saw the bristling target and the hatchets in Starke's hands. His fear compelled him to defend himself. His faith wouldn't permit him to deceive.

Faith won.

"All lost," he said. "I beg forgiveness, sir."

"Lost, how?"

"Indrissa was defended, sir. My men—"

"My children," Starke corrected him.

"Yes, sir." The interruption spoiled his timing, forced Malinke to start over. "I anticipated some resistance from the villagers. A few of them always have guns for hunting."

Starke said nothing, but as he turned to face Malinke, his eyes locked on the African's and wouldn't let them go.

"This time," Malinke said, "there was a trap. Soldiers with automatic weapons. They didn't reveal themselves at first, but—"

"Why?"

"Why, sir?"

"Why would they wait and let you kill even a few if they were hiding in the village when you first arrived?"

Malinke thought about that for a moment, frowning.

"How many?" Starke asked.

"Sir?"

"How many soldiers did it take to kill my children?"

"I only saw two men."

"Two men?"

"And one of them was white."

Starke pondered that. Kampala was on good terms with the

Western powers since Amin had been deposed and civil order more or less restored. It wouldn't be unheard-of for the army to employ foreign advisers, though the fact wouldn't be widely advertised.

"I assume you searched the bodies."

"Bodies, sir?"

"You saw this white man and another enemy. You stand before me, breathing. I assume your adversaries must be dead."

"No, sir." Almost a whisper, Malinke running out of steam.

"My children were destroyed while in your care," Starke said. "You stand before me, rank with sweat from running, but without a wound that I can see. You saw two of the men responsible for slaughtering my children, yet they live. Explain."

Malinke's shoulders sagged. He obviously knew a lie would gain him nothing. Resigned to tell the truth, he said, "My life is forfeit for the loss, sir. I have no excuse."

"Your life is mine in any case," Starke said. "Is this not true?"

"It is."

"Then tell me something I don't already know. Tell me about these men who make my field commander piss himself and run away."

Malinke flinched, but offered no retort in self-defense. "They dressed as soldiers for the jungle," he began. "The African—"

Starke interrupted him again. "What kind of gear?"

"Assault rifles."

"Both FNCs?"

Malinke thought about it, slowly shook his head. "The white man carried something else. I can't be sure. The magazine was here." He slapped the stock of his own weapon, well back from the pistol grip.

Bullpup design. That narrowed down the field. There was the LAPA from Brazil, the Steyr from Austria, the French MAS or Britain's SA-80. Figure that a weapon from Brazil would be least likely to turn up in Karamoja Province, slung across a white man's shoulder.

"What else did they carry?"

"There was little time—"

"You either saw them or you didn't. Which was it?"

"I saw them, sir. They wore web belts and bandoliers. Pistols, perhaps."

"Field packs?"

Malinke closed his eyes, replaying it. The eyes opened as he said, "Yes, sir."

"And who wears field packs, if they're setting up an ambush in a village? Why not ditch the extra weight?"

"They came from outside, then?"

Starke nodded. "Passing by," he said, "they heard your racket and dropped in to join the party. It was careless of you not to take them down."

"I fired at one of them," Malinke said.

"And missed." It wasn't a question.

"Yes, sir."

"And you only saw the two of them."

"Two, sir. But—"

"You had what? Two dozen men?"

"Yes, sir." Malinke sounded numb, a prisoner awaiting sentencing.

It's not impossible, Starke thought. Two well-armed, well-trained men with the advantage of surprise, in a chaotic situation where the hostile forces were divided. He could see it happening. He could imagine the white stranger with his own face, his shaved scalp. The blood rush ringing in his ears.

"Forget about Indrissa," Starke commanded. "You have new priorities."

Malinke stiffened to attention, faint hope sparking in his eyes. "As you command, sir."

"I want you to draw another team," Starke said. "Take all the men you need, with trackers. Use Maurice and Kashka. They're the best we have for hunting men."

"Yes, sir."

"You take your team and find these two hard cases. I want

them both alive, if possible, but you can kill the African if absolutely necessary."

"Yes, sir."

"Understand me," Starke said. "Make no mistake. I want to see the white man for myself. You bring him here to me, alive and fit to talk. I hope we're clear on that."

"Yes, sir."

"I will be very disappointed if you fail, Roshani."

"I won't fail you, sir."

"Get moving, then," Starke said. "You haven't got much time."

"We must revisit Indrissa," Malinke said, "and find out where they went from there."

"Don't bother," Starke replied. "I know their destination."

"Sir?"

Starke smiled and said, "They're coming here."

IT TOOK THREE HOURS to prepare a mass grave in the forest, fifty yards southwest of Indrissa, excavated in a natural depression where the adipose runoff from decomposing bodies wouldn't taint the village's supply of running water. Men and women from Indrissa worked with shovels, picks and garden hoes to plant and cover forty-seven of their neighbors. There was no stone in the vicinity, with which to build a cairn, but the new chief—his worthy predecessor having gone into the hole—declared that guards would watch the spot and drive away the forest's scavengers.

There was no grave for the invaders. After being stripped of weapons, boots and anything else Indrissa's stunned survivors could make use of, they were dumped together in another clearing, where they were doused with kerosene and burned. Bolan didn't attend that ceremony, having seen and smelled enough death for the moment.

On the outskirts of the village he unpacked and hastily assembled his communication unit. Several children—still afraid, but getting over it, as children do—stood by and watched with rapt attention as he opened the antenna, aimed it skyward and began dictating his coordinates into the microphone. The latitude and longitude, together with a brief message describing what had happened at Indrissa, were collected on a microchip and scrambled automatically. He waited for the satellite, checking his watch at fifteen-second intervals until it told him the appointed time. At that, he pressed a button and fired off a pulse of gibberish into the atmosphere.

With luck, the message would be logged at Stony Man before the day was out. One of the techs in communications would tap a few keys on his terminal, and Bolan's field report would be deciphered for transmission back to Hal Brognola.

And by that time, Bolan would be miles beyond Indrissa, drawing closer to his final destination. One more night, Ezana had estimated, until they were on Starke's turf. That was assuming that they met no further opposition on the way, in which case they might never get to Starke at all.

Stowing the gear, he once again reflected on the ADF lieutenant's insistence that at least one of the raiders had escaped. There had been shots exchanged, his rebel ally said, but when Ezana checked the tree line afterward, looking for a body, there was nothing to be seen.

The problem loomed in Bolan's mind. It could go either one of two ways, he decided. If there was a single member of the raiding party still alive and well, he might decide that running home to Starke with news of failure was a terminal mistake. Conversely, if Starke's hold on his disciples was secure enough to span the miles and conquer that initial fear, the runner would presumably report what he had seen.

And what was that, exactly?

Bolan couldn't know, for sure, but it was clear the survivor had seen Ezana. Whether he would recognize the ADF commando under different circumstances—minus panic, drifting smoke and flying bullets—was a moot point at the moment. They had missed the chance to run him down. The harm, if any, had been done.

The runner may or may not have glimpsed Bolan. When he understood that all his comrades had been slain, it would be natural for the survivor to assume a force of equal size or larger had been thrown in to disrupt the raid. Ego wouldn't permit him to believe that one or two men could have done such damage to God's chosen warriors.

How would Starke react when he received the word? Bolan was reasonably certain how his old friend would have handled it, back in the days when they were both on the same side. Starke was a gung-ho warrior who pursued each mission with a vengeance, stood his ground against all odds on defense and would never let a challenge back him down.

But what of Galen Starke today?

If even half of what Bolan had heard about the Lord's Vanguard was true, Starke had to be certifiably insane. That didn't mean he would have lost his edge, however. Quite the opposite, in fact, if he had managed to convince himself that he was acting under marching orders from the throne of God. He might be doubly bold.

And he would almost certainly refuse to let the massacre of his disciples go unpunished.

That raised questions of immediate security for the survivors of Indrissa. Starke might field another strike force to annihilate the village. Ezana had urged the new chief to evacuate his people and seek refuge in the nearest major town, but those who still remained were in no mood to run. Armed with the unfamiliar weapons of their enemies, they were determined to protect their homes and families.

Bolan had no time to debate the question, and he couldn't sacrifice his mission to play rent-a-cop while Starke was left to plan destruction of another village and another, unopposed. So far, the hellfire stopover had worked to the Executioner's benefit, reducing numbers on the other side without substantially delaying Bolan's progress on the trail. Three hours, give or take, should make no difference to the end result.

Indrissa's residents had tasted modern warfare now. If they

refused to leave and waited for the ax to fall again, it was their choice, arrived at in full knowledge of the risks. Bolan didn't believe they could repel a force of trained professionals, but neither could he force the villagers to flee.

His own fate waited for him, farther north.

Or maybe it was marching out to meet him.

They would need extra care from that point onward, without sacrificing speed. It was a dangerous equation, but he knew the math by heart from past experience.

Unfortunately it was never possible to guarantee the problem's outcome from one situation to the next. There were too many variables in the mix, and any one of them could spell disaster in the end.

He watched Marceau packing up her camera, a grim expression on her face, and wondered what was going on inside her mind. She had already passed the point of no return. Her choices now were to proceed with Bolan and Ezana or remain among the villagers, and she had opted to press on. As to her frame of mind and what she now expected from her interview with Starke, Bolan could only guess.

It made no difference.

His mission had no more to do with Marceau than it did with the people of Indrissa. The interrupted massacre had only made him more determined to proceed.

A former friend was waiting for him. And only one of them would walk away from the reunion.

THE PHONE CALL caught Brognola working on a sandwich at his desk. The traffic flow on Pennsylvania Avenue was normal for a weekday lunch hour. If he had cared enough to look outside, through glass that had been reinforced to stop a high-velocity projectile, the big Fed could have observed the limousine parade that signaled politicians on their way to wine and dine, wheel and deal with lobbyists, fat-cat constituents, and perhaps the occasional high-rent hooker. On the sidewalk, rubberneckers from the heartland would be checking out the

statuary, ogling public buildings that had sprouted barricades
after the Oklahoma City and 9-11 bombings, to prevent history from repeating itself.

The call was on Brognola's private line to Stony Man. He
lifted the receiver midway through the second ring and cleared
his throat before he spoke.

"Brognola."

"Chief, it's me." He recognized the sultry voice of Barbara
Price, mission controller at Stony Man Farm. "Bad time?"

Brognola pushed back the sandwich. "None better," he
replied. "What's up?"

"We have transmission from Uganda," Price told him,
speaking freely on the scrambled landline. "There's been contact at a village called Indrissa. It's not on the map. I checked.
Striker and his guide are clear. They're moving on."

"What kind of contact?" the head Fed inquired.

"I don't have details, but they interrupted some kind of
S-and-D deal, by the sound of it."

Search and destroy, Brognola translated. The killing was
still going on.

"They're still with that reporter?"

"Striker didn't say, so I'm assuming there's no change in
that direction."

"Wonderful. We get to read about the whole damn thing
next month in *True Confessions* or whatever."

"Maybe not," Price replied. "She might experience a
change of heart."

Or she might die.

A part of Brognola regretted thinking it, but he had wit-
nessed too much death—and ordered too much—to feel much
guilt about a passing thought. The French reporter was a wild
card, possibly an obstacle on Bolan's journey to find Galen
Starke, and while Brognola knew the warrior would do everything within his power to protect her, she would ultimately
have to take her chances with the rest. Ideally Brognola would
have instructed that she not be taken on the trek, but he knew

Bolan well enough to realize that it was never wise to second-guess the soldier when he was on a mission.

"What time was the message sent?" he asked.

"Almost six hours ago."

Brognola had been sitting down to breakfast at his home in Arlington while Bolan and his native guide were fighting for their lives to save a village so small that it wasn't even on the map. It was the kind of grim dichotomy the big Fed lived with every day, the knowledge that his orders regularly snuffed out lives halfway around the world, while he was shuffling papers, coddling politicians, filling up the hours of a normal business day in Washington.

The death watch kept on ticking, day and night, no matter where Brognola was or how he managed to distract himself.

"Six hours," he repeated. "Were they leaving then?"

"I'm pretty sure," Price replied.

Six hours on the trail, and if they ran into no other problems that meant twelve to fifteen miles of territory covered. Bolan should be on Starke's turf tomorrow or the next day at the latest.

Wrong.

He was already on Starke's turf. In fact, he had already clashed twice with detachments from the Lord's Vanguard. The former Green Beret was broadening his sphere of influence, annihilating anyone who threatened to oppose him—and, apparently, some others for the simple hell of it.

Two clashes with Starke's soldiers in two days, and Bolan still pressed on.

Third time's the charm, Brognola thought. Or, would it be three strikes, you're out?

"Goddamn clichés," he muttered.

"Sorry?"

"I was talking to myself," he said. "How long until the next contact?"

"Twelve hours," Price replied, "if he's in a position to transmit."

Meaning if Bolan's gear was still intact and had a clear shot at the sky.

Meaning, also, if he was still alive.

Twelve hours was a lifetime in the field for a soldier bucking killer odds on unfamiliar ground. Despite Bolan's experience and skill, each time he took another mission, Brognola lived with the knowledge that he might not see his friend again. It conjured thoughts of personal mortality that the big Fed would just as soon avoid.

"Say again?"

"I asked you," Price repeated, "whether you had a message to transmit when the satellite makes its next pass."

"Nothing from me," Brognola answered after a moment's thought.

What could he say? Be careful out there? It was Bolan's job and his predisposition to assume extraordinary risks. He had been gambling his life in games fixed by the house before Brognola met him, and nothing had changed since those early days when it had been one man against the Mafia.

Despite support staff at the Farm and secret funding out of Washington, the war still came down to a single man in practice. No one else could accurately judge the situation on the ground, react in time to make it count, and follow through on any sudden changes in the play.

One man.

The Executioner.

At times it grated on his nerves the way he had to stand at arm's length from the action and observe each play, instead of wading in to find a spot on the offensive line.

You're too damned old for that, he thought, and grimaced when he didn't even hear the small voice answer back that maybe he still had the stuff for fieldwork.

Those days were gone. He had been kicked upstairs, but the anxiety remained. One of his best friends in the world—perhaps *the* best, his wife aside—was still there, in the thick of it, risking his life while Brognola signed requisition forms and went to power lunches with the White House chief of staff.

Then again, the "good old days" weren't all that good, as he remembered them. Life in the FBI had been ninety percent tedium and ten percent blind rage or panic, when the guns went off.

In Bolan's world, Brognola knew, that ratio had been reversed. The days of rest were few and far between, the desk work nonexistent. Living on the razor's edge, 340 days a year or so, wasn't the fun and frolic some armchair commandos might imagine.

Brognola had been there, for a fraction of the time that Bolan spent on death's front porch, and he had no great urge to see that place again.

"On second thought," he said to Price, before she broke the link, "wish him good luck."

ROSHANI MALINKE KNEW he was lucky to be alive. Second chances were rare in the Lord's Vanguard, rarer still at the command level, where a mistake in judgment might cost lives and cowardice was unforgivable. Malinke had executed subordinates for breaking and running under fire. He had expected no less from Starke—had prepared himself, in fact, for absolution through the spillage of his blood—but Starke had surprised him.

The commander was full of surprises.

In one stroke he had given Malinke a new lease on life and a chance to redeem his honor. When he brought the white man from Indrissa back to Starke, Malinke thought, the stain of his transgression would be wiped away.

Malinke had some reservations about seeking volunteers to man his team. The trackers, Maurice Oji and Kashka Berhanu, would go because Starke ordered it and none within the camp dared disobey. As for the rest, word of Malinke's failure at Indrissa—and the fact that he returned, unharmed, without his men—had made the rounds with lightning speed. Many of the enlisted men now would regard him with suspicion, some with frank contempt. Those who had lost friends at Indrissa might decide that debt should be repaid in kind.

It would require a show of strength before they started on the hunt, and that meant he had zero time to spare. He rang the bell for an assembly of the troops himself instead of handing off the simple task to a subordinate. Malinke waited while the men spilled out of barracks and the mess tent, forming into ranks. He felt their eyes upon him, saw expressions ranging from simple curiosity to frank hostility. Standing rigid at the center of the camp Malinke waited for the muttering to subside before he raised his voice.

"You know—or think you know—what happened at Indrissa," he began. "Some of our comrades are no more. An enemy surprised us, and the men I led have gone to their reward in Paradise. I have returned alone to tell the tale and see to it that their heroic sacrifice shall be avenged."

Dead silence from the troops surrounding him.

"Some of you," he pressed on, "may think I should have fallen on the battlefield instead of coming back to warn our leader of the danger that approaches. Some of you may think I am a coward and deserve to feed the fire."

Some muttering at that from several soldiers to his left.

"I stand before you now," Malinke said, "because I have been charged by our commander to avenge these fallen comrades. I will lead another force to find the men responsible and punish them. Together we shall bring their leader back to face the justice he deserves."

He was surrounded and dissected by their eyes.

"Command flows from respect," Malinke said. "If any here believe I am not fit to lead, let him step forward now, with no regard for rank, and challenge me."

There was another silent moment, marked by subtle stirring in the ranks, before a tall, lean form detached itself from the nearest file of men to Malinke's left. One of the soldiers who had muttered at him earlier, no doubt. Malinke recognized the face and tried to put a name with it.

Erasto Something. Korfa? Koroli?

It made no difference now.

"I challenge you," the soldier said, raising his voice so that it carried to the farthest limits of the compound. "I say you're unfit to lead."

As he spoke, the soldier drew a long knife from his belt and held it with the blade pressed flat against his thigh.

Malinke pulled his bolo knife. It was a weapon made for hacking shrubbery, blunt-tipped but razor-edged, heavy enough to shear through limbs of trees or men. It was a simple weapon that had never let him down in hand-to-hand combat.

"There is a way to prove your point," Malinke told his challenger, as they began to circle each other.

"I shall prove it," the contender said.

He feinted with his blade, a short rush forward and a two-step back, with no real chance of drawing blood. Malinke circled counterclockwise in a fighting crouch, his bolo held well back since it wasn't designed for parrying or thrusting.

Erasto made another rush, but followed through this time. If he had managed to connect, his dagger would have skewered Malinke's belly, disemboweling him. Instead, Malinke sidestepped to his adversary's left and swung the bolo in a looping overhand. It's heavy blade connected with Erasto's left shoulder, bit deep and flung a spray of blood across the faces of the nearest spectators.

Erasto staggered, cursing, but he somehow kept his balance, even as his left arm dangled useless at his side. His wound wasn't a mortal one, though it bled freely, crimson soaking through the sleeve and shoulder of his camouflage fatigue shirt. Pain and fury mingled on Erasto's face, his lips drawn back in a bestial snarl.

Still he pressed in to the attack. Malinke felt a certain grudging admiration for this man so desperate to spill his vitals on the ground. He waited for the rush, and when it came, he once more sidestepped, this time to Erasto's right.

The bolo whipped around in a descending backhand, dropping like the oiled blade of a guillotine. It caught Erasto's knife arm, just behind the wrist, cleaving through flesh and bone so easily that his opponent's hand was on the ground, fingers still wrapped around the handle of his knife, before Erasto screamed.

That wound was mortal, if allowed to go untreated, blood pumping from Erasto's stub in a graceful arterial spray. Before the crippled man had time to think about it, though, Malinke was behind him and the bolo knife was sweeping down toward impact on the right side of Erasto's neck.

The blow staggered Erasto, sent him lurching to his left before Malinke yanked the blade free and that motion jerked him back again. Blood showered from the ugly gash, pumping from his carotid artery and jugular vein.

It was too much. Erasto took two wobbling steps and then collapsed, facedown, his body twitching as his life ran out through deep, raw wounds.

Malinke raised his dripping blade, feeling the warm blood trickle down his forearm as he turned to face the audience that was his jury.

"Who else would dispute my right to lead?" he challenged them.

No answer from the watchful throng.

"So be it. You already know my mission. I need thirty volunteers!"

8

Julienne Marceau found the march from Indrissa rough going. The terrain was no more difficult than any covered earlier, but it felt like more of a struggle, putting one foot in front of the other. Her pack and equipment seemed heavier, as if her strength were failing.

In fact, she knew, it was her will, her courage, that was dwindling with every forward step she took.

Preparing for the interview with Galen Starke had been a thrill. Travel, tropic adventure with a hint of danger and the promise of career-enhancing notoriety when she was done. A book, perhaps, and who knew, after that? She had imagined certain hardships—the inoculations, the mosquitoes, maybe blisters on her feet—but nothing she envisioned had prepared her for the slaughter at Indrissa.

Starke had ordered that, if her companions were correct. Marceau wanted to doubt them, but the soldiers they had killed weren't Ugandan regulars, nor did she think that Ezana would have fired on fellow members of the Allied Democratic Forces.

No. The truth was painfully apparent. Starke had either ordered the attack, or units of the Lord's Vanguard had run amok, striking without their leader's knowledge or consent.

As she labored along the trail behind Ezana, Marceau couldn't have said which prospect she found more frightening. She was either on her way to meet a madman or else

Starke had lost control of his disciples and couldn't protect her in his own domain.

Her only security at the moment lay in the two men marching with her. They were virtual strangers, men of violence themselves, but they were all she had.

She thought about the pistol on her hip and nearly laughed aloud. What earthly good would that do if her guardians abandoned her, if she was hunted through the jungle by a pack of bloodthirsty fanatics who knew the terrain?

Fear was an embarrassing emotion for Marceau, but above all else she hated feeling helpless, at the mercy of strangers who could decide her fate on a whim.

At home, she was a fully liberated woman and a respected professional, reasonably well-known in her field, earmarked for greater things. One day, she hoped to be an editor, if not at *Paris Match*, perhaps for some radical journal. In time, she might start her own publication. Why not? A combination of cutting-edge fashion and political dissent, with international distribution if the sales were strong enough.

Unfortunately she now understood that she was very likely running out of time. Her big break, the exclusive of a lifetime, would probably finish her life. The jungle would convert her flesh to fertilizer and bleach her bones.

The morbid turn of thought depressed her, but she was hard-pressed to find the silver lining on this particular cloud. True, they had done well against their adversaries at Indrissa, but Marceau thought there was some luck involved in that. Two men against two dozen would be suicidal odds in any normal confrontation, and the next detachment they encountered from the Lord's Vanguard might be larger still.

When their luck ended, so did hers.

Such fears aside, it also troubled her that she still had no firm idea of what her companions planned to do when they had found Starke's headquarters. She understood that they were no friends of his and could expect no warm reception from his troops.

It suddenly occurred to her that she was nothing but a pawn in their design, the key to Starke's fortress. If she got them inside, within striking distance...

It angered Marceau to think of being used that way by strangers. Still, she reminded herself, these were soldiers on a mission, using any tools at hand to get the job done. They hadn't planned to meet her on the trail, but an opportunity had presented itself. In other circumstances, standing outside the drama, she wouldn't have faulted them for their actions. Even now, with her own life on the line, she found it impossible to hate them.

But her life *was* on the line. That much was clear.

If she abandoned them, ran off from camp that night, she would be lost, no better of than on the morning they had found her. Some wild animal or one of Starke's patrols would pick her off before she had to fret about starvation in the wilderness.

By the same token, though, if she assisted them in penetrating Starke's stronghold, he would regard the act as treachery. No plea of ignorance would satisfy a man who could annihilate whole villages as if he were a pest exterminator spraying cockroaches. And if the things the American had confided about Starke's use of Ebola as a weapon were correct, Marceau might well be stricken with that gruesome plague before a firing squad could be convened to execute her.

Somehow she had been deprived of choices or, more accurately, any choices that were likely to preserve her life. The whole assignment seemed an exercise in hubris now, a mad flight of fancy that had swept her away from the realm of common sense into some uncharted land of no return.

She wondered which of her associates at *Paris Match* would be assigned to write up her obituary, whether it would rate a feature article at least. Of course, if she were simply missing, then the story had no end. Who even cared if there was one less self-important journalist in Paris?

Marceau decided she would have to wait and see what happened, if and when they reached Starke's base camp in the jungle. She had no hope of locating it alone, despite the map coordinates she'd memorized. At least with her partners there was some hope she would reach her destination more or less intact.

If it appeared to be her final destination, she would deal with the problem in turn as best she could.

Ezana had stopped in front of her. Distracted by her thoughts, Marceau almost collided with him, holding her breath as he raised a hand for silence.

Still, that sound...

He eased forward, motioning the others to follow. Marceau took her time, noting that the undergrowth had thickened, clutching at her pack and gear. It made the footing awkward, treacherous.

That sound...

A river.

Moments later, Marceau was standing on the muddy bank, with the two men close beside her. The river was dark green and sluggish. It was also easily one hundred feet across.

"We have a problem," Ezana said, pointing to the distant bank. "Our path lies there."

"We need a boat," Marceau suggested.

"Maybe not," the American said. "Did either of you ever read Mark Twain?"

MALINKE'S VOLUNTEERS were all veterans, blooded with the ADF in battles with Kampala's regulars, converted to the Lord's Vanguard when Starke showed them a better way, a higher purpose for their lives. Each man had been on cleansing missions, most of them on several. They wouldn't shrink from any dirty work as long as it was seen to serve the cause.

Malinke's main problem, he knew, was twofold. First, he had to locate the gunmen who had foiled his operation at Indrissa and surround them. He wasn't entirely sure that Starke's prediction of their course would prove to be correct. Even if the enemy was moving toward Starke's headquarters, there were at least two routes they could select and make good time. To watch both meant dividing his small force, but Malinke refused to leave himself shorthanded. He had seen what these strangers could do, and he settled for dispatching two scouts. They would watch the most common western approach while Malinke and his main party guarded the eastern trail.

And prayed that his targets didn't blaze a new trail of their own.

His second problem hinged upon the first. If he could find the enemy, he had to return with the white man alive, to stand before Starke's judgment seat. It would be difficult, he thought, perhaps impossible. The stranger knew his way around a battlefield, and he was obviously not afraid of risk. Such men often preferred to die in combat, rather than submit to torture and captivity. But if he failed to bring back the white man...

Malinke had no doubt that Starke would punish him, both for that failure and his cowardice in fleeing from Indrissa. It was possible that he wouldn't be executed, but the odds were poor—and he recalled that some of those whom Starke allowed to live were overheard to curse their luck.

Better to die than hobble through the next few years a crippled wreck, in constant pain, until some accident or confrontation with a younger, stronger soldier finished him.

The one and only way to save himself, Malinke reckoned, was to carry out his mission and present Starke with the living trophy he desired. What happened to the white man was a matter of complete indifference to Malinke, once his orders were fulfilled. If Starke kept him alive for agonizing days, so much the better, but a swift, sure death would do as well.

Malinke's soldiers carried one night's rations with them. They would have to hunt for food if they hadn't found their quarry by then. Each man among them understood that he couldn't return to Starke's camp empty-handed. The short rations added urgency to what might be their final mission for the Lord's Vanguard.

And if Malinke failed again, but managed to survive...then,

what? Should he display his dedication to the cause by going back to face Starke's judgment, knowing it would mean his life? Could he forsake his fierce devotion to the cause and thereby save himself, abandoning the unit and the man he held above all others?

There appeared to be no third alternative in the event of failure, and Malinke put the decision on hold. He wouldn't assume the worst until it stared him in the face as an accomplished fact. He would press on, locate the targets if he could and do what must be done to see Starke's orders carried out.

And if he died in the attempt a place in Paradise awaited him.

They had found the trail, if such it could be called, and split the troops so fourteen men were on each side of it as they moved southward. One of the scouts he had sent to the western approach carried a two-way radio, its frequency set to match the unit clipped on Malinke's web belt. A sighting would be instantly reported but no contact initiated with the enemy until Malinke's reinforcements could arrive.

He wished for the helicopter, but knew it would have served no purpose, hovering above the forest canopy. They had no infrared device for spotting targets on the ground, and he suspected that the helicopter's noise would do more harm than good in any case.

If the hostile force did, in fact, consist of only two men, Malinke thought it a mixed blessing. A two-man team would be more difficult to track than a larger squad, but easier in theory to outgun.

Except that he had seen these two in action, and Malinke didn't know which worried him more: the thought that two men could annihilate two dozen or the possibility that there were more like them somewhere ahead of him, waiting for battle to be joined.

More white men.

Malinke thought it unlikely. A white man in uniform these days, anywhere in equatorial Africa, meant either a hired mercenary or an adviser on loan to the government from some Western power. He ruled out the latter, because neither of the gunmen he'd seen at Indrissa wore the insignia of Ugandan regulars.

A soldier of fortune? Hired by whom? The ADF shunned white assistance on principle, since Galen Starke's defection to lead the Lord's Vanguard, and there were no other guerrilla forces of any significance active in modern Uganda.

A third possibility suggested itself as Malinke moved through the trees, with soldiers before and behind him. Suppose the men he hunted weren't soldiers, but assassins, hired specifically to execute someone in Karamoja Province. Who else could it be, but Galen Starke? Despised in equal measure by Kampala and the ADF, Starke was a bane to both and both would celebrate his death. Kampala had more resources for hiring outside killers, but the ADF wasn't exactly destitute.

Some mercs, Malinke supposed, might even take the job for the cost of expenses, using the job—if successful—to headline their covert résumés. And if they failed, it wouldn't matter whether they were paid.

A dead man told no tales and needed no cash.

The radio at his hip emitted a faint burst of static, the volume turned down to minimum level. Malinke unclipped it and thumbed down the transmitter button as he brought it to his lips.

"Repeat," he said. "Over."

"Still nothing, sir," the small, canned voice came back. "Over."

Malinke glowered at the radio. "Keep moving, then," he said. "And don't call me again unless you see something. Over and out."

He broke the connection and returned the walkie-talkie to its place on his belt. The scouts should have known better, but no harm was done. Not this time.

Two men moving northward through the forest. Who could say that they would even follow one of the established trails?

But if they didn't, then Malinke had no hope of finding them this day—perhaps no hope of finding them at all.

He settled into marching cadence, keeping every sense alert as his patrol paced off the miles.

A TEN-MINUTE diversion at the river's edge brought Bolan to a bamboo thicket suitable for what he had in mind. The cutting took another hour, twenty stout poles severed near the ground, then hacked off with machetes to a length of fifteen feet. The last phase of construction led them back into the jungle, where they cut lianas from the trees and dragged them to the river-bank. Marceau helped strip the vines for fibers, which in turn were used to lash the bamboo poles into a fairly solid raft.

At least, it seemed solid enough while resting on the river-bank. The test would come when they were well out from the shore, and by that time, if the lashings didn't hold, Bolan knew it would be a case of sink or swim.

A dunking in the river didn't worry him, per se. Most of their gear could withstand a dip, as long as they fieldstripped their rifles and handguns afterward, to dry their working parts. The satellite transmitter gave him pause, despite the guarantee that it was shockproof, waterproof and virtually inde-structible. Marceau's laptop and camera gear would be ruined, of course, but that could work to Bolan's advantage. The river's current was sluggish enough, barring any surprise un-dertow, to make swimming an option if the raft failed them, but he preferred not to soak himself if it could be avoided.

Most of all, he didn't relish swimming with the river's nat-ural inhabitants.

There was a sandbar in the middle of the river, fifty yards or so downstream, and from that distance Bolan had no prob-lem picking out the shapes of half a dozen good-sized croc-odiles. He didn't know if they were dozing, couldn't see their eyes or judge if they were on alert for prey, but logic told him that a swim from one shore to the other wouldn't be the best idea he'd had all day.

Six crocodiles that he could see—and how many more lying back in the tangled growth along the riverside, watching him?

"Let's go, if we're going," he said.

"Do we just push it out from the shore?" Marceau asked.

"Not quite," Bolan replied.

He had already used his Ka-bar to notch one of the central bamboo poles, securing one end of a liana around it as a mooring line. Two slender shafts, each more than twenty feet in length, had been stripped of their leaves and set aside as poles, with which they would propel and steer the raft.

But first they had to launch it, without giving any ideas to the crocodiles downstream.

Together, Bolan and Ezana pushed the raft across the narrow, muddy riverbank until only its stern was still on shore. At that point, both men heaved their packs onboard and Bolan turned to Marceau.

"Your turn," he said. "Take your equipment and make sure we don't lose anything before we're all aboard."

"I'm not so sure about this," she replied.

"It's this or swimming," he reminded her. "Your gear would drown you, and I wouldn't want to bet those crocs down there are vegetarians."

"We could turn back," she said, surprising him.

"Your call," he said. "Gabra and I are going on."

The redhead shrugged at that, then stepped onto the raft. The bamboo poles made shaky footing, even in her hiking boots. Marceau moved on wobbly legs to the center of the raft, then crouched between the two field packs, one hand braced on each. The long poles, lying crosswise on the raft, were wedged between the packs and her knees.

"Ready," she said.

Bolan and Ezana bent to the task of launching their raft. It was cumbersome and heavy, but the bamboo poles would bear substantial weight if all the lashings held together.

If they didn't...

Bolan held the mooring line as the raft drifted free of solid ground. He kept it from floating away as Ezana made the splashing run from shore to haul himself aboard. That done, the lieutenant lifted one of the bamboo poles and thrust it into the muddy river bottom, some twelve feet beneath the raft's prow. He flashed a smile at Bolan, as the Executioner clambered aboard and hauled the liana rope with him.

Bolan stood erect on the gently bobbing platform, half expecting the lashings to part spontaneously, plunging him into the murky water, but they held. Another moment, and he took the second pole, positioning himself to starboard, while Ezana took the port side of the raft. Marceau had her camera out, but she carefully avoided aiming it at either of her companions, instead snapping shots fore and aft as they maneuvered toward midstream.

"It's really working!" There was wonder in her voice, almost childlike.

Bolan glanced downstream, toward the sandbar, frowning as he saw that half the crocodiles had disappeared. A fourth pushed off into the water as he watched and disappeared almost without a ripple.

Going where?

"This was a marvelous idea!" Marceau was smiling as she rose from her crouch to stand erect.

Bolan was concentrating on the task at hand, wondering how they would respond if gunfire suddenly erupted from the north bank of the river, but he was still vaguely aware of the journalist's movement toward the stern of the raft.

"Be careful back there," he said.

"I'm fine," she assured him. "I just want to see—"

He never found out what she wanted to see. There was a yelp as Marceau lost her footing on the bamboo poles, instantly followed by a splash. Bolan shipped his pole and turned to find the raft empty behind him, nothing but a swirl of dark green water where she had disappeared.

Dammit!

"Gabra, hold on! She's gone overboard!"

Bolan stepped toward the stern. He was in time to see the woman break the surface, thrashing, wet hair plastered to her scalp and forehead.

"Merde!" she sputtered, clearly more angry than frightened. "My camera!"

The strap was no longer around her neck and both hands were empty as they beat the river's surface.

"Forget it!" he told her. "Swim over this way. Hurry!"

"This water tastes like muck!" she said.

"Don't swallow any more of it than you can help," he cautioned. Glancing back downstream, he saw a V of ripples trailing out behind some object moving just below the surface. Farther back were two more sets of ripples, all advancing swiftly and against the river's current, toward the raft.

"Come on, dammit!" he snapped at Marceau. "You're not alone out there."

She turned to follow Bolan's gaze, just as the nearest crocodile broke water. From a greater distance, it might easily have been mistaken for a drifting log, some twelve or thirteen feet in length. The others were too far away to judge, but any one of them could finish her. If they reached her and started playing tug of war, she would be torn apart in seconds flat.

Bolan unslung his AUG and snapped down the folding foregrip, bracing the stock against his shoulder as he rasped at the woman, "For God's sake, hurry up!"

Gasping, she launched herself into a swift Australian crawl, closing the twenty feet between herself and safety, but she wasn't going to be quick enough.

Remembering what he had learned years ago about crocodiles and alligators, Bolan lined up the Steyr's sights between the bony lumps that were his target's eye sockets. The brain was in there, somewhere, shielded by thick bone and armored hide. If he could find it—

Bolan triggered one quick round to find his mark, then two more for effect. The croc began to roll and churn the river into green froth tinged with rust, its belly flashing pale as it convulsed. Bolan squeezed off a final round into the reptile's softer underside, and then the other hunters struck their dying comrade like a pair of sentient torpedoes, long jaws snapping shut on flesh and bone.

By the time Bolan turned away from the grisly feast, Ezana had hauled Marceau clear of the water. She lay panting and dripping on the raft, her hair a tangled veil across her face.

"My camera," she said again, breathless.

"It's at the bottom of the river," Bolan said, "unless somebody swallowed it."

"You saved my life."

He set the Steyr's safety, slung the weapon once again and reached for his pole.

"I may not be in a position to next time," he said.

And then, to Ezana, "Let's get done with this before someone decides to find out what the shooting was about."

HIS NEMESIS WAS on the way. Starke knew it with a certainty that he couldn't explain, the way he knew things when the Lord was speaking to him, sharing prophecies. It was a gift, though sometimes incomplete.

He couldn't see the hunter's face. Starke knew he was a white man—why else would a European or American be found in Karamoja Province at the present time with a paramilitary guide? The question of identity was foremost in his mind, since motive was already clear to him.

The white man and his escort had been sent to bring about Starke's death.

Someone, in Kampala, in the ADF, perhaps even in the United States, had decided that Starke was too dangerous to live. The enemy had weighed his commitment to cleansing the planet and assessed his capability of fulfilling his orders from God. The plotters knew that if he wasn't cut off soon, it would be too late for them to frustrate the Lord's will. His death had been decreed the same way men of power always dealt with their rebellious underlings. It was a practical decision, businesslike, dispassionate.

But they had failed to reckon with Starke's immortality.

The truth had come to him some weeks before after a mamba found its way among the soldiers of his bivouac. The ten-foot snake had bitten half a dozen soldiers in the wild gyration of its fury. Two more had been shot and wounded by their comrades, trying to dispatch the serpent with automatic weapons.

Starke had arrived in time to seize the reptile as it struck again, jaws gaping, toward another soldier's face. Outraged, the mamba turned and sank its fangs into his naked arm. Before Starke tore it loose and snapped its neck, he gazed into the flint-black eyes of death and understood that it wasn't for him.

The medics in his troop had panicked, driven to Starke's tent at gunpoint by Malinke, after they insisted that an adult mamba's bite was certain death. They were correct, as far as Starke's six bitten soldiers were concerned. The neurotoxic venom paralyzed their lungs and suffocated them while Starke remained alert and paced his tent, issuing orders to his aides.

The bite had barely fazed him. Some discoloration near the puncture wounds, a headache that persisted for the next two days, but nothing more. Malinke thought perhaps the mamba had expended all its venom on the first six victims, but Starke knew better.

The Lord had smiled upon him, blessed him for his dedication to pursuit of God's most perfect will. He had been made invulnerable. Neither man nor animal could stop him now, at least until his task had been completed.

After that...

It made no difference what became of Starke's body after his work was done. He knew his soul would be transported to Paradise. If it was God's will that he be reborn someday, to reign upon an earth remade to order, so be it.

If not, he would be happy with whatever lay in store for him.

But first, he had to deal with his nemesis.

God loved to test his faithful warriors.

Starke knew his enemy was coming, and he couldn't shake a feeling that he knew the man. That smacked of madness, even to his own mind, since he had cut off most of his links to civilized society long years before. He was a loner, sharing his private thoughts with no man prior to the day when God had smiled upon him, opening his eyes.

A hunter from his past, perhaps?

Who could it be?

Starke searched his memory and came up empty. There had been too many in the old days, when he served generals and politicians like a zombie, trained to kill upon command. Many of those who'd been his friends were dead, as were the vast majority of Starke's known enemies. Who was there left to reach out from the past and send the shiver of anticipation racing down his spine?

A warrior, clearly. One who wasn't frightened of the jungle or the challenge. One who honestly believed he could complete the task, and that it was a job worth doing.

Kneeling with his eyes closed, Starke couldn't suppress a smile. All would be clear to him in time, sooner than later. Any day now, it would be revealed.

A test was coming.

And the Lord's warrior wouldn't allow himself to fail.

9

The jungle registered each movement of its visitors and dwellers, large or small. There may be no truth to the adage that the beating of a butterfly's wings in Brazil ultimately affected the climate in Tokyo, but within the closed system of the rain forest, every change had an impact, producing reactions. Some were microscopic or invisible, and they passed unnoticed. Others brought life shrieking to an end.

Bolan registered the silence at a subconscious level, before his mind took notice of it. Bringing up the rear of the parade, with Ezana on the point and Marceau between them, he couldn't have said exactly when the birds and monkeys ceased their noise, or why. It was entirely possible his party had disturbed them, as the passage of large predators often did.

Silence could mean anything. A leopard on the prowl, its musky scent transmitted by the breeze, yet imperceptible to human senses. It could be a simple lull in mating calls and squabbling over food. Perhaps the wind had changed direction in the canopy above, though they would never feel it on the ground.

Or perhaps some danger was approaching—but from which direction? In what form?

Bolan couldn't call out to Ezana without risking even greater peril. If he hurried to catch up, it would mean startling Marceau, and there was no predicting how she would react.

Give it a minute, Bolan thought. Be sure.

He didn't have a minute. As it turned out, he had no time at all.

The warning shout came from in front of them. It drew a startled gasp from Marceau.

"Stop there!" a male voice ordered. "Drop your weapons!"

Bolan waited while the order was repeated in another language. It sounded like Swahili, but it didn't matter. Bolan used the fleeting time to scan his flanks, detecting movement on the left that might have been a man or something else.

The choice was simple: disarm and submit to an unknown adversary or risk resistance.

It was no choice at all.

Gabra Ezana had to have felt the same. He opened fire an instant before Bolan did, raking the trees in front of them with his FNC assault rifle. Bolan couldn't tell if Ezana had a clear target or not, but he had his own problems.

"Get down!" he barked at Marceau, spinning to fire a short burst from his Steyr at the man-sized shadow on his left. There came a grunt and a responding muzzle-flash, but it was angled skyward as his target fell.

One down, but not necessarily out.

Bolan dropped into a crouch behind the largest available tree. It would be pointless if they were surrounded, but it still beat standing in the open, acting as a magnet for converging streams of fire.

So much for silence. The forest rocked with the reports of automatic weapons. They all sounded like 5.56 mm rifles, no distinctive Kalashnikovs among them. It told Bolan nothing in a region where the Belgian FNC his comrade carried was the standard military arm. He couldn't count the rifles, but he guessed there were at least a dozen sounding off at any given moment.

It could be army regulars, although he was betting on another detail from the Lord's Vanguard. There would have been time for a straggler from Indrissa to connect with reinforcements and come back to settle up the score. Or maybe it was just another chance encounter in the jungle, one of

Starke's patrols out looking for some action while their leader concentrated on his dreams of prophecy.

Whatever. Bolan had to move before the gunners managed to encircle him. The fact that he was still alive, with no rounds drilling through his back, told him the enemy was concentrated to their front, with gunners circling left and right. It was a fair set for an ambush, and it still might work if Bolan didn't get his act in gear.

He risked a glance around the tree, looking for Marceau, but she was nowhere to be seen. He had no time to search for her, compelled to trust her own survival instincts for the moment. If she got clear of the ambush, he could focus on her whereabouts another time.

If he was still alive.

He rolled out to his left, hoping the wounded gunner on that side had been alone or else that his companions would be taking extra care to keep their heads down. In the present circumstances, Bolan wished they could have been in thicker jungle where the undergrowth—though far from bullet-proof—would offer better cover. As it was, he had to take his chances in a rush from tree to tree, hoping that no one nailed him with a lucky shot while he was crossing open ground.

Somebody tried. The initial burst was high and wide, the product of a jerky trigger finger. Nice and easy wasn't always feasible in combat, but a soldier who habitually rushed shots at moving targets seldom lasted long in the field.

Bolan was hunkered down behind another tree before the shooter found his mark. Too late to make up for the wasted rounds. He had Bolan sighted.

Reluctantly Bolan unclipped one of his frag grenades and pulled the safety pin. He had a rough fix on the shooter. It wasn't clear enough to risk a duel. Ezana was clear of any flying shrapnel. As for the woman...

Do it!

Bolan lobbed the grenade side-handed, timing his release to put a slight curve on the pitch. Counting down the seconds in his head, he was prepared for the explosion, waiting out the squall of shrapnel.

Covered by a pall of smoke he went to find the enemy.

ROSHANI MALINKE FELT a flash of panic when the shooting started. He had briefed his men before they left the base camp, hammering the message home that anyone who killed the white man would be mercilessly punished. It was one thing to receive an order and quite another to come under fire from deadly adversaries without firing back.

His task now was to salvage something from the first chaotic moments of the confrontation and to save himself from suffering the consequences of an error by his men.

It would have been much easier if members of his team had been equipped with headsets for communication at a distance. That kind of battlefield technology eluded the Lord's Vanguard. Soldiers were compelled to make do with equipment captured from Ugandan regulars. Even the supply of simple two-way radios was limited, but Malinke used his now, recalling the two scouts he had dispatched to check the western trail.

He could use every available man at the moment to surround the enemy and cut off their retreat. Before the shooting started he had glimpsed three targets moving through the forest. Two of them were white and one of them—unless his eyes were failing him—was female.

That could pose an unexpected problem of another sort, but there was time enough to think about it when the prisoners were in his hands. Meanwhile he needed to control the gunfire his men were pouring through the trees before a lucky burst brought down the white man he was sworn to take alive.

Malinke started shouting, calling for a cease-fire in Swahili, trusting that the foreigners probably wouldn't understand him. He wanted the shooting to stop before the trespassers were slaughtered, but Malinke knew it would embolden his enemies if they knew he was under orders to preserve their lives.

If he could kill the African who served as point man for the party, or even the woman...

The woman.

What was it that nagged Malinke at the back of his mind? Why did the white woman's presence strike a chord of memory, elusive but insistent?

There was no time to work it out. The soldiers nearest to him heeded Malinke's cease-fire order with visible reluctance. The rest fought on, having either failed to hear him or decided to ignore the command. He smoldered at the thought of mutiny among these handpicked troops, the prospect of a new—and terminal—humiliation in the face of Starke's rage.

Galvanized by a mental image of himself bound to a wooden stake, flames gnawing at his legs, Malinke brushed past the nearest soldiers, circling to his left. He kept his head down, ever conscious of the bullets hissing past. A head shot would be quicker than the fate Starke would prescribe for him if he should fail to bring the white man in alive, but Malinke didn't plan on dying.

He reached the next soldier in line, came up behind him and clapped a hand on the rifleman's shoulder. Startled in the midst of a short burst downrange, the soldier turned on him, whipping his weapon around. Malinke blocked the muzzle with his own FNC.

"Stop firing!" he hissed through clenched teeth. "Remember your orders!"

The soldier blinked at him, then swallowed hard and nodded, acknowledging the command with a muttered "Yes, sir."

A pair of soldiers were blazing away at his next stop, one of them dropping a spent magazine and reaching for a fresh one when Malinke grabbed his wrist to stop the move. He elbowed the other rifleman, putting enough force behind it to stagger him. When both men were facing him, Malinke repeated his cease-fire order and held their eyes until it was acknowledged.

Moving on.

It was laborious and dangerous. Worse yet, he would be forced to circle back and repeat the procedure on the west side of the trail when he was finished with the soldiers on the east.

A sudden movement in the forest to his left startled Malinke, distracting him from his purpose. Was it an animal startled by the gunfire?

No.

He could make out a human form, running in a crouch, but the clothing appeared to be soiled khaki rather than the camouflage garb worn by Malinke's troops and their enemies alike. A flash of auburn hair surprised him.

The woman!

She was running for her life, leaving the two men to fight on while she fled. Malinke couldn't tell if she was armed, but it was clear she had no stomach for the battle.

Inspiration struck him like a slap across the face. He could catch and bring her back.

The smile that pulled Malinke's lips back from his teeth could easily have been mistaken for a snarl. With a final shout of "Cease fire!" in Swahili, he abandoned his goal of restraining the troops and took off at a run through the trees, pursuing the slender woman.

Take her alive, he thought, and poured on more speed.

It didn't matter if she heard him coming now as long as Malinke could catch her.

GABRA EZANA WASN'T sure that his initial burst had found its target, but the result had been none the less striking for that. All around him the jungle had exploded with muzzle-flashes, streams of automatic fire converging as he hit the dirt and scrambled for the cover of a large tree's stiltlike roots.

The ambush would have been more lethal if his enemies hadn't called out a warning to surrender. That was their mistake, and they would have to live—or die—with it, now that the battle had been joined. Ezana wasn't optimistic in regard to personal survival, and he meant to take some of the bastards with him if it was his time to die.

He got his first chance seconds later when one of the ambush party shifted to obtain a better field of fire. The movement only exposed him for an instant, but it was all the lieutenant needed, triggering a short burst from his FNC that rocked the gunner on his heels. Before he could recover Ezana fired another burst and took him down.

The hostile fire seemed to redouble after that, though Ezana fancied he could hear a harsh voice somewhere in the background calling for the ambush party to stop shooting. He could make no sense of that and consequently didn't try. They were surrounded on at least three sides, perhaps by now cut off from all retreat. If someone on the other side wanted to give them breathing room, Ezana would take advantage of that generosity as far as possible. He gave no thought to laying down his own gun, not while he still had strength to aim and fire.

Ezana glanced back from his skimpy shelter, caught a glimpse of the American firing from behind another giant tree, but there was no sign of Marceau anywhere. On the one hand, that could be good news. She wasn't lying dead or wounded in the open, and had thus presumably escaped the first barrage of hostile fire. Conversely, he hoped she hadn't run panicked through the trees.

A bullet gouged the bark beside Ezana's cheek, stinging his face with splinters. He hunched lower, squirming back among the roots as thick as his thigh, grateful that no snakes or scorpions had nested there. He had enough to deal with at the moment, coping with his human enemies.

Dismissing Marceau from his thoughts, Ezana concentrated on survival. It wasn't by any means certain that he would last another minute, much less manage to escape the trap alive. He and Bolan were outnumbered ten or twelve to one, by the sound of it, and surprise was on the side of their enemies this time.

Ezana picked out another target among the trees and fired

a burst of 5.56 mm rounds. He saw his adversary stagger, drop from sight, but he couldn't be sure it was a kill.

He ducked back as more angry fire spattered around him, gnawing bark and gouging divots in the soil.

Why call for a surrender if they mean to kill us anyway?

Ezana had been the first to fire, but that was only natural. He knew the Lord's Vanguard, had seen what they could do in service of their master, and he didn't need the American's vote to tell him that surrender was a bad idea. If this turned out to be his dying day, Ezana could at least dictate the method of his death. And he would take a bullet over slow, protracted torture anytime.

It was unfortunate that they might never finish what they'd started, never have a chance to deal with Starke. In retrospect, the mission seemed like madness, two men marching off to face an army. It had turned surrealistic when they met the Frenchwoman and granted her permission to accompany them. The rest of it—Indrissa and this final showdown in the jungle—seemed a fitting climax to the folly of their march.

I'm not dead yet!

As if to punctuate that thought, the blast of a grenade sent shock waves pulsing through the forest. Ezana craned his neck and saw the smoke cloud billowing, a man-shape lurching in the midst of it, cut down by automatic fire an instant later. The American charged out from his hiding place and rushed the site of the explosion, milking short bursts from his Steyr AUG.

Both of them were still alive and fighting back.

For how much longer?

The lieutenant jettisoned the thought and concentrated on survival. If his adversaries rushed him they would kill him. That was guaranteed. He couldn't stop them all.

But he wouldn't go quietly or make it easy for them.

If this was the end of his road, the closest he would ever come to Galen Starke, at least he could whittle the number of soldiers available to Starke for his next raid against a helpless village, and the next after that.

It was little enough to ask of his life's final moments.

A lull in firing on the east side of the trail surprised Ezana. It made him instantly suspicious. He braced himself for an attack, all the while staying low to avoid continuing fire from the western flank.

A diversion from the main attack?

Ezana braced himself for battle.

JULIENNE MARCEAU had panicked at the first sound of gunfire. She had already seen enough killing for one day—one lifetime—and it didn't help to realize that any contact with the enemy on this isolated game trail meant that she and her companions were the targets.

It would have shamed her, wishing death on hapless strangers rather than herself, but she was too busy trying to save her own life.

That was no easy proposition when bullets started flying from three sides, the snipers hidden by huge trees and shadows. Her first move, an instinctive one, was to flatten herself at the base of a massive tree, trusting its bark to screen her from the worst incoming fire. It helped a little, lying with her eyes tightly closed, but her body still twitched involuntarily with each report of gunfire, quivering as if she were afflicted with a tropic fever.

In her mind, she was transported back to the smoking charnel house of Indrissa. This time, instead of nameless darkskinned strangers scattered on the ground, she saw her own face everywhere she looked. Marceau was still oppressed with a sense that each moment, each breath, might be her last.

She had to do something or she would start to scream, and once the screaming started, Marceau was worried she might never stop, until a storm of bullets cut her down.

She felt the Mauser automatic in its holster, unaware that she was reaching for it, and at once withdrew her hand. She had eight rounds of small-caliber ammo to contend with an untold number of soldiers firing hundreds of rounds per minute. The pitiful side arm would pass unnoticed and accomplish nothing more than leaving her unarmed.

She needed another plan.

She immediately ruled out staying where she was and waiting for the storm to pass. There was no reason to believe her two companions would survive the firefight, as skillful as they obviously were, and if their adversaries didn't kill her outright, even worse than death might lay in store for Marceau. She didn't relish the idea of being held for days or weeks by a platoon of madmen, subject to their every sadistic whim.

If it came down to that, she thought, the pistol might be useful, yet.

What if the ambush party captured her alive, unharmed, and carried her to keep her rendezvous with Starke? Marceau might yet obtain the front-page, headline interview she had come looking for, the story that could make her journalistic reputation once and for all.

At what cost?

The question startled her, even as she hugged the earth and mouthed silent prayers, with bullets hissing overhead. She had come prepared to hear Starke's version of events, record his story with an open mind, and even craft a sympathetic portrait of the hermit warrior, should such a portrayal seem feasible. That had been before Indrissa. Before the stories of Ebola and attempted genocide.

She was now uncertain whether she could even smile at Starke without betraying the revulsion that she felt for him. Could she pretend to listen objectively? Restrain herself from blurting questions that would lead inevitably to her screaming death?

Why was Starke attacking innocent, apolitical civilians? Why did his soldiers slaughter women, children and the elderly? Why—if it was true—had he unleashed a plague that had no cure in a nation formerly exempt from the disease?

They were hard questions and courageous ones.

The kind that got reporters killed.

Marceau quickly decided that she didn't have that kind of courage. There had to be another option, some means of escape wherein she simply got away, leaving her companions to the fate she couldn't change.

That thought did shame her, but her survival instinct took over, surprisingly powerful in a city girl who had never faced real hardship or danger in her life before she came to Uganda on a quest for journalistic glory.

Running—if she managed to survive the first few minutes—meant that she would be alone in the jungle again, wandering lost. She still couldn't navigate, and she had precious little food.

Would she die there?

Most likely. But at least she would have done her best, and when the time came—if it came—she had the Mauser on her hip. She would be spared the threat of torture, rape and humiliation at the hands of savages.

The decision made, Marceau turned her thoughts to the mechanics of escape. It seemed to her that the incoming fire was concentrated on those points where her companions had concealed themselves while fighting back. Stray rounds still snapped around her and made her flinch, but she didn't believe the enemy snipers were firing at her deliberately.

If she was quick enough...

Marceau spent another precious moment hyperventilating, willing her muscles to obey any sudden command from her brain. When she leaped to her feet, the surge of adrenaline hit her like an amphetamine rush, propelling her across the trail and into the dark forest.

She heard shots behind her, had no idea if they were meant for her, and wasted no time looking back to see. Her lungs burned with the frantic panting rhythm of her respiration. The rapid-fire throb of her pulse nearly muted the sounds of automatic weapons behind her growing farther way by the heartbeat.

She had made it!

Marceau's lips were drawn back into a triumphant smile

when someone clapped a calloused hand across her mouth and sudden, crushing weight propelled her into stunning impact with the forest floor.

THE SOUNDS OF GUNFIRE had begun to taper off, starting on the east side of the trail. Bolan, whose actions had been concentrated on the western flank, didn't believe Ezana could have wiped out their assailants on the other flank.

Not yet.

He lay beside the still-warm body of a stranger he had killed ten seconds earlier. If he had placed a hand upon the shooter's chest, there was a chance he may have felt the heart still fluttering, reluctant to shut down. It made no difference, since the stranger's brain was scrambled by a 3-round burst dispatched from point-blank range.

The dead man couldn't tell him what was happening, and there was no one else to ask.

A decent head count might have let him second-guess his enemy's intent, but as it was, the Executioner could only speculate. Assuming a majority of the assault force was alive and fit for combat—knowing he had taken out no more than four of them himself—he had to assume that they were cutting back on aimless, probing fire to save their ammunition for some other enterprise.

A rush, perhaps, if they were able to pinpoint Ezana's position and his own. If they were quick and cool enough about it, Bolan guessed they had the manpower and firepower to overrun him and finish the play in a minute or two of frantic action that would leave him dead or dying.

This is what it comes down to, he thought, but strangely felt no sorrow or despair. There was a sense of loss, for friends whom he would never see again, but they would carry on without him, waging the good fight.

That knowledge helped.

It made him stronger somehow.

Bolan wasn't giving up. He had mentally prepared himself

for such a moment from the first time he had tasted combat. Every time the guns went off, he knew it could be the last time.

That knowledge beat some soldiers down and dulled their fighting edge, but Bolan found it oddly comforting. Each time he walked away from a hellfire confrontation, he experienced a sense of calm that a religious person might have labeled beatific.

Bolan, for his part, was simply grateful for the rest.

It was work time now. He kept track of the shadows moving in the forest, to his left and front. He held his fire, preserving ammunition for the moment when he needed every round to break a wave of charging enemies—or to fight clear and find another angle of approach to his intended target.

Even in his present straits, Bolan didn't forget his mission. He had come to Karamoja Province with a purpose and the work was incomplete. If he could manage to survive the next half hour, there was still a chance that he could see his plan through.

"My friends! My friends, please hold your fire!"

He didn't recognize the voice, but it was speaking English with an accent he could only classify as African.

Bolan waited silently, hoping Ezana would do the same. He did.

"My friends!" the stranger called again, from somewhere off to Bolan's front. How far away? He couldn't tell. "I have someone who wants to speak with you!"

What the hell?

It clicked before he heard the other, more familiar voice. A quick sweep of the trail, as far as he could see, and there was still no trace of Julienne Marceau.

"Please stop the shooting now!" her strained voice called to Bolan from the forest shadows.

There had been no shooting for the better part of ninety seconds, but he let that pass. Waiting. There was no mystery to what would follow. He could only wait and listen to the ultimatum that he knew was coming.

"She is very beautiful," the strange voice offered. Closer, now. "And very wise. We mean no harm to you."

Bolan weighed the odds that Marceau's capture was simply a way to lure Ezana and himself from cover so they could be shot without a fight.

"White man!" the voice called out. "Our commander wishes to speak with you. Surrender means safe passage. I can also spare your friends if you cooperate. The choice is yours."

Is it a choice at all? he wondered. Marceau was in the bag. She could be dead in seconds flat if he stood mute. Ezana was still prepared to fight, but for how long? Could Bolan make his guide's choice, either way?

It was a gamble.

And it seemed to be the only game in town.

"I can only speak for myself," the Executioner replied, raising his voice just enough to be heard at a distance.

"You agree, then?"

He slung the AUG, stood and stepped from cover, braced for the impact of incoming fire.

"I agree," Bolan said.

"And I," Ezana echoed an instant later. He emerged from hiding, still holding his rifle, with its muzzle pointed at the ground.

"A wise decision," the stranger replied, stepping into view with Marceau before him, a knife at her throat. "You may put down your weapons now."

10

Galen Starke knew Malinke had captured the intruders before word was radioed back to the camp. He couldn't have explained how he knew, but the certainty was absolute. Another revelation whispered in his ear by God?

Those flashes grew more frequent by the day—and more illuminating. Starke could sometimes read the thoughts of those about him, although he tried to let them have a modicum of privacy.

It was fascinating, staring at a man and *through* him, listening to what went on inside his skull. Not merely idle thoughts, but to synapse-crackling function of the brain itself, blood pumping through the arteries and veins, hopes and dreams stored up as humming electricity.

A few short months ago, before he was touched by the finger of God, Starke would have thought he'd lost his mind. The masters he had once served when he cashed an Army paycheck would have written him a Section Eight and dropped him like a scorching spud. Some of the men who'd hired him as a mercenary might have had him killed—or tried to, anyway.

It was that kind of power. It frightened everyone it touched, Starke included, but he was getting used to it.

The others never would, and that was fine.

It was dangerous—even sacrilegious—to become too comfortable in the presence of the Lord.

The radio told him that Malinke had lost several men before capturing the strangers. Starke didn't care. His children were expendable resources, easily replaced. Sometimes he thought that he could conjure reinforcements from his mind, by will alone.

He hadn't put that theory to the test, so far.

Three prisoners, the radio had said, and one of them a white woman. Starke knew who she had to be, although he had spared little thought for the French scribbler since agreeing to an interview. There were always other pressing matters on his mind, demanding his attention as he moved toward cleansing of the planet in the name of God.

Her name would come to him when it was time. God would provide. The Lord spared his anointed servant from embarrassment in such things. It was one fringe benefit of working full-time for The Man Upstairs.

An hour before Malinke's patrol returned to the camp, Starke retired to his quarters and put on his dress uniform. It pleased him now, this crazy quilt of styles he had once found absurd. The red-coated outfit impressed his men, too. It set Starke apart, in the same way his towering rage made him someone to fear.

Head freshly shaved, he buttoned the swallow-tailed coat and adjusted the fit of his old green beret. Years of service in inclement climes had taken their toll on his headgear, but Starke refused to replace it.

His next headgear would be a golden crown, placed on his brow by God Himself.

The hub-cap mirror stretched Starke's reflection. He was convinced that no man had a single face, worn all the time. Even drooling idiots had some degree of guile and could adapt themselves to different situations, smiling at need for a handout, snarling when it came to self-defense. How much more complex was a servant of God with the Lord's hand upon him!

None of his children knew Starke deep down.

But they would know him one day soon.

The radio squawked once more when Malinke's patrol was two klicks out, alerting the sentries to look sharp and hold their fire. Starke gave it ten more minutes, loitering about his quarters, then went out to take his place for the impending ceremony.

Three trespassers.

Starke didn't care about the African. Malinke could take care of him, extract whatever information the intruder might possess by any efficacious means.

As for the other two...

The woman had been promised special treatment. Her manner of arrival was bizarre, marching with gunmen who had killed Starke's children at Indrissa and along the trail. In truth, he didn't blame them for the latter incident, but he still had a reputation to uphold. In any case, the woman—Julienne, her name was!—had been compromised beyond the whisper of a doubt.

All bets were off.

And finally, most critically, he was concerned about the white man who had traveled half a world or more to find him, kill him, see his righteous dreams ground into dust. That was the one he needed to examine closely.

Satan wouldn't have come himself. That was ridiculous.

But he might well have sent another fallen angel in his place. Starke wondered if it would be possible to stage an exorcism, cleanse the warrior's soul and thus recruit him for the Lord's Vanguard.

What a magnificent victory that would be!

First things, first.

Starke trusted his emotions, hunches and impulses. They came from God, and since he had been touched Starke understood that any errant thought might be a pearl of wisdom, worthy of examination. He devoted hours to the study of those pearls. They taught him so much that his skull could barely keep it all inside.

Right now, he had an overwhelming sense of déjà vu. Before Malinke led his troops into the compound, Starke could see them, and he felt the mixed emotions emanating from the ranks. Fatigue. Pride. Anger at the loss of comrades. Hope for a reward.

All things to those who wait.

Malinke led his captives to a place before Starke's throne, trail-weary guards fanned out behind them. He made a little speech, which Starke ignored. It had been interesting the first time, now it simply grated on his nerves.

Starke raised a hand for silence and could feel Malinke's surprise, with a dash of resentment for flavor.

Not bad.

He studied the faces of his prisoners, beginning with the least important first. The African seemed calm, as if he had accepted death and wouldn't give his enemies the satisfaction of displaying fear.

We'll see.

The woman would have been a beauty, bathed and dressed to compliment her body. As it was, she had a certain quality that made Starke question his resolve to be celibate. Perhaps he had been hasty, misunderstanding God's instructions. Maybe the command hadn't been to abstain entirely, but to watch and wait until the proper helpmate was provided.

He met the white man's eyes and felt a shock. There was something...

It felt like staring down into an empty grave and knowing it was meant for him.

Those eyes.

Starke frowned, leaned forward on his wicker throne and said, "I know you."

"I DON'T think so," Bolan replied.

He tried to keep it casual, trusting the surgeons who had redrawn his visage twice since Bolan's last meeting with Starke. Elsa Bolan wouldn't recognize her son if she were still alive.

Still, there was something in Starke's eyes that gave him pause.

"I don't forget a face," Starke said. "But yours..."

The founder of the Lord's Vanguard unfolded from his

wicker throne, seeming almost to levitate rather than rise by mere action of muscle and bone. He stood erect, his military bearing still apparent even in the costume he'd affected for their welcoming. The getup reminded Bolan of something from a fox hunt in a lunatic asylum, but he felt no urge to laugh.

"There's something," Starke went on, stepping down from the dais that supported his chair, planting himself in front of Bolan at arm's length. "It'll come to me soon. What's your name?"

It required a force of will to keep Bolan from seizing the moment—and seizing Starke's throat in his hands.

He might not get another chance, but if he failed to kill Starke instantly the others would surround him, beat him down.

"Belasko," Bolan answered. "Mike Belasko."

If the initials triggered something in Starke's disordered mind, so be it. It was the long shot of all time.

"I don't think so," Starke said. "We'll work on that. You've traveled far to see me dead."

A murmur rippled through the camo-clad crowd surrounding them. It sounded like a lynch mob warming up.

"What makes you say that?" Bolan asked his one-time comrade.

"I see things. Feel things. You're not the first who's tried to take me out."

"That tell you anything?"

Starke laughed, throwing his head back, hands on hips. The moment passed and he replied, "It tells me that I'm doing something right. A man is judged by his enemies. In this world, the more, the merrier."

"So everyone's against you?" Bolan said, probing.

"Hardly." Starke was smiling, opening his arms. "I have my children all around me and the Lord above is my commanding officer. It makes the opposition seem less daunting."

"I suppose it would."

"Shall we discuss who sent you?"

"Don't you know?"

Starke blinked at that. "My visions aren't continuous or comprehensive," he replied. "The Lord helps those who help themselves, but He won't do it all."

"And if I tell you no one sent me?"

Starke advanced another step. "Consider the scenarios," he said. "An American soldier shows up in Karamoja Province with a native guide who's also paramilitary. Is he a hunter?" Starke smiled and shook his head. "The weapons are wrong for big game. He's got no porters, no equipment to speak of. Prospecting?" Another head shake. "Still no gear, no support. What's left?"

Bolan stood silent, letting Starke study his face.

"Maybe he wants to join the Lord's Vanguard," Starke said. "But if that's true, why has he killed off thirty-plus prospective comrades on his way to join? It wouldn't sell in Hollywood, my friend. It won't sell here."

"I brought them," Marceau announced. "They are my bodyguards."

Starke turned his smile on her. "And what a fine body it is," he said. "Your story's bullshit, though. Two natives, maybe. If you brought a white man with you, I'd expect one who's a bit more froggish. You're a mercenary or assassin, if there's any difference. I've been both. I know the look."

"It sounds like you're projecting," Bolan offered.

"Psychobabble, now? Am I supposed to think you've traveled all this way, armed to the teeth, to give me therapy? A little TLC? Group hug?" Starke's smile took on the aspect of a grimace. "Shrinks and politicians. I'm hard pressed to tell you which I hate the most."

"But you're okay with killers stalking you?"

"Why not? It's honest work. If I can't hold my own, the Lord will find someone who can. Meanwhile, if there was no one out to grease me, I'd assume that I was doing something wrong."

"That's a unique perspective," Bolan said.

"Exactly. I'm in a unique position. Who else do you know who's felt the hand of God and heard His voice?"

"No one at all," Bolan replied.

Starke didn't take offense. "You're skeptical, of course. Who wouldn't be? You see all this—" another broad sweep of the hands, encompassing the ragtag camp "—and you must think you've fallen in with lunatics."

"It crossed my mind."

"If you were a coward, you'd deny it," Starke said. "Even if I'm required to make the last days of your life a long, protracted scream."

"Is that the plan?"

"I'm not sure yet. You're holding information that I need, and I suspect you won't let go of it without resistance. I'd rather educate than destroy you. The choice is ultimately yours."

"What kind of education did you have in mind?"

"The purest sort there is," Starke said. "Enlightenment from God Himself. He speaks to me, through me."

"You say."

"That's right." The smile acquired a brittle edge. "I say."

"And if I was to ask God whether that's an accurate assessment of the situation, would He answer me?"

"You reek of cynicism, Michael. You don't mind if I call you Michael? Is there some other name you'd rather use?"

"Mike is fine."

"In answer to your question, then, although you spoke facetiously, the Lord is free to speak with anyone He chooses in His wisdom. I obey His orders, Mike. It's not the other way around."

"Suppose I said He sent me here to tell you you're off base and you should let it go?"

"I'd know that you were lying."

"Ah."

"Beware of false prophets who come to you in sheep's clothing. Inwardly they are ravenous wolves. That's good advice, I'd say."

"Convenient, anyway."

A frown. "Meaning?"

"You say God speaks to anyone He chooses, but if some-one else's message disagrees with yours it doesn't count. These men—your children—have no more free will than if you shackled them together in a cotton field."

"God doesn't contradict Himself," Starke said. "He's flaw-less, Mike. Infallible. Once vengeance is decreed He doesn't change His mind."

"Vengeance for what?" Bolan asked.

"That's the question, isn't it?" Starke half turned, beckoning to Marceau and Bolan. "You two come with me." Glancing at Ezana, almost as an afterthought, he told his second in command, "Take that one to the shop and find out everything he knows."

THE CAMP HAD startled Marceau, its cleanliness surprising, but she was still unprepared for Starke's personal quarters. From outside the structure looked like one of those do-it-yourself storage sheds on steroids, inflated to double or triple the usual size. Its outer walls—aluminum?—had been painted with a kind of wraparound mural that combined camouflage and art. It was all forest tones, greens and browns and grays.

The interior of Starke's quarters was as different from the outside as night from day—literally. The walls and ceiling had been painted navy blue, then sprinkled with white specks to create the illusion of stars. It took a moment for her to rec-ognize the first complete constellation, belatedly under-standing that the artist had spent days—perhaps weeks—recreating a perfect night sky.

"Your work?" she asked.

"A hobby," Starke replied. "I'm fascinated by the stars. They may not rule our fate, but they are still His awesome work."

The furnishings, by contrast to their background, were routine. A hammock sprawled across one corner of the room, between the Big and Little Dippers. Plastic crates and empty ammo boxes had been stacked along one wall to form a nest of cubbyholes for folded clothes and other things. A sun-bleached skull peered out from one crate on the top row.

Marceau's eyes moved on. An ornate standing screen, decorated with fire-breathing dragons, occupied the corner nearest Starke's hammock. His lounging furniture consisted of a folding camp chair and a wooden stool.

"You won't mind if I change," Starke said, not asking their permission. The journalist watched him unbutton the swallow-tail coat and shrug it off, stifling a gasp as he revealed his naked torso.

Galen Starke was covered with tattoos from his shoulders to the point where various intertwining designs vanished into his breeches. The complicated body art covered his chest, stomach and back. His arms were bare and tan below the elbows, bright with vivid ink above.

Tattoo artists called total-body coverage a "suit." It was favored by some Asian gangsters and mystics alike, Marceau recalled, designed to be concealable beneath everyday clothing. Untold hours of agony had been endured to gain the end result—worse if traditional bamboo needles had been used in place of modern tattoo equipment.

"That must've hurt."

Starke smiled at her before he stepped behind the screen. "Pain is a state of mind," he said. "It's also very educational. I'd never want to lose it."

"So," Bolan said, "what is this all about? Sharing the pain?"

Starke didn't answer for a moment. He was changing pants, balanced first on one foot, then the other. Marceau found herself wishing the screen were transparent. Her interest was purely academic, of course.

"It's not about sharing anything," Starke replied. "It's not about warnings or lessons. We're past all that, Mike. Mankind has failed the test *again*. It's not the first time, if you know your Bible. Eden. Noah's flood. Sodom and Gomorrah. We keep screwing up, my friend, and we're fresh out of second chances."

"This isn't political," Bolan stated.

"Only in the universal sense."

"You don't expect someone to pay you off?"

"No, Mr. Bond, I expect you to die." Starke watched them for a moment, deadpan, then flashed a smile. "Gert Frobe. *Goldfinger,* 1964. You people need to keep up with the classics."

"This is all about destruction, then?" Bolan said.

"It's all about *cleansing,* Mike. Mankind was His greatest creation, His favorite of all the universe, but we've turned our own backyard into an open sewer time after time. He's given up on the unworthy. As for me, I'm just following orders."

"Where have I heard that before?" Bolan asked.

"The Germans got it wrong," Starke said. "They got hung up on all that nonsense with the Jews and went down a blind alley. Millions paid for their mistake. Imagine what an army with that kind of prowess and determination could accomplish if its leaders took their marching orders straight from Him!"

"Most of the Nazis thought they did," Bolan said. "We're back to state of mind."

Starke's smile evaporated in a heartbeat. "Hitler blew his shot. He had a mission, but he stumbled on the sin of pride. It's lethal."

"You're immune, I take it?"

"I've been purified." Starke frowned, eyes narrowed to study Bolan's face. "It may not be too late for you to join the winning side."

"And all I have to do is—what? Acknowledge you as God's mouthpiece?"

"Acknowledge *Him.* I'm just his messenger."

"That's where I hit the snag," Bolan responded.

"You find it unbelievable, God speaking through a man?"

"I've never given it much thought, but if I did I'd keep in mind what you said earlier, about false prophets."

Starke emerged from behind the standing screen. He had changed into camo fatigues and an olive-drab T-shirt, the cuffs of his pants tucked into combat boots.

"I can't fault your skepticism," he told Bolan. "I resisted

for months when God first started talking to me one-on-one. It takes a private revelation, sometimes."

"I imagine it would."

"I *do* know you," Starke said. "I still can't put my finger on it, how or when, but I'll get there eventually."

"Take your time."

"Time's not my problem, but it could be yours. I'm all for gradual persuasion in the proper circumstance, but when you live at Defcon Four it's basically shit or get off the pot. You know what I mean?"

"I've been there," Bolan said.

"I can see you have."

Starke turned to Marceau and said, "I don't mean to neglect you. We can talk about that interview while we eat dinner. How'd that be?"

"There's still our friend," Bolan reminded him.

"He won't be joining us." Starke's face was blank, eyes cold and flat. "He already has more than he can handle on his plate."

IT TOOK MALINKE half an hour to extract the subject's name. That was pure willful stubbornness, of course. Real soldiers knew that name, rank and serial number were legitimate questions under any code of international law. The stalling was an insult and deliberate affront to Malinke's authority.

Unless the subject was a spy.

Malinke took a break to let the hand-crank generator rest and put his thoughts in order. Starke was sure these strangers had been sent to kill him, either by Kampala or the ADF, but what if he was wrong? What if the two men were supposed to watch and gather information for their masters, thereby threatening the Lord's Vanguard itself, and not one individual?

Starke was the founder and commander of the movement, certainly—but if the Lord stretched out His hand to call Starke home before the work was finished, someone else would take his place. Malinke had aspired to that exalted post on more than one occasion, then chastised himself for yielding to the sin of pride.

Killing one man wouldn't derail the movement if another stood willing and able to replace the fallen hero. To destroy the Vanguard their enemies would need details on membership, numbers, precise location of the base camp and supply dumps, and above all else the plans for future cleansing actions.

Information that a lurking spy could store inside his head and carry back to those who bought his soul.

Malinke didn't think the man who slouched before him, straining the ropes that held him upright, was much of a spy. More likely he had been employed to guide the others, based on knowledge of the province and his military skill. Admittedly he had killed many of Malinke's men—and while that seemed to clash with the covert intelligence scenario, Malinke reckoned some agents were too weak or self-righteous to avoid meddling, even when it jeopardized their mission.

The mission was blown now. All Malinke had to do was pin down the objective and find out what that mission was.

Break time was over.

"You're a stubborn man," Malinke told the slouching, naked figure. "I admire that. You've met your match in me, however. You will never leave this place unless you tell me what I want to know."

"Then I will die," a raspy voice replied.

"The time and manner of your death is still a matter unresolved."

"Do what you will."

Malinke stepped in close. "I don't need your permission! Within these walls I make the rules."

"That might surprise your master."

Glancing to his left, Malinke saw the soldier crouched behind the hand-crank generator frowning at him. Malinke commanded loyalty—or had, before the bloody business at Indrissa stained his reputation. What if this one muttered to his fellows in the ranks? How might Malinke's innocent, unthinking comment sound when it got back to Starke?

Enraged, he swung a fist into Ezana's face. The sagging figure shuddered, spitting blood. Malinke turned away, fuming, so that his flunky couldn't see him flex his aching hand.

"You are a clever man, as well as stubborn." Pleased to hear no tremor in his voice, Malinke forged ahead. "You seek to twist my words and turn them back against me."

"Are you frightened of me?" Ezana asked. He forced a bloody smile.

"Frightened of you? You're finished, little man. The only matter unresolved is how and when I will permit your soul to flee the useless form in which it now resides."

"Please wake me when you finally make up your mind."

Malinke's cheeks were flushed with anger. "If you have the strength to joke," he said, "you can provide the answers I require."

"Unlikely." Ezana spit into the dust, saliva flecked with blood.

"There is no doubt that you will speak. Perhaps if I place the electrodes...here?"

He spent a moment with the shiny alligator clips, adjusting them, then stepped back from the stake and nodded to his aide. The generator's whirring sound was followed instantly by thrashing and a high-pitched, ululating squeal.

Malinke smiled. Sweet music to his ears.

Defiance always had a price. He wondered how much this one was prepared to pay.

Gabra Ezana gave a final spastic lunge against his bonds and slumped insensate, drooling down his chest.

"Enough."

Malinke dared not kill the spy before he had extracted some useful information. He had managed to regain a measure of respect from Starke by capturing the trespassers, but he could lose it just as quickly if he failed in his assignment.

There was time.

Outside, he knew, the troops were on their way to dinner. Starke and the two white captives also would be dining. He could take leave of the grilling now and join them, but Malinke feared what Starke might say. He pictured the commander's blank face and felt himself quail inwardly at having no response.

Malinke let another moment pass before he stepped up to his prisoner. The latex gloves he wore made contact with the sweat-drenched face somehow unreal. Detached.

Malinke took an ear in either hand and twisted them. He could have ripped them from Ezana's skull, but that wasn't his plan. A variation in the pain would bring his subject back to him, chastened, perhaps more willing to cooperate.

The hostage sputtered, fighting back to consciousness against his better judgment. Only suffering and death awaited him, but he couldn't resist the call.

"Is that your best?" Ezana asked through deeply bitten lips.

"Not yet," Malinke promised. "Are you a religious man?"

"You want to save my soul?" he asked, grinning.

"It may be too late for that. You've sinned outrageously against the servants of the Lord and offer no repentance when your crimes are pointed out to you."

"It's hell, then? I will see you there."

Malinke kept his face deadpan. "I simply wondered, if you were religious, whether you had any scruples about going whole into the ground."

Ezana blinked at that, confused.

"You're such a stubborn man," Malinke said, "that I'm afraid you've beaten my first line of questioning. That's tedious for me—and bad for you, if your have any craving to be buried in one piece."

"Do what you will," the hostage responded. Malinke noted that he spoke with less resolve this time.

"The bag," Malinke said.

His aide got up and fetched it from a corner near the door. It clanked with every step he took, again when it was set down at Malinke's feet.

Malinke crouched and reached inside the bag. His captive's brimming eyes were riveted on stainless steel: skewers and blades, a corkscrew, heavy shears, a compact saw.

"I'm sorry you have made this necessary. Is there anything you wish to say?"

Ezana shook his head, sweat raining down his face.

"I feared as much," Malinke said. "Let us begin."

11

The compound's mess hall was an open tent some twenty yards long, with mismatched tables scattered throughout. Most of the seats were low-slung camp chairs that left diners peering over the edge of their respective tables as if they were standing in foxholes. In other circumstances it would have been funny, but the faces of Starke's soldiers, tracking Bolan and Marceau with dead eyes, killed any vestige of humor the setting possessed.

The mess kitchen consisted of two side-by-side fire pits and a squarish brick oven. Something was baking when they reached the tent, its aroma conjured images of nothing Bolan recognized. Black kettles hung above the fire pits. Two of Starke's commandos on KP were sweating into pots of rice and stew.

Delicious.

Marceau went pale as Starke picked up a metal plate and ladled her food, taking his own in turn.

"We're over here," he said, proceeding toward the only table that had three chairs of approximately normal size. Given the empty space around the table, Bolan reckoned that it had to have been reserved for brass.

The stew looked gamy, smelled about the same, but he had eaten worse. Bolan would need his strength for whatever was coming next. His battery of shots before he left the States had included one for botulism. He didn't think the food was dangerous. The soldiers he had seen before looked strange in some respects, including some of their tattoos and glassy stares, but none of them seemed weakened by disease or malnutrition.

He sat across from Starke, with Marceau on his left. Their table had folding metal legs and a fiberboard top that was starting to warp. A card table once, he supposed. Someone had written two words across one corner in heavy black felt-tipped pen. A name perhaps? Bolan couldn't read it.

He tasted the stew, thinking back to survival school days. Was it monkey or snake?

"You've joined us at a busy time," Starke said between mouthfuls of stew. "We've stepped up the program dramatically the past few weeks."

"More slaughters like this morning?" Marceau asked.

Starke smiled. When he replied, his tone reminded Bolan of a kindly pedant, taking time out from his scholarly research to answer questions from a child.

"My dear," he said, "when I described my orders and their urgency, I didn't mean to say that I'm without free will. Tactics are flexible. That's why the Lord selected one of my experience."

"More shootings, then," she said.

"He means Ebola."

Starke froze for a heartbeat, with the spoon poised halfway to his open mouth. He set it down again, sat back and smiled.

"You've done your homework, Mike. Or should I say someone has done it for you?"

"It's true, then?" Marceau asked.

Starke didn't seem to hear her, cold eyes locked on Bolan's face. "Who are you, really?"

"Someone who's not ready to be 'cleansed' out of existence."

"You assume you have a choice," Starke said.

"We all have choices."

That produced a smile from Starke. "True enough, within limits," he said. "A man facing execution can try to escape or commit suicide. On rare occasions he's granted an opportunity to redeem himself and change the course of history."

"One man's redemption is another's damnation," Bolan replied.

"Touché." Starke frowned then, leaning forward with his elbows on the table, making it shift from his weight. "I will remember where we've met. I promise you."

"Your revelations must be slipping."

"This isn't from the Lord." Starke raised a hand and tapped his temple with the index finger. "Everything I need is right in here."

"Retrieval getting rusty?"

"We have time," their host replied. "It would be rude to send you on your way until we've cleared up the loose ends."

Bolan didn't suppose that Starke was thinking of a pleasure cruise. What modes of execution were available to send him "on his way"? A firing squad? Then again, Starke might devise something more original—more protracted—for a fellow countryman dispatched to murder him.

Marceau cleared her throat. "What about our interview?"

"We're having it," Starke said. "Ask anything you like." Before she had a chance to speak he pointed his spoon at her plate and asked, "Is everything all right?"

The journalist poked at the turgid mass with her spoon. "Oh, fine," she said. "It's been a long, strange day. I've seen so many things...some of them not conducive to a hearty appetite."

"I understand," Starke said. The perfect gentleman, if he hadn't been certifiably insane. "You're not accustomed to the rigors of a war zone."

"Is it war?" she asked him pointedly.

"What else?"

"This morning when your men were killing unarmed villagers it looked like genocide."

Bolan gave Marceau high marks for courage, but her instinct for discretion left something to be desired.

"I wouldn't quarrel with that," Starke said, "as long as we agree on proper definitions. "'Genocide' comes from the Greek *genos,* for 'race.' In standard usage it describes the efforts of one ethnic group to liquidate another. Nazis killing Jews. Turks and Armenians. Tutsi and Hutu. In that context, we regard it as an evil act."

"You disagree?" She was in a journalistic mode, her curiosity sincere.

"The concept has been hijacked and perverted," Starke stated. "It's been trivialized to the point of becoming cliché. Whatever happened to the real genocide, meaning annihilation of the human race? More the point, who has a better right to wipe man off the planet than Almighty God, who put him there?"

Bolan could almost feel the heat behind Starke's eyes. Fanaticism burning bright.

"God tried before, you may recall," Starke told them, forging on. "He drowned the planet with a mighty flood, but he was merciful to Noah and his family. With all respect, that was the Lord's mistake. Those bastards barely found a place to moor the boat before they started fornicating, piling up their list of brand-new sins."

Starke pushed back from the table, smiling radiantly.

"All right, then," he said. "Who wants dessert?"

GABRA EZANA KNEW he was alive because his body hurt from head to heels. The pain seemed to have infinite variety. His head throbbed from the sick hangover of electric shocks and stunning blows. His broken nose pulsed with a slightly different ache. Each time he drew breath, cracked ribs drove short, sharp blades into his lungs. His genitals felt scalded, flayed. The weakness that he felt from loss of blood was almost a relief—if only it would tip him back into unconsciousness.

No! Stay awake!

The darkness beckoned him. If he gave in to its pull, Ezana knew there was a fifty-fifty chance that he would plummet through that no-man's-land until he lost himself entirely and could never find the light again.

Would that be bad?

He had to think about the answer for a moment, even knowing in advance what it had to be.

You must survive to take revenge.

The mission had become intensely personal for Ezana in the past few hours. Embarrassed by surrender, separated from his comrades, he had been debased and violated to the point where nothing remained except pain and a simmering hatred. He had pledged himself to kill his torturer and to avenge himself against the man who gave the order.

Starke.

It was a victory of sorts that he could still recall the name. His thoughts were jumbled, hazy, drifting in and out of focus through a fog of suffering. He didn't know the name of his interrogator, but that face was etched forever in his memory. Ezana reckoned he could track the man by scent to the far ends of the earth if necessary.

But he would have to stay alive to do that.

And he had to free himself somehow.

They'd left him bound, more or less upright, to the post in the interrogation chamber, sagging in his bonds so that the ropes chafed his skin and competed for attention with the other, greater pains that haunted him. He knew his legs would soon begin to cramp—he could already feel it starting in his calves—and then it would become a challenge not to scream anew.

Slowly, determinedly, Ezana started working on his bonds. It was a challenge, since his arms were bound behind the wooden stake that chafed his back, fingers clumsy from restricted circulation. The ADF lieutenant couldn't reach the knots at first. He squirmed and twisted, chafing his wrists to the point where they bled. The new pain seemed to help somehow, the warm trickle of blood across his palms and knuckles helping resurrect the feeling in his hands.

Once he had found the knots, untying them became the challenge. Ezana couldn't see the knots or pluck at them directly due to the awkward placement of his hands. Instead, he had to scratch blindly and hope one of the knots would loosen if he kept it up.

How long, assuming it could work at all?

He had no clue.

The worst part, pain aside, was fading in and out of consciousness. Three times after he started picking at the knots, Ezana jerked awake with fresh pain in his head and no idea of how much time had passed. He didn't know when his interrogators would return or what else they might ask. But if they started in on him again, Ezana knew he would tell them everything.

They had already broken him—or had they? In his ragged, jumbled thoughts, Ezana remembered babbling between the screams. He had no clear-cut memory of what the questions were or which ones he had answered. Were there any secrets left to him, before the darkness fell?

Belasko!

Had he doomed the tall American by spilling what he knew about the ADF's involvement with Kampala in the plot to silence Starke? And did it matter if he had? Starke seemed to recognize them as assassins from the moment they had walked into his camp. Would simple confirmation shorten or prolong the final hours of their lives?

And why am I not dead?

That question stopped him picking at the knots for several moments, then he shook it off and resumed his work. He was alive because his captors didn't wish to kill him yet. As for the reason, who could say? Perhaps he *had* withheld some information they still wanted to extract. Or maybe they preferred his execution to be public, an amusement for the troops.

He might surprise them if he could only—

The lieutenant stiffened at the sound of footsteps drawing

closer. When the door to his cell opened, it was all that he could do to keep from screaming his frustration.

As it was, he couldn't stop the scalding tears of rage from spilling down his cheeks.

MARCEAU HAD PROTESTED when Starke sent the American away with two guards to his quarters, but Starke had insisted they have time alone.

"For the rest of your interview," he'd said. "It's only fair."

Back in the hut he occupied, beneath the artificial starry sky, they sat in camp chairs facing each other. He permitted Marceau to use her tape recorder.

"May as well keep everything in context, yes?" he said.

Before she had a chance to ask him any questions Starke leaned forward, elbows on knees, holding her eyes with his own. "I sense that you're disturbed," he said, "by what you've seen since you arrived."

Instead of mocking his pretentious tone she said, "You're right. Communications with my editor, assurance of safe passage and so forth, were taken in good faith. I understood that you'd consented to an interview. Now, here I am, delivered under guard, a prisoner."

"My prisoners wear chains," Starke said, eyes flicking over her body, "or they wear nothing. If you were my prisoner, Julienne, you'd be talking to my second in command right now. Not willingly, perhaps, but he can be persuasive when he concentrates."

She flashed on Ezana being led away. "Is that where—"

"Speaking of good faith," Starke interrupted, "I don't normally expect reporters who want interviews to show up with a couple of assassins hired to kill me. Is that what they're teaching now in journalism school?"

"I've told you how that happened. I was—"

"Stranded by your porters. I remember." Starke made no attempt to hide his skepticism. "And first thing you know, two heroes happen by to save you from the perils of the big, bad jungle. Better yet, you share a common destination with your heroes. Serendipity."

"I needed help," she said.

"Were you their prisoner?"

"Excuse me?"

"Did they force you to accompany them? Or were you free to leave their company?"

"I could've left," she said.

"You have the same freedom with me. By all means, take your things and go."

She blanched. It hurt to speak the words, "I can't survive alone out there."

"And yet," he said, "you chose to come here for an interview, knowing the dangers of the journey. On the way, you met my enemies and welcomed them with open arms. Now, when I offer you my hospitality, you call yourself a prisoner. Is that objective journalism, Julienne?"

"I was deceived by your agent in Paris," she said. "He lied to me and to my editor. He called your people freedom fighters."

"So we are."

"Whose freedom?" she demanded.

"God's freedom to enforce His will as He sees fit," Starke said. "It's really best for all concerned, you know. What kind of lives do people really have today, stewing in sin and blasphemy? They have so much to answer for on Judgment Day, it's only merciful to cut them off before they run up any more transgressions on the tab."

"You're doing them a favor, then?"

"That's right. You could say it's a blessing in disguise."

"You bless them with machine guns and Ebola?"

If her sarcasm affected Starke, he hid it well. "I use the most efficient tools available to carry out God's work," he said. "The ancient Israelites used swords and spears to cleanse the Promised Land. We've learned a thing or two since then."

He smiled. His gaze felt like a lizard crawling on her skin. "You're proud of this?"

"Serving the Lord with every means at my disposal? Certainly. Who wouldn't be?"

"The villagers killed at Indrissa this morning, what sins had they committed?"

"Specifically?" He shrugged. "I wouldn't know. Scripture tells us all men have sinned and come short of the glory of God."

"Including yourself and your men?"

"*Especially* myself and my children," Starke replied. "But we've been rescued, pardoned and we serve God now."

"As He reveals Himself to you."

"That's right."

"Why weren't the people of Indrissa rescued, too?"

"That's not my job. I've been commanded by the Lord to carry out specific duties in the final days. The cleansing has begun. Repentance and salvation happen here." An index finger tapped his chest, above the heart. "It's private, known but to the sinner and to God. The righteous have nothing to fear from Judgment Day. Nothing to fear from me."

"You've said you plan to murder everyone on Earth."

"Not murder," he corrected her.

"All right, then. Cleansing."

"Better."

"You intend to *cleanse* the innocent along with everybody else."

"No one is innocent. The righteous and redeemed will be called home to God. I'll see them there. They should be grateful for my help in crossing over."

Marceau's recorder clicked, a signal that Side A of the cassette was full. She popped it out, reversed it and thumbed the button to record. A red light winked, voice-activated, as she spoke.

"I'm curious about logistics."

"Ah." Starke didn't seem surprised.

"We're sitting in the middle of the jungle. You've cleansed how many by now? Two hundred? Three?"

"Who's counting?" he replied with that infuriating smile.

"You have three hundred men or so?"

"That's close."

"You see the problem? With three hundred men—three hundred Africans—how can you hope to kill eight billion all around the world? Even with the Ebola it's a hopeless task."

Starke frowned. "It seems that way," he said, "because you're steeped in disbelief. God deals in miracles. Noah and half a dozen members of his family repopulated earth after the flood. Creating life has always been more difficult than ending it."

"But Noah and his family were sinners," she reminded him. "You told me so, yourself."

Starke blinked at her, then rose, ending the interview.

"We'll talk again before you leave," he said. "It's too much to expect that you'll report our message favorably. I'll be satisfied if people know what's happening. Each sinner has a chance to seek redemption now, before the end."

He snapped a finger at the doorway and two guards appeared.

"These men will take you to your friends," Starke said. "Tomorrow, before you leave, we'll give you something more to think about."

"WHAT ABOUT THE WOMAN?" Malinke asked. He watched Starke pacing restlessly about his quarters, never still.

"She's a reporter," Starke replied. "She reckons I'm insane but she'll print what she's seen and what I told her, anyway. That's all we need."

"Publicity." The word had a sour taste on Malinke's tongue.

"You were opposed to it, I know. It's for the best." He paused and met Malinke's gaze. "It's done."

"Yes, sir."

"There'll be no interference in this matter. Understood?"

"Of course."

"Some of the men don't understand about Indrissa," Starke

went on. "You silenced them with your display out on the yard, but doubts remain."

"In your mind, sir?"

Starke turned away, resumed his pacing to and fro.

"If I doubted your loyalty, you'd be dead. As for your courage..."

Biting off the first reply that came to mind, Malinke said, "What about my courage, sir?"

"I was always taught discretion was the better part of valor," Starke replied. "If I thought you were yellow, I'd have busted you."

Before Malinke could relax, Starke added, "It's the men you have to think about. Do you expect one of them to step up and challenge you each time you take a squad into the field?"

"No sir!"

"I hope not, son. Your future could depend on it."

"Yes, sir. What about the prisoners?"

"You put them together like I told you?"

"Yes, sir. But the African—"

"What was his name?"

"Gabra Ezana, sir."

"That ring a bell for you? Someone we used to know?"

"He's from the ADF, sir, as I told you."

"It rings a bell for me, but I can't place it. ADF you say? That must be it."

Starke paused. Malinke rushed into the momentary lull.

"I think we ought to separate the prisoners," he said.

"Why's that?"

"Leaving the three of them together may cause problems."

"Spit it out," Starke ordered.

"They've conspired to kill you, sir. Why trust them now?"

"I'm not convinced the woman is part of that," Starke said. "Besides, they're unarmed, under guard and outnumbered sixty-to-one. What do you think they've got in mind?"

"If I knew that—"

"Don't let it worry you. I've got something in mind."

"Sir?"

"We can sort it out tomorrow," Starke replied. "Two birds, one stone. We solve our problem with the unbelievers, send the woman on her way and get back to work."

"But, sir—"

"We'll have to pull up stakes, I know." Starke looked around his quarters, at the painted sky surrounding him, and frowned. "First thing tomorrow, then. Right after breakfast."

"Sir?"

"What is it?"

"If I'm to help you, I should know the plan."

"You will, in time."

"But the arrangements, should I—"

A long stride put Starke in his face, their noses almost touching.

"I said you will know in time!"

Malinke kept his eyes open, despite warm flecks of spittle on his cheeks and forehead. Showing weakness now wasn't an option. He wouldn't survive it. There was madness in Starke's eyes, a crazed look tilting over into mindless savagery.

"Yes, sir! As you say, sir!"

"*Exactly* as I say." Starke took a short step backward, swivelling his head as if to ease a muscle cramp or swallow something stubborn. "Are we finished here?"

"Yes, sir!"

Malinke held a crisp salute until it was returned, then fled Starke's quarters feverish with rage, his dignity in tatters.

Starke blamed him for Indrissa. That was obvious. He was excluded from decisions now, despite his role as second in command. Starke's hints of insurrection in the ranks were meant to rattle him and undermine his confidence. But to what end?

Starke claimed to know the white assassin who had come

for him. The prisoner denied it, but Malinke took for granted that he lied. Ezana had known nothing of a link between Starke and the stranger when Malinke questioned him and broke his will.

Was Starke mistaken? Was his recognition of the stranger a hallucination?

Was there something else?

Malinke didn't like surprises. He was troubled about whatever Starke was planning for the next day. It made him nervous, wondering if Starke and the American had something planned between them.

Something, he feared, that violated Starke's pledge to the Lord.

Scowling, he walked back to his quarters in the dark, then detoured past the armory.

He would be ready with his own surprises in the morning. Just in case.

"I'LL BE all right," Ezana said.

"You're tough," Bolan replied, "but you're a long way from all right."

He couldn't judge the full extent of the lieutenant's injuries through clothing, and the African refused to strip in front of Marceau. Ezana's face was badly bruised, his lips split and swollen. There were bloody rope burns on his wrists. The way he moved—reluctantly—and hissed in pain each time he changed positions, Bolan knew he had to have been through hell. The upside was that Ezana's limbs were still intact and functional. He had both eyes, he was coherent and he hadn't suffered any major loss of blood.

"I don't think you can fight."

"I can!" Ezana insisted, narrowing his eyes.

"We'll see."

"What do you mean, fight?" Marceau demanded. "Fight with what? Against three hundred men?"

"There aren't that many," Bolan said. "Two hundred and a handful seems more like it. They've been whittled down a bit, the past few days."

Ezana smiled at that. The lady rolled her eyes.

"Oh, that makes all the difference!" she said. "There'll only be a hundred men with guns for each of you to kill bare-handed."

"You make it sound unrealistic."

"Oh? I meant for it to sound insane."

"It beats the chopping block or whatever Starke has in mind for us. I'd rather go down fighting, if it's all the same to you."

"Me, too," Ezana echoed.

"And you?" There was more pity than scorn in the journalist's tone as she faced Ezana. "You can barely walk, for God's sake!"

"For my *own* sake," Ezana said. "I've done enough harm as it is. They won't drag me to slaughter like an animal."

"You did okay," Bolan assured him. "No one beats interrogation in the long run."

"Better to have died than to be broken."

"Or if you look at it another way, payback's a bitch unless you're still alive."

"Payback?" Marceau sounded confused. "What can you possibly accomplish now?"

Bolan had checked the hut for bugs as soon as he was left alone after the evening meal. Unless Starke had devices more sophisticated than his budget and the general decor suggested, it was clean. He had no qualms about responding honestly to Marceau's concern.

"We have a problem, Julienne. That's obvious. Starke can't afford to let us live." He tipped his head toward Ezana as he spoke. "I don't know what he has in mind for you."

"I'm free to go," she said. "He promised me, tomorrow."

"Did he mention any escort back to town?"

Her forehead crimped at that. "We didn't talk about details."

"Maybe he'll keep his word," Bolan said. "Maybe not. At least you've got a chance. Gabra and I, we're done whether we fight or not. It seems a shame to let Starke have it all his way."

"What will you do?"

"Depends on what he's cooking up."

Bolan had seen the charred spots in the middle of the compound, blackened stumps of logs protruding from each one. Before he went that way, Starke's men would have to best him down, hog-tie him, tape his mouth to stop him snapping at their throats.

"He has too many soldiers."

"It's a challenge, I admit."

"You're so sure of yourself."

If only that was true, he thought. "I'm sure that anything Starke wants from me, he'll have to take by force."

There was something else he hadn't mentioned even to Ezana. Something in the way of a surprise. Starke's men had confiscated his communications gear along with Bolan's weapons, and the Executioner took for granted that someone in camp would tinker with the set sooner or later. When they did, unless they used the sign-on code Bolan had memorized at Stony Man, the transmitter would beam a silent long-distance alarm, nonstop until its battery was dead. Two days, perhaps.

And Jack Grimaldi would be listening, prepared to lead an air strike on the transmitter's coordinates if Bolan didn't countermand the signal.

Bolan planned to let it run, no matter what.

"What have you done?" the woman asked.

"What could I do, in here?"

She frowned and shook her head. "Give me another chance to speak with him. I'll change his mind."

"Don't waste your time. He's always been the stubborn kind, and going crazy didn't help."

"You *did* know him before!"

"It doesn't matter."

"Yes! It troubles him!" She was excited now. "I've seen it in his eyes. Tell him the truth and buy some time."

Bolan pictured the war birds lifting off, heavy with rockets, bombs, napalm.

"I'll play the hand I've got," he said.

"Men are such stubborn fools!"

"So I've heard."

Footsteps. Bolan was on his feet before the guarded door opened, admitting Starke.

"I hope I'm not intruding."

"Not at all," Bolan replied. "Pull up some mud and take a load off."

"Thanks, but I'm not staying. You'll need rest before tomorrow. I want you to be prepared."

"Prepared for what?"

"You've questioned my commission from the Lord."

"I think you're nutty as a fruitcake, if that's what you mean."

Starke smiled. "Tomorrow, you'll have your chance to prove it."

"Oh?"

"I'm setting up a trial," Starke said.

"Where'd you dig up a jury of my peers?"

"Trial by ordeal, I meant to say. Your faith against my own."

"The best man wins?"

"Is that a problem?"

"Not for me."

Starke fairly beamed. "It's done, then. Get some sleep. We'll have an early breakfast and a festive day. God rest your soul."

Jack Grimaldi had been sleeping with the radio receiver since he got back to Kampala. It was nothing personal. The set was cute enough, of course, but Grimaldi was more inclined toward curves than hardwired circuits when it came to recreation.

This was work.

The set he had plugged in beside his cot at the Kampala air force base couldn't receive Bolan's broadcasts to Stony Man. It had no scrambler and in fact was so precisely specialized that it would—in theory—receive only one signal. It had been tested and had performed without a hitch. If the alarm built into Bolan's commo gear went off, Grimaldi's set would pick it up and let him track the tone—inaudible at Bolan's end—back to the source.

As long as he got there within six hours.

That was fine. Six hours was beyond the fuel capacity and cruising time of any aircraft on Kampala's military runway, and beyond the range of Bolan's last-ditch hurry call as well. Grimaldi could be in the air and riding down that alarm, unloading everything he had within a fraction of that time. His orders called for nothing less.

That was the problem.

If he got the call, he was supposed to scramble with one thought in mind: annihilation of the target waiting for him at the other end. He'd been instructed that the sound would mean Bolan had located his primary target but was in no shape to deal with it himself. Destruction of said target took priority over any and all personal concerns.

So he had waited, hoping there would be no alarm. No news was good news. He didn't know where Bolan was, what he was doing, whether he was even still alive, but if Grimaldi never heard the call to scramble he could live in hope.

He didn't want to be the one unloading doomsday hardware on the forest, maybe on his friend.

He didn't want to spend the next few decades wondering if he had taken out Bolan.

Grimaldi could've used a beer or ten, but coffee was the strongest drink he would permit himself under the circumstances. He had slept sporadically since his return from dropping Bolan over Karamoja Province, but he hadn't left his stuffy two-room quarters. Meals were brought to him, and Grimaldi picked at them and sent them back. He had a toilet and a shower, but he washed up at the sink instead, afraid of missing the alarm or losing precious seconds in the rain room.

He could shower later.

If he was forced to fly against his friend and Bolan wound up missing, there would never be enough soap in the world to wash him clean.

He read newspapers while he waited—stared at them would be more accurate. The stories blurred and ran together, making no sense to him. He paced the room, wishing he smoked or had some other nasty habit that would help him kill the time. His mind sketched images of Bolan—in the jungle, in a cage, dead on the ground—but none of them were reassuring.

No news equals good news, right?

Grimaldi would've rather had the worst confirmed and put it behind him, get on with the healing process of scorched-earth revenge, than to wait in a silent void of uncertainty.

Bolan should've located Starke by now. Five days and counting for an estimated four-day march was stretching it for someone of the Executioner's abilities. Grimaldi thought about the things that could've slowed him, and all of them were bad.

Hell, most of them were lethal.

He'd confirmed with Stony Man that Bolan had checked in on time the first three days, then nothing. Silence in itself meant nothing either way. There were a hundred different ways equipment could malfunction in the jungle without damage to the operator.

The first thing Starke and company would do, if they had captured Bolan, was to strip him of his gear. That would in turn cut off his broadcasts, but it didn't mean he faced a hopeless situation, much less that he had been killed. If someone at the rebel camp began to monkey with the transmitter, it would trigger the alarm and send the pilot on his way.

He would never know if Bolan was alive before he made his bombing run. That haunted him, but he could live with it.

Better my call than someone else who didn't even know him and wouldn't feel the loss.

Grimaldi made a conscious effort to snap out of his blue funk. Bolan had walked away from confrontations where it seemed a lead-pipe cinch he had no chance at all. He had defied the odds a thousand times and left his adversaries lying broken in the dust.

But how much luck did one man have?

Enough. Please God, just let it be enough.

Though he had been expecting it, the squeal of the alarm still made Grimaldi jump. He spilled his coffee, cursing as he sprinted from his quarters, down the empty corridor and out to the runway.

The McDonnell Douglas Av-8B Harrier was waiting for him, gassed up and fully loaded. He had already checked the Paveway II smart bombs that hung beneath its wings, two thousand pounds of searing death in each payload. There was a twin to the receiver in his quarters waiting for him in the cockpit.

He was good to go—or as good as it got, when his best friend may be sitting at ground zero, waiting for hellfire to rain from the sky.

"You bastards!" he muttered, running for the plane.

BREAKFAST WAS STEW again, left over from the night before. Bolan supposed he'd seen the best of Starke's menu, and he kept it down despite the bitter, cloying aftertaste. He needed strength for what was coming.

Trial by ordeal.

It was vague enough that he couldn't imagine what Starke had in mind. That would've been the plan, to keep him guessing, losing sleep, a little psywar in advance to wear him down. Instead of worrying about the problem, though, he sized it up and let it go.

There were two kinds of trial by ordeal. One involved a solitary player forced to undergo some test of his endurance, while the other featured some more active challenge. Bolan didn't know which kind Starke planned for him, but he would find out soon enough.

Meanwhile, he had Ezana and Marceau to think about.

"How are you feeling?" he asked Ezana. "Well enough to run if you have to?"

The lieutenant surveyed their cramped quarters and frowned. "To run perhaps," he said, "but not to knock down walls."

"That may not be a problem."

Marceau touched Bolan's arm. "What do you mean?"

He didn't want to lay it out in detail, but he owed them something. Hedging, he replied, "I think it's probable that Starke will want you front and center for his little show this morning. That puts you outside."

"Unarmed," Ezana reminded him. "Surrounded by an army."

Bolan nodded. "Even so, it's possible something may happen to distract them. If you see an opening, don't hesitate. Don't wait for me."

"What are you saying?" Marceau sounded worried now.

"If something happens and you get a chance to run, just do it. Don't look back. Don't hesitate. Cover as much ground as you can, as rapidly as possible."

"How do we recognize this thing you cannot name?" Ezana inquired. A half smile played across his swollen lips.

"It should be obvious. Just make the best of it. Do what you can."

"Why won't you tell us what it is?" Marceau asked.

"Because it wouldn't help," he answered truthfully. "It may not happen. If it does, the warning will be minimal."

He could have added, and you may be blown to bits before you realize what's happening, but what would be the point? Their future was already bleak enough without him dumping on their slender hopes.

"How can we be prepared—"

"You can't. Just keep your eyes open and don't relax too much."

"Relaxing's really not an option at the moment," Marceau replied, withdrawing her hand from his arm. "I can't imagine what Starke's planning."

"Don't bother," Bolan said. "Imagination's what he's counting on. It wears you down before the opposition makes a move, unless you keep a lid on it."

"But you can't plan your defense."

"You play the card he deals you," Bolan stated. "That doesn't necessarily mean playing by his rules."

She frowned at that, not understanding, but she let it go and changed the subject. "Do you think he'll keep his word to me?"

Meaning, did Bolan think Starke really planned to spare her life and set her free. He thought of sugarcoating it, then changed his mind. They were in desperate straits. He owed the lady as much honesty as he could spare.

"He may be serious, but then again, he's also crazy. If I had to guess, I'd say the odds are eighty-twenty that he'll send you on your way."

If Marceau was reassured by that, her face concealed it.

"What you have to think about," Bolan continued, "is whether his subordinates will let you go."

"But surely, if he orders it..."

"The rank and file are likely to obey," Bolan agreed. "It's not the grunts I'm thinking of."

"Who, then?"

"His second in command—the guy who brought us here— isn't as far out in the stratosphere as Starke. I won't pretend he's Mr. Rationality, but you can see him thinking, wondering. He may not favor the publicity."

Marceau looked stricken, as if treachery within the Lord's Vanguard hadn't occurred to her. "You think he would ignore Starke's orders?"

Bolan shrugged. "He's under some kind of a cloud right now, the way Starke treats him. I don't know what's on his mind, but if he's getting itchy, something like a layout in the press could be the thing to tip him over."

"Thanks. I'm feeling so much better now."

"Better to think about it in advance than to find out when you're five miles down the trail."

She glared at him. "I thought you said imagination was the enemy."

"I never said you should ignore the obvious. There's a world of difference between worry and being prepared."

"I wish you'd tell me what it is," she said.

"That's easy. Worry breaks you down, preparation makes you stronger."

"Ah. And how should I prepare for escorts who may want me dead?"

"It may not come to that."

"The mystery again."

"Sorry. It's all I have."

"I don't think so."

"Think what you like, but stay alert today. You owe it to yourself."

"And you?" she said. "Are you ready for what may come?"

"As ready as I'll ever be."

STARKE STOOD before the polished Caddy hubcap, intently studying his reflection. The face looked familiar, of course, but there was something out of place behind the eyes.

Something...

Could it be fear?

He scowled at the notion, watching wrinkles squirm across his forehead. When he'd shaved that morning, he had nicked himself for the first time in months. The dribbling stream of blood had fascinated him, tracking the planes and angles of his profile to answer to gravity's draw, dripping from his chin.

An omen?

No.

Starke put his trust in God. With Him there were no mystic signs or omens, only revelations to the faithful. Dabblers in the arts of divination were condemned to the eternal lake of fire.

But there was something....

He had dreamed of the American overnight. In Starke's dream the assassin was a changeling, fluid-faced, his features melting and reforming almost faster than the eye could follow. Once, between changes, Starke thought he'd glimpsed a face he recognized.

So much for dreams.

Malinke knocked and entered on command. Starke noted the reflection of his second in command's salute and waved it off.

"It's nearly time, sir."

Starke knew that. He didn't wear a watch but always seemed to know what time it was.

"What happened with the transmitter?" he asked.

Malinke's frown looked almost comic in the hubcap-mirror. "Access must be coded, sir," he said. "I've tried, but—"

"Never mind. We've got no one to talk to anyway. They'll hear us when it's time."

"Yes, sir. About the contest?"

"Have they finished breakfast?"

"I don't know, sir."

Breaking eye contact with himself, Starke turned to face Malinke. "You don't know?"

He felt a cold smile twitching at the corners of his mouth. His hands were twitching, too, a sudden urge to strike.

Not yet. Save it.

"Why are you here," Starke asked in his most patient voice, "if they're not ready for me yet?"

"I thought you'd wish to be there first, sir."

"Arrive before my guests? That would be rude, Roshani. Have I taught you nothing? It would also be bad theater."

Malinke frowned at that, but only for an instant. He was trying not to blow it, the Indrissa incident still fresh in mind.

"Go back and find out if they're ready for me now," he said. "And don't come back again until they are."

"Yes, sir."

"And Roshani?" Starke caught him in the doorway.

"Sir?"

"Don't leave those baskets in the sun."

"No, sir."

Starke saw the glimmer of resentment in Malinke's eyes and reckoned he'd have to deal with it soon. Today might be a good time, while the men were still on edge about the losses at Indrissa and Malinke coming back without a scratch. He had survived one challenge, granted, but Starke had a rather different game in mind.

First he meant to test himself with the American. It galled him that he couldn't place the stranger, work out when and where they'd met before. Starke wouldn't let it distract him when the stakes were life and death.

He finished dressing for his day, choosing comfort over pomp and circumstance. The camo pants were standard-issue, loose enough to let him move, the cargo pockets empty so he wasn't thrown off balance on a crucial move. The spit shine on his boots was fresh, although he knew it wouldn't last ten seconds once the contest started. There was something to be said for pride. He topped the outfit with a black T-shirt that was a size too large—again, for practicality and comfort.

One more turn before the Caddy hubcap. When he had the green beret positioned on his shiny scalp, Starke knew he was ready to go.

The test he had devised wasn't new. Starke guessed it had been used among the native tribes for generations, maybe centuries. He had observed it for the first time at a tiny village in Busoga Province, south of Lake Kyoga, and it stuck with him, lurking at the back of his mind. This would be his first time to play the game himself.

Perhaps the last?

Starke smiled at that. His faith in God was absolute. If he was judged and found wanting, the Lord could reach down and replace him anytime He felt the urge. Starke wouldn't argue—but until he got the word from God, he meant to carry on as leader of the Lord's Vanguard and do his duty as it was revealed to him.

Which didn't mean he couldn't have some fun along the way.

Starke hoped his guests enjoyed the contest he'd prepared for them. He knew his soldiers would appreciate it. They could use some entertainment and diversion, considering the losses they had suffered lately. After he was finished with the American, Starke would let them have the African assassin—and perhaps Malinke, too.

The more he thought about it now, the more Starke was convinced it was high time for him to choose a new second in command.

His struggle in Uganda would be finished soon. It would be good to have new personnel beside him, new ideas to supplement his own.

Starke drew his Ka-bar from its sheath and found the whet stone in a cubbyhole among his plastic crates. He sat in one of the camp chairs and began to stroke the blade's cutting edge with loving care.

There was no need to rush.

He had all the time in the world.

MARCEAU WAS THANKFUL for a breeze as they were herded from their quarters. It was stifling in the prison hut, no ventilation to speak of, and her shirt already showed dark patches at the armpits.

There was no such thing as haute couture in rural Africa, she had decided. It was strictly rough-and-ready wear, pith-helmet chic.

In fact, Marceau wished that she had a pith helmet right now or the hat she'd lost in the river when she was saved from the crocodiles. The central portion of Starke's compound was a clearing, and the nets strung overhead for camouflage did less to screen the tropic sunshine than the forest canopy a few yards distant. When the breeze died down, as it was sure to do, Marceau would start to sweat in earnest. Some of that, she realized, was due as much to nerves as to the morning heat.

So much for self-composure in a crisis.

Starke's men were assembled in the middle of the compound, waiting for them like an audience. In fact, she thought, they were exactly that. Starke had prepared some spectacle for the amusement of his troops, with the American as the centerpiece. Marceau still didn't know what he had planned, but common sense told her it had to be bad news.

Their escort marched them toward a patch of barren ground some thirty feet across. Ezana was limping, but he kept up well enough. Starke's men edged back to let them pass. Marceau could feel them watching her, eyes crawling over her like groping hands.

Apparently admission to the Vanguard didn't require a vow of chastity.

She thought again about Belasko's words, saying she

couldn't trust Starke—or his subordinates—to let her leave the camp alive. It occurred to her, not for the first time, that her jeopardy wasn't confined to simple death.

And if the American managed to survive the challenge Starke had planned for him, then what? Would any of them stand a chance surrounded by at least two hundred enemies?

She searched her soul for anything resembling optimism, but the only thing she found was dread.

Starke hadn't joined them yet, but when she glanced toward his quarters she noticed two baskets sitting in the shadow of his wicker throne. They seemed identical, each roughly two feet tall and eighteen inches in diameter, their lids tied down with twine. One of them seemed to bulge slightly, then settle back into its normal shape before Marceau could be sure it had moved at all.

She knew Starke was approaching when the whisper stream of conversation in the ranks dried up, replaced with nothing but the sound of boot heels crunching soil. She'd thought Starke might put on his redcoat uniform again for the festivities, but when she saw him in the black T-shirt and camo pants her heart lurched.

Their host wasn't content to watch the trial by ordeal. He would play some part in it.

Was that good news or bad?

If the American defeated him, would they be better off—or worse?

Why was her stomach clenched as if she were about to lose her greasy breakfast in the dirt?

"I'm happy you could join us," Starke said, beaming, as he reached his throne. "I think you're going to enjoy the contest I've prepared."

He crouched behind the baskets, drew a knife and cut the twine that held their lids in place. Marceau waited for something to burst forth, then reminded herself to breathe when nothing happened.

Starke sheathed his knife, grabbed each basket by a handle on one side and lifted them as he rose, moving toward the center of the clearing. The baskets seemed heavy, making the muscles stand out on his deeply tanned arms.

"I hope you rested well," he said, addressing himself to Bolan. "You'll need a firm hand and a steady eye this morning. Or, I should say, we both will."

He tipped the baskets, shook them both at once. The lids dropped off, spilling their contents on the ground in front of him. For an instant Marceau wondered why anyone would bother coiling old rope in a basket, then she gasped and took a long step backward.

Two fat, dusty-looking snakes were writhing on the ground in front of Starke. They separated, hissing at each other, as he tossed the empty baskets carelessly behind him. It was difficult to say, but the journalist guessed that each snake measured close to eight feet long. She watched them coil and raise their heads a meter off the ground, necks flaring the width of her hand.

"These are forest cobras," Starke said. "I can promise you they're lethal. Certain native tribes use them as dueling weapons when there's an affair of honor to be settled. I thought we might follow their example, if you've no objection."

"IT'S DIFFERENT," Bolan said. "I'll give you that."

"I thought you'd like it." Starke was grinning like a child on Christmas morning.

"Are there rules?"

"Pick out a snake. Try to make sure it bites the other guy."

"So, I don't have to dance or play the flute?"

"Maybe next time," Starke said. "You game?"

"Why not."

"My man! You want first pick up?"

"Be my guest."

Starke dropped the smile and focused on the nearer of the cobras, crouching slightly as he moved in closer to the snake. He kept his hands well out to either side, the left one moving, fingers wiggling to distract the reptile, while he waited for an opening.

Bolan watched Starke, reviewing what he knew about venomous snakes. There were basically two kinds on Earth, excluding sea snakes. Vipers had long fangs that folded back inside their mouths like jackknife blades, and they injected hematoxic venom that produced internal hemorrhages. Elapid snakes—the cobras, mambas and related species—boasted shorter fangs and neurotoxic venom that induced paralysis of heart and lungs. Drop for drop, the worst killers were native to Australia, but that wouldn't help him if his cobra got a decent bite and sent its venom coursing through his blood stream.

Bolan nearly missed Starke's move, it was that fast. The cobra made a swooping lunge for his left hand, and Starke's right caught it close behind the head, lifting the serpent as he rose from his crouch. The cobra gaped and twisted in his grasp, trying to reach his fingers, while the whiplike body coiled about his arm.

"Your turn," he said.

Bolan moved up behind his cobra. It was watching Starke but felt the tremor of Bolan's footsteps, pivoting to face him with a warning hiss.

I hear you, Bolan thought. This isn't my idea.

Snakes were deaf, he remembered, and some had poor eyesight. They "heard" by picking up vibrations through the ground and "smelled" by tasting the air with their flicking, darting tongues. Performing cobras swayed in time to the movement of a snake charmer's body, not the sound of his flute—and many of them, unlike Starke's, had their fangs or venom glands removed for safety's sake.

No such luck.

He judged the cobra's striking distance as the length of body it held poised above the ground, about three feet. After watching Starke's pet, he knew the snake could lash out forward or loop around to one side, but a strike left it unbalanced, surging forward while the rest of its body followed, without the swift recovery time of a coiled viper.

He could use that, perhaps, if he found an opening.

Distract it.

Fanning the air with his left hand as Starke had done, Bolan circled the reptile, making it turn to follow him. It lunged at him twice before he was ready, making Bolan sidestep and duck back a pace. Someone cackled in the crowd behind him. Bolan did his best to ignore the audience, focusing on the snake that was his adversary and his weapon, all rolled up in one.

Crouching slightly, feet well apart for balance, he braced himself for the grab. Split-second timing was required. If he missed the snake—or even if he grabbed it too far back—the deadly jaws could round on him and fasten on his arm. It wouldn't matter if he killed the cobra. By the time he snapped its neck and pried it loose, he would've absorbed enough venom to kill a half-dozen men.

He didn't stop to think of what would happen if he won the contest, whether Starke's men had been ordered to stand back or open up with everything they had. He didn't think about his transmitter or Jack Grimaldi.

Bolan focused on the snake.

The cobra had no eyelids and no ego, so a stare-down wasn't practical. Bolan would have to follow Starke's example, plant his grip as close behind the serpent's head as possible and hang on for dear life.

He hoped his palm was dry but couldn't check.

He ducked lower, leaned forward, reaching out with his left hand. Instead of wiggling his fingers, Bolan kept them clamped together, waving from the wrist like Queen Elizabeth. He had the snake's attention for the moment, but he had to time the move exactly right.

When the cobra's head swept forward, Bolan twisted at the waist, drawing his left hand back and out of range. His right hand moved at the same time, shot forward in a modified karate strike, his fingers cupped to grab instead of clenched to kill.

He caught the snake an inch or two behind its head and it began to thrash at once, hissing and whipping Bolan with its lower body. Although slender, no more than two inches in diameter, the cobra was pure muscle, writhing in a frenzy as he straightened and lifted it.

He had a moment of surprise at finding it was too long for his arm. To lift it fully off the ground he'd have to hold the cobra's head a foot or so above his own. Instead, he grabbed the middle of its lashing body with his left hand, feeling angry muscles flex against his palm.

"Not bad," Starke said from somewhere to his left. "I wasn't sure you'd get it."

Bolan turned to face his enemy. "I'd hate to disappoint you."

"That's the spirit," Starke replied—and rushed him with the cobra's jaws thrust out toward Bolan's face.

13

Marceau recoiled from Starke's advance as if the cobra's fangs were aimed at her instead of at Bolan. She collided with Ezana, almost knocking down the wounded man. She caught him in time to keep him upright.

Behind her, someone laughed as if the whole scene were the most amusing thing on Earth. Marceau was tempted to lash out at those around her, but she couldn't tear her eyes away from the combatants armed with snakes.

Starke's first rush missed but drove Bolan backward, dodging as Starke pressed ahead. The reptile squirming in his grasp was difficult to handle but at least Bolan kept the fangs clear of his flesh. The journalist was no expert on snakes, but she knew cobra bites were routinely fatal without proper treatment. The American's problem was twofold—avoiding Starke's live weapon while keeping control of his own.

How could he hope to win?

She had her answer seconds later when Starke made a feint to his left, then rushed toward Bolan once more. This time Bolan stood his ground and tossed his snake at Starke, as if it were a living lasso. Cursing, Starke raised both hands to deflect the airborne cobra, but it slithered down one arm and draped across his shoulder, hissing like a punctured tire and lashing out at him before it slid to earth.

Had Starke been bitten?

If so, he gave no indication of it. As Bolan's cobra pooled around his feet, Starke kicked out blindly, flinging it away from him. Infuriated but unharmed, the reptile glided toward the front ranks of the startled onlookers directly opposite where Marceau and Ezana stood. As if afraid to kill it when their master might still have some mission for the snake, Starke's soldiers scrambled to avoid its hissing strikes.

Cursing and shoving broke out in the crowd across the compound, fists flying while the cobra struck at various legs. Marceau had no time to assess the chaos, drawn back to the deadly action in the center of the makeshift ring.

Starke pressed home his attack with grim determination now, oblivious to what was happening around him. Bolan, empty-handed, circled with him in a wrestler's crouching stance, hands well apart, the fingers hooked like talons.

Bolan had to avoid the fangs of Starke's reptile yet somehow find a way of dealing with his enemy. He couldn't dance around the ring indefinitely, and Starke showed no signs of breaking off pursuit. If anything, the grimace on Starke's face bespoke fanatic dedication to the effort.

"We should help him," Ezana whispered to her.

"How?"

He didn't answer that, but she could feel him turning, studying the soldiers who surrounded them. She had no doubt they'd open fire if Ezana tried to seize a weapon, and she wondered if he'd risk it.

More to the point, she wondered whether it would help.

Across the clearing, someone squealed and started slashing at the ground with a machete, but it seemed the frantic cobra managed to evade the blows, still striking out in all directions as it zigzagged through the crowd. One man was down, she saw, and clawing at his ankle, another clutched one hand as if it pained him, cursing bitterly.

She guessed those were two soldiers who would never raid another helpless village. She was stricken with a sense of satisfaction that alarmed her. Marceau had never honestly wished death on anyone before her trip to Africa, but now it had become a nasty habit.

And she meant it fervently.

Returning her attention to the main event, she saw Bolan stumble, lurching backward as Starke pressed home his attack. Just when she thought he might be finished, she saw him drop deliberately, lash out with his feet and cut Starke's legs from under him.

Starke cried out as he fell. He couldn't catch himself with outflung hands, but bent his arms instead, so that his chest and elbows took the brunt of impact. As it was, the fall brought Starke's face within inches of the cobra's dripping fangs. Bolan rolled well away and sprang back to his feet.

Bolan moved to take advantage of the moment, but Starke recovered swiftly. With a jerk and twist that left him sitting upright, he propelled his cobra toward his adversary, looping through the air. It fell between Bolan's feet and lashed out with a strike that snagged his pants. Marceau couldn't tell if the fangs had met his flesh, Bolan shuffling through a jerky little dance routine that finally dislodged the snake and flung it several yards away from him.

Starke was already on his feet by then, drawing the knife from his belt sheath. "So much for ritual," he said. "We'll do this the old-fashioned way."

"Suits me," Bolan said. "I never had much fun at sideshows anyway."

"I'd offer you a knife," Starke said, "but I don't seem to have a spare."

"Why am I not surprised?"

Marceau felt Ezana step away from her, knew he was up to something, but the sound of heavy impact from behind her came as a surprise. Turning, she saw a startled soldier clutching at his throat, eyes bulging, while Ezana stripped him of his bolo knife and pistol. Even as the gasping soldier shuddered to his knees, Ezana turned, calling Bolan's name, and tossed the knife into the ring.

She saw him catch it, as if he and the lieutenant had re-hearsed the move for days. She saw Starke's smile inverted in a heartbeat, turning into a scowl.

A shot rang out behind her, quickly followed by another. Marceau dropped to a crouch, arms raised in futile self-defense. She caught a glimpse of movement from the ring and saw the cobra streaking toward her like a sentient torpedo.

She was opening her mouth to scream when an explosion rocked the compound and its shock wave sent her sprawling in the dirt.

BOLAN WAS STARTLED by the blast. It shook him to his knees, but he didn't release the knife Ezana had thrown to him. He saw Starke wobble on his feet, almost go down, keeping his balance by sheer force of will. A splash of crimson on Starke's shoulder marked a superficial shrapnel wound.

"You're done," Bolan informed him in a voice that sounded hollow in the aftermath of the explosion. "That's the cavalry."

"Too late for you," Starke said.

"We'll see."

Bolan had no idea if Jack Grimaldi would be on his own or leading other war birds, no fix on the ordnance he was packing.

The first blast had been a stunner, taking out the mess tent and surrounding real estate, leaving a number of Starke's soldiers sprawled in crumpled, writhing heaps. That could be Bolan, when the next bomb fell. Survival meant departure from ground zero, but he had to nail Starke or log his mission as a failure.

Not that Starke was going anywhere—except for Bolan's throat. He seemed oblivious to pain or danger, trusting God to see him through. He came at Bolan with relentless strides, his knife blade weaving little figures eights in front of him.

Distract him, Bolan thought. "So, did you figure out where we met before?"

It worked. Starke blinked and hesitated.

"What?"

"I thought you would've got it by now." Bolan spoke softly, voice low-pitched for privacy.

"It you want to take that knowledge with you," Starke replied, "that's fine with me. You're almost done."

"First time," he said, "Strategic Hamlet 419."

That froze Starke in his tracks. "You're full of shit," he said.

"Think so? How would I know the scar on your left shin comes from a pungi stake?"

Starke studied his face as if trying to see through the muscle and flesh to the skull underneath, maybe X-ray the brain. Something dawned in his eyes, his taut lips going slack.

"They sent *you?*"

"Looks that way."

"You're a dead man," Starke whispered.

"Not yet," Bolan said. "Here's your chance."

Above them somewhere, whistling down, another bomb was on its way. Bolan knew the rule of thumb—if he could hear it coming he was probably okay—but if the charge was big enough and shrapnel was involved, a direct hit wasn't needed to score kills. He held his breath, counting, waiting to see if Starke would make his move before it hit.

At the last instant, Bolan hit the dirt and rode the numbing shock wave of the blast. It deafened him. He didn't know if there was damage to his eardrums, but a brass band could've marched within a yard of him and Bolan would've been no wiser in the aftermath of the explosion.

Struggling to his feet, covered with mud and flecks of shredded jungle vegetation, Bolan looked around for Starke. Where had he gone? The epicenter of the blast was off to Bolan's right, among the sheds that served as barracks for Starke's soldiers. More of them were down, torn and bloody—some still moving, others perfectly inert—but there was no sign of their chief.

Dammit!

There came a tug at Bolan's sleeve and he was turning with the bolo in full swing before he recognized Marceau. Her lips were moving, but he couldn't hear a word she said. Tapping one ear, he shook his head and tried to say, "I can't hear you." His own voice sounded like a whisper at the bottom of a mine shaft.

Grimacing, she pointed past him through the swirling smoke and dust. He turned and caught a glimpse of Starke's retreating form, running full-tilt across the devastated compound.

Bolan felt an urge to let him go, take solace in the fact that he was beaten, with his compound shattered and his troops in disarray, but he knew Starke would never let it rest. His one-time friend was somewhere in a private twilight zone where God dictated marching orders and commanded Starke to purge the earth of human life. And if he knew one thing about Starke, then or now, it was the man's wholehearted dedication to the task at hand.

Having accepted the assignment, even from the lips of a hallucination, he would never let it go. Starke wasn't capable of turning back.

Fixing the point where Starke had disappeared, Bolan turned back to Marceau. Hoping that she could somehow hear and understand him, he told her, "Find Gabra. Get as far away from here as possible. Go now!"

She tried to answer, clinging to him, but he had no time to waste. Shaking her off, he turned and started after Starke at a dead run.

One of Starke's men stepped up to intercept him, brandishing a pistol, but his nerves were shaken by the bombing and he stalled too long to save himself. Bolan slashed at him with the bolo knife and dropped his twitching gun hand in the dirt. A backhand caught the gunner's throat and freed a crimson geyser as he staggered out of range, trying to stop the blood flow with his one remaining hand.

Bolan was almost to the spot where Starke had disappeared

when another bomb exploded in the middle of the compound, hurling him facedown into the mud. He felt as if his head were trapped inside a kettle drum with King Kong beating out a frantic march.

Dizzy and vaguely nauseated from concussion, Bolan lurched upright and reeled off in pursuit of Galen Starke.

GABRA EZANA RECKONED he was dying, and the strange part was he didn't seem to mind. The pain left over from his earlier interrogation hardly fazed him now. It was as if the bomb blasts had eclipsed all other feelings when the first one picked him up and hurled him right across the compound like a rag doll, tumbling through the ruins of the camp.

Somehow he had survived, and he had kept the pistol liberated form his enemy. That struck him as an omen. He could still fight, even if his time was running out. Ezana wouldn't lie down and die without inflicting losses on the enemy.

He scanned the smoky camp in search of Starke, Bolan, Marceau or either of the soldiers who had tortured him. Spotting no friends and no specific enemies, Ezana decided to do what he could with what he had. It wasn't much, granted, but if he used his wits it just might be enough.

Starke's men were everywhere, panicked, heedless of Ezana's presence in their midst. He might have had two heads and still they would've passed him by, focused as they were on self-preservation.

It gave him an edge and he took full advantage, leveling his pistol at the two nearest soldiers, dropping each one with a shot to the head. The gunshots barely seemed to register with anyone around him, so he shot another of Starke's men, and yet another.

Number five had spotted him, raising an automatic rifle to his shoulder, but he wasn't fast enough. Ezana squeezed off a double tap into his face and caught the rifle as his adversary fell. The pistol still had two or three rounds left, so Ezana eased down the hammer and tucked the weapon in his waistband.

He felt better with the FNC assault rifle.

It almost seemed as if he had a fighting chance.

Two shaky-looking soldiers passed by, shooting nervous glances at him, and Ezana cut them down. One of them wore a bandolier that the lieutenant had appropriated for himself. He might not have a chance to use the extra magazines, but wearing them made Ezana feel more like a soldier than a walking wreck.

For the first time since his capture, he felt complete again. He could repay his enemies for the humiliation and pain he had suffered.

Ezana glimpsed the man who had interrogated him, a profile flitting through the crowd. Inflamed, he sprayed the crowd in front of him to cut a path, rushed through it over twitching bodies to pursue his quarry.

Ezana lost sight of his tormentor for a moment, cursing as his injuries prevented him from making any better speed. An instant later he saw the man again and raised the liberated rifle to his shoulder. He would trust ballistics when his muscles failed him, every time.

His finger was tightening on the FNC's trigger when he was struck from behind, staggered, his aim thrown off target. The shot went wild and Ezana rounded on his enemy, confronting a young soldier who looked as startled as Ezana felt.

No matter. Ezana shot him in the chest before he could recover and left him squirming in the dirt.

He turned back to follow his primary target, worried that Starke's second in command might have fled while Ezana was distracted. He was unprepared to find the man no more than twenty feet in front of him, aiming a pistol at him in a firm two-handed grip.

The first shot struck Ezana in the chest, off center, ripping through a lung. Ezana squeezed off a long burst from the FNC as he was falling, but he knew the rounds were wasted, even as a double tap from his assailant tore into his abdomen.

The ground rushed up to meet him and the darkness followed swiftly after. He barely had time to curse the fates that robbed him of his last chance for revenge.

MALINKE WAS AMAZED the battered assassin had come so close to killing him. It was a fluke and would've been impressive under different circumstances, but he had no time to waste on admiration of the dead. Another bomb might strike at any moment.

He heard the whistling sound and hit the deck, mouthing a desperate prayer. The blast lifted Malinke, held him airborne for a split second, then dashed him back to the earth. He sputtered to draw breath, face caked with dirt, and felt a moment's panic when he thought he'd lost his pistol, only to discover it was still clutched tightly in his tingling fist.

Get up and run!

It was the only way to save himself. He could do nothing for the others, and running away seemed less shameful somehow, after Indrissa. If the Lord wanted his blood this day, Malinke reckoned it would make no difference what he did or where he tried to hide. If he survived, it was a sign from God approving his escape.

Malinke scrambled to his feet, still dizzy from the last explosion. It had taken out Starke's private quarters and an untold number of disciples. Bodies and their smoking remnants had been strewed about the camp like the scattered remains of a mannequin factory.

Malinke's nerves were stretched nearly to the breaking point. If he didn't escape soon, it would be him screaming among the dead and dying soldiers, shrieking until his throat bled and his mind went numb at last. The enemy could step in close and finish him, if he hadn't been blow apart by one of their infernal bombs.

As if in answer to his thought, another blast erupted on the far side of the camp. Malinke had lost count of the explosions, taking this one in staggering stride as he fled toward the jungle. Bits of shrapnel stung his flank, but he ignored them. They were no worse than mosquito bites, less likely to infect him with disease.

The slug that burned a track between his biceps and his ribs was something else.

The impact made Malinke stumble, clutching at his side. He felt the draw of gravity and let it take him down, instinctively aware that if he stood his ground a second shot might finish him.

Malinke lay unmoving where he'd fallen for a moment, feeling blood soak through the camo fabric of his shirt. His mind was racing, ticking off alternatives. If it had been a stray round fired at random, he was wasting precious time. But if the shooter had selected him deliberately, wisdom dictated that he let his enemy believe he had been killed or incapacitated, at the very least until he could identify his foe.

The shot had been both lucky and unlucky for him. On the upside, he was still alive and only grazed. It was a painful wound, but one which he could easily survive. The downside was logistics. He was lying facedown in the dirt, with his head pointed in the opposite direction from whoever shot him. There was no safe way for him to rise and turn to face his enemy.

Lie still and wait.

If it was a deliberate shot, the triggerman would very likely try again—in which case he might very soon be killed—or else approach Malinke to find out if he was dead. Plan B afforded him a chance, however slim, to take the gunman by surprise and turn the near miss into victory. Conversely if the shot had been a stray, he would lose nothing by remaining where he was for several moments longer, testing the hypothesis.

Unless another bomb was hurtling toward him.

Malinke tried another prayer. His faith was ebbing with the slow, warm pulse of blood beneath his arm, staining his garments and the soil. Had he been judged on high and found to be unworthy? Had the Lord abandoned him?

With his ears ringing from the bomb blasts and sporadic gunfire, Malinke realized it was unlikely that he'd hear an enemy approaching him, even if one were so inclined. He started to imagine an advancing sniper, weapon poised to finish him. What was the sneaky bastard waiting for?

Malinke kept his eyes closed with an effort, tried to modulate his breathing, so a careless adversary wouldn't notice he was still alive.

He started hoping for another bomb. It would wreak havoc with his comrades—those who still survived—but it would also be his one best chance to make a move.

The whistling sounded small and distant to his ringing ears. Malinke clutched his pistol tightly, every muscle in his body tense, awaiting the blast that would either liberate or kill him.

When it came, he thought it was the loudest yet. The earth convulsed beneath him, helped him rise on trembling legs. He turned, the pistol held before him in both hands, his finger taut around the trigger.

It had been a stray shot. Malinke started to relax.

Until the muzzle of a weapon kissed his moist nape.

Though nearly deafened, he still heard and recognized the woman's voice. "You killed my friend," she said.

Malinke offered no reply. His brain was humming, thinking through a move that just might save him, if his timing was precise. He'd have to crouch and spin, corkscrew his legs and whip his left arm back, deflect her weapon even as he aimed and fired his own.

Tricky, but not impossible.

"Goodbye."

Before the words had time to register, a fireball hurtled through Malinke's brain and sent him spinning into darkness.

STARKE HAD A LEAD, but Bolan followed him on legs that trembled dangerously, threatening to fail him. He ran through a drifting pall of smoke and dust, past nightmare scenes of broken bodies, walking wounded, craters painted crimson. Near the outskirts of the camp he saw one of the cobras coiled about a feebly struggling soldier, striking furiously at his face.

Bolan moved on.

He had a fix on Starke's direction, but the odds of overtaking him outside the camp were minuscule. Starke could run until he dropped or find a hiding place secure from prying eyes. Bolan could track him through the forest for a lifetime without ever getting close enough to make the kill.

A heavy sound of impact from behind him brought the Executioner around in a defensive crouch. He was in time to see Starke rising from all fours beside the tree where he had hidden, watching Bolan pass.

Starke drew the Ka-bar from between his teeth and smiled. "I couldn't let you go without a thank-you," he declared.

Bolan relaxed a bit and rose from his crouch.

"Oh, yeah? For what?"

"Isn't it obvious? For showing me the error of my ways."

"Your mind's all clear now?"

"Crystal," Starke replied. "My mistake was trusting others when I should have carried out the program by myself."

"World cleansing? That would keep you busy for the next millenium or so."

"With God all things are possible."

"You'd better take it one step at a time."

"That's why we're here, old friend."

Bolan stood easy, with the bolo knife at his side, waiting for Starke to make a move. Instead of rushing him at once, Starke inquired, "You mind if I ask something?"

"Be my guest."

"How did you pull it off? New face, new life. I wouldn't mind a deal like that."

"Too late," Bolan replied. "It's a long story, and you're out of time."

"I always liked your confidence. We need to test it, though."

"Ready when you are," Bolan said.

Already moving, circling to his left, Starke said, "It's too damned bad."

"What's that?"

"The day I heard you'd bought it, I broke down and fucking cried."

"I'm born again."

"Have to see if we can fix that, buddy."

Starke came for him in a rush, his right arm blurred from slashing back and forth. Bolan waited for him, sidestepped at the last instant and blocked a cutting backhand with his bolo knife. The blades struck, creating sparks and vibrating from the impact. Starke leaped back as Bolan countered with a disemboweling sweep.

Starke's smile was fierce and bright.

"I should've known it was a setup," Starke exulted. "All those reports, pretending that a bunch of mobsters took you out. That's my job!"

With the final syllable he rushed again, slashing at Bolan's throat. The Executioner slid underneath the thrust and swung his blade behind Starke's forward leg, its sharp edge biting deep behind his knee.

"Goddamn it!"

"That's a no-no," Bolan said. "Don't take His name in vain."

"Smart-ass."

Starke grinned and forced himself upright, hobbling toward Bolan with his blade outthrust. He launched himself into a hopping charge, the last few yards, his face contorted to emit a wordless battle cry.

Bolan stepped to his right this time and swung the bolo knife with everything he had. The blade sank out of sight below Starke's ribs and came back dripping crimson, while the stricken man stumbled to all fours.

Bolan stood over him and kicked the Ka-bar out of reach.

Starke shuddered to a kneeling posture, rocked back until he was sitting on his heels. The camo pants he wore were soaked with blood.

"I guess negotiated settlement's out of the question, eh?" Starke tried to laugh and wound up coughing raggedly, blood gleaming on his chin and chest.

"You want to finish it," Starke asked, "or let me have a fighting chance for old times' sake?"

"I'd never have another moment's peace," Bolan replied.

"You got that right." Starke grimaced, breathing hard. "All right, get on with it, you miserable bas—"

He swung the blade from Starke's blind side and felt Starke shudder with the impact. Bolan needed both hands to extract the bolo knife and let Starke fall. There was no need to check his pulse. Each heartbeat loosed a flood from Starke's severed carotid artery, feeding the thirsty soil until the source ran dry.

BOLAN FOLLOWED his nose back to the camp. Tendrils of smoke crept through the trees to beckon him, helping him stay the course. There were no more explosions, no more gunfire. Bolan thought he heard the dwindling sound of a jet's engines overhead, but it could just as easily have been phantom echo.

Halfway back to camp he picked up on a sound that was indisputably real. Footsteps approaching on the trail in front of him, the unseen hiker making no attempt at stealth. He waited in the shadows, stepping forth at the last moment to a startled gasp.

"Jesus! You frightened me!" Marceau announced.

She looked okay, all things considered. Better than okay, in fact. After the first fright passed, she let the pistol in her hand rest by her thigh, its muzzle pointed at the ground.

"Where's Starke?" she asked.

"Back there." He nodded toward the trail behind him. "Gabra?"

"Dead."

There was no time to mourn. There were still soldiers to watch out for.

"You want to let me carry that awhile?"

"I'm done with it, I think," she said.

He put the pistol in his waistband and tucked the bolo through his belt.

"What now? Where do we go?"

Too many questions, but he answered anyway. "Maroto's south of here. With any luck, we ought to be there in a week or less."

"A week." She shook her head and smiled. "There goes my deadline."

"For the interview, maybe. You've got another story now."

"But I can't tell it, can I?"

"Most of it," he said. "Why don't we talk about it on the way?"

"Sounds fair."

The jungle slowly started coming back to life around them as they made their long way home.

Epilogue

"I like the tan," Brognola said.

"Next time around," Bolan replied, "I'd rather go to the Bahamas."

"That makes two of us. I'll see what I can do."

"Meanwhile?"

"Meanwhile—" Brognola nodded in agreement "—it's congratulations for another job well done."

"They're getting squared away, out of Kampala?"

"More or less. The ADF's considering a cease-fire followed by negotiations, if nobody drops the ball."

"That's a big if," Bolan said.

"Not our problem, either way. Starke was the bogeyman, for us. He's finished, thanks to you. Whatever happens next, at least it won't rebound on Washington."

"One problem," Bolan said. "We never got around to sharing on the subject of Ebola. There was nothing in the camp resembling any kind of lab, as far as I could tell."

"Turns out he had a separate facility," Brognola said. "It was a few miles east of where you ran him down. I guess he didn't want his people blundering around and spilling anything by accident."

"You know this, how?"

"Ugandan regulars moved in after Jack smoked the camp," the big Fed said. "They flushed out some stragglers and ran them down. One of them talked. The lab is history, or so I'm told."

"You don't sound very confident."

He shrugged. "Kampala isn't interested in spreading plague among the population," he replied. "Whether they'll torch the stash or keep the bugs on ice somewhere, who knows? We've got the white coats on it now, World Health and CDC."

It could be worse, Bolan decided. Starke or one of his lieutenants could have slipped away with the Ebola virus to begin another round of cleansing. As it was, with organized surveillance from assorted global agencies, it seemed unlikely that a twitchy colonel in Kampala would unleash the next apocalypse.

Unlikely, right—but not impossible.

"Kampala's sitting on the whole Starke deal?" the soldier asked.

"Affirmative. They brought him in, remember. He was on their payroll when he split to join the ADF, and moved from there to start the Lord's Vanguard. Nobody wants to claim him, and they can't start pointing fingers without stepping in the mess. Call it a standoff."

"No survivors from the Vanguard then?"

"None in a position to be holding coffee klatches with the press," Brognola said. "Kampala thinks a handful slipped the net, but they're too busy running to give interviews. Besides, what could they say? They either come off sounding crazy or confessing to a string of war crimes that could put them up against a wall."

That didn't mean that some of them weren't carrying the word, of course. Starke's word. The call to Armageddon.

Religions had begun with less. One of the biggest in the world had started out with only twelve believers.

"There's something on your mind," Brognola said.

"Just *Paris Match*," Bolan replied, ducking the rest of it.

"Turns out there's no match, after all. Your friend went home and told them that she couldn't get the story she was looking for. I understand they're working on another angle.

Mad messiah in the jungle, modern *Heart of Darkness* or some damn thing. But I've got something here the editor passed on."

"Oh, yeah? What's that?"

Brognola delved inside one of his pockets and retrieved an envelope. It was off-white, about the size normally used to mail wedding invitations, slit along the left-hand seam. Bolan accepted it and extracted a note handwritten on expensive stationery, folded once to fit.

It wasn't long. He read it over twice, Brognola watching him. When he was done he folded it and slipped it back inside the envelope.

"You need this?" he asked.

"It's yours." There was a twinkle in Brognola's eye—or was it merely the reflected sunlight?

Bolan pocketed the note and said, "Looks like we're covered, then."

"Seems so. I take for granted that she didn't know the inside story anyway, but this is better."

"I'll be interested to see her angle on the story," Bolan said.

"Since when do you read French?"

"I get by. And I've got a program on my laptop that can translate."

"Ah. The marvels of technology."

That brought his mind back to Ebola hemorrhagic fever and the lab Starke had established in the wilds of Karamoja Province. Busting it was one thing. Soldiers in Kampala maybe holding back the stash was something else.

"The virus was airborne?" he asked.

"Apparently," Brognola said. "World Health and the Department of Defense are looking into it. Nobody's sure how Starke finessed that part. There was a Russian CBW man who disappeared out of Sudan last year, but no connection's been established. He was never found."

CBW. Chemical and biological warfare.

It was just like Starke to shop around and take the best—

or worst—from any source available. Bolan thought it was safe to say the Russian had gone missing for eternity, his bones perhaps recycled on the wheel of life in Karamoja Province.

The Russian's fate was no concern of Bolan's, either way. What worried him was simple science and the laws of probability. If a zealot like Starke could get his hands on a mutated killer virus, even breed it under primitive conditions, what would stop another warlord and another from doing the exact same thing in Africa, Asia or the United States?

Nothing at all.

He put the problem out of mind for now. Worry, in his experience, was a down payment on disaster that might never come to pass. In the meantime, there were other threats and enemies to think about in present tense.

Brognola checked his watch and frowned. "I'd better roll," he said. "I've got a meeting back at Justice, after lunch."

"Okay."

"You ought to take some time, unwind a little."

"Maybe."

"All right," Brognola said, as he stood. "I'll be in touch—but not too soon, I hope."

"You've got my number," Bolan said.

They shook hands, skipping the goodbye routine. In Bolan's line of work he never knew when partings would be final, but he didn't like to press his luck. It was the closest that he came to superstition, anyway, but it had worked for him so far.

It was a three-block stroll to reach his rented car. Bright sunshine all the way, and warm. He thought about the note tucked in his pocket. It had come from Marceau and read:

> Your secret shall be safe with me. Next time, perhaps, an Ocean view?

Next time, he thought, smiling.
Why not?

Stony Man is deployed against an armed
invasion on American soil...

DEEP RAMPAGE

In this brand-new episode, Stony Man comes up against
the shkval—a supersonic underwater rocket with stunning
destructive capabilities. Elusive arms dealers have put it up
for sale, making it available for any terrorist group with a
cause…or a grudge. Racing against the clock, Stony Man
hunts for the elusive arms dealers selling blood and death.

STONY MAN

*Available in
December 2002
at your favorite
retail outlet.*

Or order your copy now by sending your name, address, zip or postal code, along with
a check or money order (please do not send cash) for $6.50 for each book ordered
($7.99 in Canada), plus 75¢ postage and handling ($1.00 in Canada), payable to Gold
Eagle Books, to:

In the U.S.	**In Canada**
Gold Eagle Books	Gold Eagle Books
3010 Walden Avenue	P.O. Box 636
P.O. Box 9077	Fort Erie, Ontario
Buffalo, NY 14269-9077	L2A 5X3

Please specify book title with your order.
Canadian residents add applicable federal and provincial taxes.

GSM62

DEATH LANDS®

Destiny's Truth

**Available in
December 2002
at your favorite retail outlet.**

Emerging from a gateway in New England, Ryan Cawdor and his band of wayfaring survivalists ally themselves with a group of women warriors who join their quest to locate the Illuminated Ones, a mysterious pre-dark sect who may possess secret knowledge of Deathlands. Yet their pursuit becomes treacherous, for their quarry has unleashed a deadly plague in a twisted plot to cleanse the earth. As Ryan's group falls victim, time is running out—for the intrepid survivors…and for humanity itself.

TAKE 'EM FREE

2 action-packed novels plus a mystery bonus

NO RISK
NO OBLIGATION TO BUY

James Axler
Outlanders

EQUINOX
ZERO

As magistrate-turned-rebel Kane, fellow warrior Grant and archivist Brigid Baptiste face uncertainty in their own ranks, an ancient foe resurfaces in the company of Viking warriors— harnessing ancient prophecies of Ragnarok, the final conflict of fire and ice, to bring his own mad vision of a new apocalypse. To save what's left of the future, Kane's new battlefield is the kingdom of Antarctica, where legend and lore have taken on mythic and deadly proportions.

In the Outlands, the shocking truth is humanity's last hope.

Or order your copy now by sending your name, address, zip or postal code, along with a check or money order (please do not send cash) for $6.50 for each book ordered ($7.99 in Canada), plus 75¢ postage and handling ($1.00 in Canada), payable to Gold Eagle Books, to:

In the U.S.	**In Canada**
Gold Eagle Books	Gold Eagle Books
3010 Walden Avenue	P.O. Box 636
P.O. Box 9077	Fort Erie, Ontario
Buffalo, NY 14269-9077	L2A 5X3

Please specify book title with your order.
Canadian residents add applicable federal and provincial taxes.

GOLD EAGLE®

GOUT24